TRANSITION
OF
POWER

by Karen D. Bradley

Ambrosia Sands Books
Dolton, Illinois

Transition of Power
Published by:
Ambrosia Sands Books
PO Box 827
Dolton, Illinois 60419
www.ambrosiasands.com

Transition of Power © Copyright 2019 by Karen D. Bradley
Trade Paperback ISBN: 978-1-7336089-0-9
Digital ISBN: 978-1-7336089-1-6
LCCN: 2019907340

Cover Art by: Woodson Creative Studios
Interior Design by: Lissa Woodson www.naleighnakai.com

Manufactured and Printed in the United States of America

TRANSITION OF POWER

◆ DEDICATION ◆

For the warriors whose roars are forcing the world to take notice and to the ones who fight battles in silence. I see you. I love you and I appreciate you. Someone is watching and being inspired to do more and be more. To the gladiators who have fallen too soon and have gained their wings, you will be missed but your legacy of courage, love, and fierceness lives on.

♦ ACKNOWLEDGEMENTS ♦

To my family and friends and core group of readers, thanks for supporting me through the ups and downs of this unexpected writing expedition. Most of what I have accomplished has been due to your excitement and encouragement that has provided fuel for a journey I wasn't sure was mine to take.

A special shout out to my sister, Jenetta M. Bradley, for her part in getting my books off the shelf where they were collecting dust. I appreciate you reading my stories over and over again without complaint.

English and Grammar were never my strongest subjects but the stories in my head didn't seem to care about that fact. Thank to my developmental editors Lissa Woodson (Naleighna Kai) and J.L. Campbell for your energy and efforts in strengthening the weakness in my writing, challenging me to be better and improving the novel. The process was brutal and painful at times but hopefully the end result is the creation of a book that readers will love.

To my beta readers Crystal Baltimore, Debra Mitchell, and Michelle D. Rayford, I appreciate your constructive feedback. Your comments and questions were essential to putting the final touches to the story of my favorite character thus far.

A special thanks to J. L. Woodson for a cover that is beautiful yet edgy. To NK's Tribe Called Success—you rock!

Finally, thank you to everyone who purchases a book, know your support is appreciated.

CHAPTER 1

Cameron Stone sat in a black Dodge Charger looking at her parents' house. She took a moment to prepare herself before she entered the three-story, blonde brick building with white trim around the windows. Visiting her mother, sometimes put Cameron in an odd place. She had battled men three times her size, conversed with some of the most intelligent people around the globe, yet she couldn't deal with her 5'2" mother on certain days. Her mother, ever the campaigner, always tried to do one of three things—mend fences, make a lady out of Cameron, or marry her off. She hadn't been successful at any of the three.

Cameron tightened the black bandana over her braided hair before sliding out of the driver's seat. She didn't plan to stay long because it was too close to dinner time and she had no intention of being there when her father arrived. Since the incident that led her down the not-so-straight and narrow path of the underworld of Chicago, she had only laid eyes on him a few times.

The light oak door opened as she climbed the concrete stairs. *What the hell was he doing there?* Cameron fumed as the youngest of her brothers stepped outside. She selected today to visit because her mother was supposed to be alone.

She scowled, taking in the tawny skin that was so much like their father's. Her brother, Jason, was several inches taller than her. "Didn't know you'd be here."

"Or what?" Jason snapped, face morphing into a frown that matched her own. "You wouldn't have come?"

"Pretty much." Cameron crossed her arms over her chest. "I'm not in the mood for your legendary lip service or lectures."

If Justin and Jaime Quinn were also present, she'd definitely leave and come back another day. She stared at Jason, knowing the days of getting back the brother who once knew all her secrets were long gone. In his place was "daddy junior" with his father's judgmental expressions, searing stares, and his knack for being an authority on everything.

"The lifestyle you're living isn't right," Jason scolded, his hazel eyes squinting and his nose crinkled as though he smelled something rotten.

"As I remember, my brothers introduced me to my current lifestyle." The last thing Cameron wanted to do was rehash a painful past but she also wouldn't let him forget his role in her current situation.

Jason leaned in the doorway, blocking her path. "Yeah, but *we* got out. What's your excuse?"

Cameron tried unsuccessfully to keep the anger out her voice as she moved back. "If memory serves me right, your *father* got you out."

"He's your father, too," he countered, pulling the silver doorknob forward and stepping further onto the porch. Cars swished by on the street behind them.

"Technically, he's my sperm donor." She sighed, hating this bickering session that occurred every time they were within a few feet of each other. She'd once considered herself, Jason, and their cousin, JD, like a three-cord rope, hard to break apart. "Tell Mom I'll stop by to see her another time."

"Jason, is that Cookie?" their mother's soft voice called from beyond the door.

"Yeah, it's her," Jason answered dryly.

"Then let her in." She ambled from the hallway and pushed Jason out of the way. "How's my baby girl doing? Not good, seeing those dimples have disappeared."

"I'm fine." Her family claimed her dimples vanished whenever she was angry. Cameron gave Jason the evil eye as she slid past him into the house. If Jason wasn't standing there, Caroline Stone would have said something about Cameron's black jeans and baggy sweatshirt not being feminine enough. She would be right.

Cameron had her mom's light, barely-there complexion and oval face, but her curvy shape was a replica of her Aunt Renee's infamous one. Her height came from the other side of the DNA strand. Each of her brothers' square faces, varying shades of tawny brown skin and hazel eyes were their father's contribution. The rest of their features had a strong resemblance of their mother's African-Native American side of the family.

Lavender perfume tickled Cameron's nose as Caroline's arms wrapped about Cameron's waist, then the petite woman pushed her toward a rose-gold couch. "I was telling your brother that your Aunt Renee was worried about JD."

Jason frowned as Cameron claimed a seat next to their mother. "I'm looking into it."

"I'm trying to catch up with him, too," Cameron said, ignoring Jason who loomed over her, as though wishing he could put a muzzle on her.

"She'll be glad to hear that," Caroline said as the phone rang. "Let me get that."

Caroline hustled toward the kitchen. The only people who called the house phone were church folks and older family members. It had taken forever to get Caroline Stone used to a cell phone.

Jason waited until their mother was in a full-blown conversation before growling, "Cam, don't get involved."

She chuckled, since she had no idea what he meant. "In what?"

"JD's back in trouble," Jason whispered, glancing at their mother who was still in an animated conversation which wasn't a good sign given her body language.

Cameron rose, put a hand on her chest and schooled her expression into a more innocent one. "I didn't—"

"He's safe for now but don't interfere. Trust me," he said in a low, almost raspy timbre.

"Trust you," Cameron snapped, shoving his shoulder and daring him to do something. "Six of us were there that night when you were shown the error of your wicked ways. You, Que, and your two friends were redeemed, and JD and I were not. Trusting you is not an option."

The Stone clan had grown up in the south suburbs of Chicago and would sometimes catch the train into the city. When Quinn and Jason found a new set of friends, the trips became more adventurous. What started as a dare to shoplift small items from department stores without getting caught, then spiraled into procuring high-end merchandise.

"It wasn't my choice to leave you behind bars," Jason argued, adopting a wide stance with his chin jutted out.

"No, it was your *father's* choice," she countered, glaring at him. "You accepted it. Reaped the benefits. Now, you want me to trust you." She tried not to relive the shock and betrayal of Jake Stone getting Quinn and Jason and their friends out of jail and leaving Cameron and JD in that cell as though they didn't matter. Her brothers didn't even attempt to reach out to her after "the incident." Therein lay the separation of the black sheep from the flock.

"JD's life may depend on it." Jason angled himself so he had a better view of the kitchen. "I know what's going on and it's being handled. FBI's all over it."

All of her brothers had followed in her father's footsteps, embracing some form of law enforcement. She, on the other hand, found herself entangled in the darkness and shadow of the criminal world. Despite his assertions, she didn't trust any of them to do right by JD. "Then let's work together," Cameron suggested.

"Our cousin needs to find a job that doesn't have ties to organized crime and stop dragging you into his mess."

"I can't sit idle while you all try to figure it out," she shot back.

Cameron scowled more, not wanting to let Jason know his words hit home. Both JD and her lives would be different had JD had the confidence to fight for his dream of being an artist when he was young. Unfortunately, his friends convinced him that his artwork was trash and would never make real money. Then they introduced him to Bishop, who could make them all wealthy men and JD went to work for him. Nothing was the same after that.

"Let the proper authorities handle it." He shifted his gaze toward the sound of their mother's laughter. "I'm serious, Cam. Leave it alone."

Cameron edged forward until mere inches remained between them. "Don't you wish I would."

"More than JD's life is on the line here," he shot back. "If I find out you're in the way, I'll arrest you in a heartbeat." Jason stared her down, daring her to defy him. He retreated a few feet as their mother's head peeked out from around the dining room wall that had finally been painted in that eggshell color their father hated. She'd finally won that tug-of-war that had been going on for at least three years.

Cameron balled her fist and silently counted to ten. "You would, wouldn't you? Like father, like son."

Jason frowned with an air of dismissiveness, something that also made him more like his father. "Don't start that."

"I'm saying bye to mom. I'll see you around." She walked over to the pint-sized woman, kissed her moist cheek, and whispered a farewell.

"Cameron," he called after her, but she ignored him.

Her mother covered the mouthpiece and whispered, "See you tomorrow?"

Cameron gave a noncommittal shrug, then shifted her focus into the living room in time to see Jason blocking the path to the door. She was tempted to leave out the back way but all he'd do is slide out the front and plant his behind on her Charger.

"Bye, Jason." She brushed past him, knocking into his shoulder, then grabbed the knob, swinging the door open. As Cameron attempted to close the door, Jason caught it.

He trotted to catch up as she raced to the curb. "The best I can do is update you on JD's status."

Realization hit her. Jason not only knew where JD was, but who he was with. "You've got eyes in the organization." She was so angry she hadn't been listening to what he *wasn't* saying.

"I can't comment on that." Jason's face went blank, same as when his father caught them doing something they weren't supposed to do. They all knew anything said could be twisted, turned, and used against them.

Cameron deactivated the locks on her vehicle. "You don't have to bother, brother dear." She slid behind the wheel and pulled away, leaving her frustrated brother standing on the curb.

CHAPTER 2

The instant Jason Stone heard JD was with The Warden, he'd been waiting for his baby sister to make an appearance. Cameron didn't disappoint. The smell of fresh garlic wafted through the air as he walked across the beige carpet toward the kitchen. His mom had to be making her infamous creamy garlic butter Tuscan shrimp for dinner. Jason realized his early appearance had ruined his mom's plan to set up Cameron.

He walked into the kitchen, remembering how the white cabinets with mint-green accents had always gotten him and Cameron in trouble. The doors were the perfect canvas for their Picassos, whether it was with dirty hands or crayon drawings. Unfortunately, Jake Stone didn't appreciate the artistry the way their mother had.

"You came over early for a reason. Sweetie, what's going on?" Caroline asked as she stirred the sauce in a silver pan.

"Just seeing if you'd heard from Cam." Jason leaned on the marble counter near the stainless-steel stove. "And to let you know I hadn't forgotten about JD."

"You shouldn't *have* to come to me to find out about your sister."

She grimaced, setting the spoon down on the holder in the center of the stove, adding spinach to the white mixture.

The day the six of them were thrown in jail changed everything. Caroline was so angry with Jake's actions, she packed up and moved out for the summer to stay with Cameron at Aunt Renee's until Cameron went off to college. She'd come over every day to check on him and his brothers, but their sweet, pushover mom became a quiet storm. He'd never heard their parents argue so much.

Jason stood straight, knowing a lecture was coming next. "I'm going to let you get back to cooking. The rest of the gang will be here soon."

"I haven't stopped cooking but it's obvious you want to run off." Caroline grabbed his arm as he passed. "We'll talk about it later."

Jason nodded and escaped to the back porch, perching on the deck's wooden steps, and enjoyed Chicago's warm weather while it lasted. His mom was right. He shouldn't have to go through her, but his father told them to stay out of the situation with Cameron and he did. At the time, he agreed with what his father had done. Cameron needed to learn how to lead, not follow, especially with plans for college at such a young age. Besides, being on his dad's bad side was never a good experience.

Some days, Jason wanted a do-over to change how he'd handled things. The year he was graduating from high school, JD's lawyer contacted him and requested he visit shortly after he'd gotten arrested, stating it was important. Since JD seemed to attract trouble, Jason didn't rush. Now, he wished he had. By the time he finally got around to visiting a week later, it was too late. Cameron had made a deal with the devil.

JD had been roughed up in jail and Cameron went to Bishop, the man JD worked for, to secure some protection since the judge refused to grant bail. Bishop was rumored to be a Crime Lord but neither the police, FBI, DEA, or ATF could ever nail him on anything. Cameron's interactions became even colder toward the men in the family after that. Now Jason didn't even know how to bridge the gap between them. He became FBI, hoping to take Bishop down but having Cameron mixed up in it would mean risking completely alienating her from the family and breaking his mother's heart.

The sound of someone getting smacked caught his attention. When "Ow" echoed, he grinned. His dad had to be in the kitchen trying to taste test the food. Caroline Stone didn't play that.

Jason stood and dusted off his jeans before heading to the back door.

"For my birthday, I want a dinner with the *entire* family." Caroline turned off the burner.

Jason stopped in his tracks, watching his parents through the screen door.

"Cookie won't come." Jake Stone opened the fridge, grabbed a bottled water, and grimaced because his wife had replaced his preferred Guinness beer with water.

She pressed the door closed, glaring up at her husband's tawny, brown face. "What you did to her was wrong. Why don't you put aside that stubborn pride and apologize?"

Jake lovingly shifted her out of the way. "I was trying to—"

"You treated her like you do the boys but she's a girl, a woman now." She snatched the bottle of Fiji out of his father's hand like she used to do when Jason and his siblings were younger, to make sure their complete focus was on her. "While she'd roughhouse like one, she processes and responds differently to the way you handle her."

"I did what I thought was best." He grabbed another water.

"Bullshit." She slammed the bottle on the counter.

Jason froze, taken aback. He'd never heard his mom curse. He leaned on the bricks, trying to decide whether to go in or wait until they finished. Waiting seemed best. This fight was like a ticking time bomb that could explode at any moment and reduce his family unit to ashes.

"Parents are supposed to balance each other. Men tend to be hard on their boys and soft on their girls and women are usually the reverse." She grabbed five dinner plates and the cabinet banged closed. "But you—."

"You've made it clear. I failed her," Jake huffed, rubbing the back of his salt-and-pepper fade.

"No." Caroline slowly turned, facing her husband. "You're *still* failing her."

He put the Fiji bottle down, clasped his wrist with the other hand as though trying to restrain himself. "What?"

"Man up, like you're always telling your sons to do." Caroline moved forward, scowling up at him. "And admit to your daughter you were wrong. She's just as stubborn as you."

"I'll apologize," he shot back. "Not for what Cameron *thinks* I did but the mistake I made in honoring *your* request." Jake issued Caroline a steely stare. "So, are you ready to come clean to our daughter about the part *you* played in her going to live with your sister?"

The room went so quiet, Jason held his breath for fear of being heard. He was glad the burner under the food was off otherwise dinner would have been charred.

"Always silence," Jake said in a lower tone. "You made me a villain and it cost me a relationship with my daughter."

"You should have never left her in jail," Caroline roared, turned toward the counter, and shifted the plates. "Just say you're sorry."

"Dammit. My decision may have laid the foundation but your choices gave Cookie the bricks to build a wall between us. Two years of poor decisions." He waved two fingers in front of her face. "You could have easily corrected our daughter's misinterpretation of the situation. You've no idea what damage your *filtered* information did to her life."

"Damage?" She swiped his fingers away as the doorbell rang.

"You should have fixed this before it spiraled out of control."

"If you'd done what I asked, it—"

"Absorb the blame, so you could remain untarnished in her eyes." Jake leaned down, staring into her eyes. "You and I both know Cookie would've required a full explanation to move past this grudge."

The doorbell rang several more times in the midst of their standoff. Jason remained rooted to his spot on the back porch absorbing this new piece of information.

"You didn't even try." She whirled to face Jake.

"How many times did I try to see my daughter? I trusted you to make things right." Jake leaned down in her face. "By the time I realized what you were doing and decided to take matters into my own hands, our daughter was —"

"Jason, quit eavesdropping and get the door," Caroline snapped, not taking her eyes off Jake.

The screen creaked as Jason stepped into a kitchen that suddenly felt much smaller than its large size as he avoided eye contact with his parents. He rushed past the dining room and living room then peeked through the small glass rectangle in the wooden door into Jaime Quinn Stone's chiseled face staring back at him. Justin, or Hawk to friends and family, stood three feet behind Quinn, resting his narrow behind on the black railing.

"What's wrong?" Hawk asked as he stood to his full height, which was about two inches more than Jason's 6'2"

Jason didn't respond, but stepped aside to let them in. They'd feel the tension once they hit the dining room.

Quinn wore a worried frown as he made it over the threshold. "Does it have anything to do with mom's request for us not to bring a guest?"

Even though Quinn's girlfriend wouldn't be in attendance, Jason thought Hawk's wife would still manage to come. She tended to think the rules of their family didn't apply to her. "Mom and Dad were arguing about Cam," Jason said, as Hawk cleared the doorway.

They had plenty of disagreements over Cameron but this was the first time he'd heard more than the words *Cameron* and *apologize*.

"Dinner's ready," Caroline called out.

Jason followed his brothers into the dining room, taking a seat at the oak table that accommodated ten people.

"Jason, could you get the salad from the fridge?" Caroline placed the serving utensil in the large red bowl filled with bowtie pasta.

Jason detoured into the kitchen and was surprised to see his father close on his heels.

Jake grabbed one of the bottled waters off the counter. "A friend contacted me today to let me know Bishop's name popped back up on the radar."

"He's dead," Jason replied, frowning as he opened the fridge.

"But his actions live on." Jake untwisted the top and took a swig. "Have you heard any chatter?"

"No." Jason lifted the salad bowl. "I've been busy with my latest case."

"Has JD gotten himself in trouble again?" The question came with an intense stare down. "He's determined to end up in prison like his father."

Jason hesitated to answer. The last thing he needed was to have his father involved. "Umm I'm—"

"Gentlemen, stop yapping and get your butts back to the dining room," Caroline yelled, interrupting Jason's attempt to side-step his dad's question.

He exhaled. Jake wasn't known for dropping a subject, especially if he thought the person wasn't being honest.

Hawk said, "Yeah, Jas. Hurry up."

"We can't eat until we've blessed the food," Quinn chimed in, once again being the one in a hurry to dig in. Where he put all that food was a mystery.

Jason retrieved the salad dressing and let the fridge door shut. "In that case, I'm going to take my sweet time," he joked before he and his father returned to claim seats at opposite ends of the table.

As his mother prayed over the food and family, Jason grew more determined to keep his sister out of this situation with JD. Cameron was willing to go to extremes to protect their cousin, because the two of them bonded due to their closeness in age, shared trauma, and mutual dislike of their fathers. Now, he had to make sure her stubborn behind didn't end up in prison or worse – dead. Truthfully, it would be easier to dive into the belly of a whale, cut out a piece and swim back out, than it would be to get Cameron to shift once she dug in her heels.

Prayer ended and Jason said, "So is anyone going to let us in on the real reason Cam's been estranged from the family?"

Everyone froze as Jake and Caroline glared at him. Under his father's intense infuriated stare, Jason found himself on the hot seat realizing this might not end well for him.

"The disrespectful tone of that question will *not* be tolerated in this house." Jake shifted the chair back, angling his body toward Jason. "I may not have kicked your sister out ... but I'll throw your grown ass out without blinking an eye."

His father's words weren't a slip of the tongue. Jake had a sly way of passing on information to him and his brothers when Jake couldn't officially speak on something but he wanted them to know. Jason was barely able to process what his dad said, when his mother shot him a displeased glare that sent chills down his spine.

Caroline's eyes narrowed with jaw clenched and lips pressed together. She rose from her chair, throwing down her napkin. "Jason Warren Stone, kitchen now." She extended an index finger at him then swung it to the door.

Jason glanced over to his brothers searching for some kind of support.

Quinn lifted his shoulders and twisted his lips up as if to say 'bruh, you're on your own' before averting his gaze.

"It's been nice knowing you," Hawk patted him on the back.

Jason realized he'd pissed off the one person who was known for neutralizing situations to get everybody talking and laughing again.

Jake's eyebrow lifted and mouth turned down, he gazed at Jason as if he felt sorry for him.

Shit. If his father was feeling empathy for him, Jason had really messed up. Caroline looked at him as if she was three seconds from kicking his ass and that was before she ripped him a new butt hole.

The moment he crossed the threshold into the kitchen, he wished he'd kept his mouth shut. Caroline waved an index finger for him to come closer. The second he was near, she reached up, snatched his shirt, pulled his face closer then adjusted her hold around the collar.

"Ma." Jason grabbed her hands but couldn't pull away without choking himself or hurting her.

"Let me establish this. You ain't *that* grown," Caroline fumed, tightening her grip. "Do that again and all 6'2" of you will realize, I can still whoop that ass."

"I was just asking." He tried to pry her fingers from his shirt.

"Something you had the opportunity to do before your father or brothers arrived, instead of blurting it out like a five-year-old with no control of his mouth," Caroline's fist flew open as she released his collar. "You were trying to put me on the spot."

"Why not just respond?" He rubbed the area on his neck where the shirt had dug into his skin.

"You answer the question, Jason. Take responsibility for your actions." Caroline stepped back near the knife block, giving him a once over. "You're trying to place blame when you need to accept the part you played. Trust me, I learned *that* the hard way."

"Part I played," Jason huffed, frowning as she chuckled as if he told a joke. "I didn't do anything."

"Once you came of age, you lost your ability to blame our parenting for your life and your relationships." Caroline leaned on the counter with a smug stare. "You became accountable for making the choices you wanted. Certain things that you didn't like, you had the ability to change them."

Jason was planning to repair the relationship with his sister. He needed to keep her out of prison and alive to do so. "I'm not trying to point fingers, I just…I want to understand."

"Again." Caroline stared up at him. "Answer your own question."

"I don't know."

"Ready to swallow this truth?" Caroline moved closer to him. "Your father told you stay out of grown folks' business, he never said stay away from your sister. That was your choice. So tell me son, why are *you* estranged from your sister?"

Caroline gave him one last searing glare before patting him on his chest and sweeping out of the kitchen.

The devasting blow his mother issued felt ten times worse than when he was shot multiple times.

CHAPTER 3

Most days, Cameron was an upstanding citizen. Nights, not so much. She spent those reclaiming stolen items and returning them to their owners for a hefty fee. The pieces she retrieved came from private collections—stolen property purchased off the black market or poached during war times. Her services were critical since the victims couldn't make police reports. Cameron's current assignment was one of many she and her team, Greg, Rob, and Trenton, completed over the years. They all used to work for Bishop, who dabbled in everything illegal. Today, she was doing a recon in downtown Chicago, preparing for a job they would execute later that evening.

People milled about on their lunch hour, soaking up the touch of warm weather before the Chicago chill returned. Cameron rested a manicured hand on top of her fake pregnant belly as she made use of the outdoor seating at a Pub on Wabash Street. The view of a particular brick office building, not the food, was her reason for being in one of the most uncomfortable guises she'd ever donned. She scanned the streets in a slow, casual manner.

"Need anything else?" the waitress asked, picking up the cash payment Cameron had left for the bill.

"No, but thanks," Cameron replied, shifting the wicker chair toward the black, metal fencing around the seating area.

Her gaze was focused on the door where the client would exit, but her mind was on leaving the business. The dangers didn't make for a life-long career. She did a double take as a woman bearing a striking resemblance to Kathleen Frost passed her. Kathleen was one of the few women Bishop had allowed into their inner circle.

Cameron's cell vibrated. She slid the hands-free buds into her ears as her attention shifted to a bald man with a beer belly, stepping out of the dull-brown office building. Her client, Mr. Arthur, was on the move. She already knew what restaurant he was heading to and what he'd order. Being a creature of habit was dangerous.

She answered Rob's call. "Hey, hon, I'm sorry. Got your message. It's okay to place the order."

"Greg is calling him now," Rob replied.

The sound of a call trying to connect let her know Greg had put the phone on speaker so she could listen in via Rob. Cameron increased the volume to tune out the chatter of an older couple sitting nearby, the city sounds, and the rumbling of the train overhead. The stoplight changed and Mr. Arthur crossed to the other side. She heard the client answer. A tall, spiky-haired man walked past Mr. Arthur, blocking her view of his mouth. The chubby man continued his journey without a cell in his hand.

"We may have a problem," Cameron said as she rose to her feet, maneuvering past the fencing and waddling down the street. She reached Mr. Arthur before he made it to the building that housed the restaurant Heaven on Seven. He had no hands-free set and Greg was still on the line with the client. *Who was pretending to be Mr. Arthur?* "Track the person on the line location now."

The Gu, a 12th Century metal piece—one of thirteen works stolen from the Gardner Museum in 1990—had been in Mr. Arthur's possession from a black-market purchase. The Museum offered a ten-million-dollar reward for the recovery of the thirteen pieces. They were worth more on the black market. Someone had stolen the Gu from Mr. Arthur, killing his wife in the process. The police report corroborated the break-in and murder.

Cameron had a feeling that old man missed the artwork more than his wife. Last week she had let herself into his private museum, which was hidden behind the bar in his basement. Pictures with him standing next to the Gu were splayed in the vault, but barely any of his deceased wife. The "client" who stated he had located the Gu and wanted it retrieved and now was currently making final arrangement with Greg on the phone, was clearly not Mr. Arthur, but someone hired to eliminate her team.

She changed direction, heading toward a Honda Civic parked near the Pub. Minutes later, she slipped behind the wheel. One thing she learned from her first failed job was to prepare to be double-crossed and to expect anything from anyone.

The memory had been seared in her brain when Neil, who had been the look out, spotted trouble on a job. On what should have been a simple heist, armed men arrived while Cameron was removing a valuable painting. Neil rushed in, warning them seconds before bullets sprayed the room. Neil was hit three times. Greg took a bullet to the shoulder. Cameron had to eliminate four guys to clear the way for them to get down the fire escape to their car.

Neil died on the way to Bishop's medic.

After that night, the depth of Bishop's assignments changed. She vowed to do whatever it took to protect her teammates and the people she loved. This was not the time to have any issues showing up at her door step, especially with retirement once again on her mind. She definitely couldn't handle her team going to prison, or ending up on the wrong side of the grave.

The cell vibrated as Cameron cut through Madison Street to the expressway. "Are you on speaker?"

"Yeah," Rob replied.

"We're both here," Greg confirmed.

She increased the volume from a button on the steering wheel. "Where did the call originate from?"

Rob huffed, "Somewhere near the house with the Gu."

"What's the move?" Greg asked.

"Hunt or be hunted. We're about to return the favor." Cameron honked at a cab driver who cut her off and slowed a little to accommodate his unwanted presence. "Get my gear and make sure the business cards laced with the knockout drug have been restocked. I have a feeling we're going to need it."

"Got it," Rob said.

Cameron peeked at the newly-freckled face, with brown eyes, and short black hair staring back at her in the rearview mirror. She wanted to pull off the wig, wipe away the freckles, and get back to her normal self. "Make sure the van with the motorcycle transport rig is ready."

"We'll be prepared to rock and roll when you get here." Greg said.

Cameron disconnected as she merged into the stop-and-go traffic, her mind crafting a strategy for tonight. The plan to deal with the issue wasn't without risk, but adapting to these new developments was necessary to handle the situation.

♦ ♦ ♦

This had been her life for too many years. Retirement needed to become a priority. The team received confirmation the targeted house was vacant. Several hours later, Cameron's Yamaha motorcycle rolled over the grey porcelain tile of the pool deck. Other than the sounds of the neighbor's dog barking in the distance, it was quiet. Her gaze roamed the area as she unclipped her gun holster.

Her communication unit clicked, and Rob's voice came through the ear piece. "Clear, you can enter."

Cameron's microphone was melded into the collar of her bodysuit under a black hoodie to prevent her from losing it in any physical confrontations. She quickly moved past the pool to the door. Rob had hacked the digitally advanced house with no problem, giving her immediate access.

Her gloved hand pulled the bronze handle of the doorknob. The warm air inside clashed with the cool atmosphere outside. She crossed the threshold, eyes shifting up to stars twinkling from the skylight then back down to navy-and-white furniture surrounding the indoor swimming pool. She crept into the luxurious space.

"We've got your bike and we're moving into position," Rob said, to a backdrop of rustling noises. "What's your status?"

"Looking for the entrance. Check back in five." Cameron slowed her pace, moving along the interior wall. A crack of light on the floor between the couch and the pool caught her attention.

"Trigger the switches in the room one by one," Cameron whispered.

The lights above went off, then the ones in the pool and the floor flickered. "Switch that last one back on."

Her gun led the way down the stairs to a private museum with three aisles of artwork. The row to her left was filled with paintings, the middle one held statues, and to the right, items ranging from chairs, vases, to masks had been exhibited. Cameron didn't have to slide too far down to find the Gu. She pulled the clear case off the black pillar, sweeping the Gu off the stand then scanning the other cases. She was fairly sure the piece she snagged and some of the others weren't the real deal.

A distinctive bronze statue gleamed on a pedestal. She knew someone who had been searching for it. Cameron set the Gu on top of the stand next to it, grabbed the other statue, quickly wrapping and putting it in her transport bag, then slid the bag's strap back over her head. The door swished open and she grabbed the Gu and made a quick dive to the concrete floor. She scrambled to the end of the aisle and stashed the Gu between two black pillars.

"I've got an exit issue," Cameron whispered as she peered around the base of the black marble that hid her position. Clicking sounds were the only response. The room must have been designed to jam signals.

Five men emerged from a door in the wall near the miscellaneous items. She quickly crawled to the row of artifacts near the opening, angling to run if necessary.

"It's already gone," one of the men said.

Cameron peered around the display to the shortest of the group, who remained too close to the exit for her to slip away.

"Find them. We know they're still here," someone yelled. "The system has only been down less than fifteen minutes."

She pulled out one those special business cards and flung it down the aisle. The short man grunted the moment it made contact with his chest. He stumbled to the wall before crashing into a chair on display. Cameron was grateful that Bishop insisted her aim be perfect when throwing cards even more so than a gun. Firing a weapon would have immediately revealed her location and decreased the chances of a successful exit.

"What the hell?" One of the men nearest him yelled as several pairs of feet shuffled across the polished concrete floor. Cameron darted to the opening, taking the stairs two at time. She turned, pulling the trigger, and firing on the man who entered at the base. She heard a thud as she neared the top. The white door cracked open. Her heart thumped as she swung her gun upward toward a bronze face with locs peeking out of a skull cap.

"Greg." She pushed him out of the way seconds before bullets sprayed the closing door.

Greg pressed his 6'3 frame against the wall. "How many?"

"Three." She nudged him, pointing toward the back entrance.

Their feet pounded across the stonewashed oak planks. "We're on our way out," Greg said.

"More company coming up the rear," Rob shot back.

Shuffling on his end meant he was moving into the driver's seat. "I'm swinging around front," he said.

They reversed direction, hesitating at the basement's threshold as they raced to the front. The door hinge creaked, and Cameron hopped onto the plush carpet in the living room with Greg fast on her tail. A bullet shattered the glass main door that had been ahead of them. She slid the bag over her head, handed it to Greg then kneeled, rolling onto the wood floors before firing three shots. Two bodies dropped as one dove into the kitchen to take cover. She paused, listening for movement on the ceramic tiles. One man stepped from behind the kitchen door but quickly retreated when she fired twice.

Cameron scrambled to her feet as Greg fired a shot across the living room. She turned as a man grunted and pitched forward onto the carpet. "Get to the van."

Greg sprinted to the door with the bag in hand as she backed over the threshold, constantly scanning in both directions.

Wheels screeched in the driveway. Four armed men ran across the yard.

Rob hopped from the van, immediately lifting his weapon and took out one of the four as Greg slipped into the driver's seat.

Cameron turned and ran for the van, alarmed. Her heart sank into her stomach. *Rob doesn't have his vest on.*

"Got to go. Your gift's on its way." Rob pulled out his other firearm as the side door slid open.

A fifth man running across the lawn was squarely in Rob's blind spot aiming for his back. Cameron launched her body in front of Rob, pulling the trigger as she sailed through air.

"No," Rob yelled at the same moment the bullet hit her square in the chest.

CHAPTER 4

Cameron's body slammed onto the lawn, knocking the breath out her lungs. Rob scooped her up and laid her on the floor of the van. The side door slid into place as Greg peeled away from the driveway. The bullets pounded the sides of the van, sounding like marble-sized hail.

"Is she okay?" Greg asked.

Cameron moaned as Rob unzipped her jacket. "I'm going to be sore, but at least I didn't break a rib this time." She stared at the bullet lodged in the Kevlar mere inches from her heart.

Rob sighed and let out a deep breath as his head tilted forward. Cameron sat up, taking the seat next to the Yamaha situated at the rear of the van. Greg decreased his speed. She winced while buckling up. "What did I tell you about always wearing your vest?"

"Won't happen again," Rob replied, sounding regretful as he should. He, of all people, knew how quickly these jobs could become deadly. His cell rang as he slipped into the passenger seat.

Whenever Rob was restricted to the van as support, he felt he didn't need a vest. Nights like these were the reason she was constantly on him and everyone to wear one when they were on a job.

Rob glanced back at her. "The gift has arrived. Right now, they're confiscating his collection."

Cameron didn't bother to ask whether Rob tipped off the FBI or the local authorities. She was grateful the man they thought was their client wasn't on the phone when they checked or this night could have ended very differently.

"Did you see that she still got us paid?" Greg asked, cracking the window to let in the cool Chicago breeze.

She slid the hoodie off her head. "Call Paul in the morning and tell him we finally found his statue."

"Three mil." Rob grinned, rubbing his hands together at the prospect of a three-way split of so much cash. "Sweet."

"Naw. He doubled it last time we spoke." Greg snatched the cap off his locs that flowed down the middle of his back.

"Man, that's even better."

Cameron leaned back and closed her eyes as Rob and Greg talked, and the slow jams wafted from the speakers.

Minutes later, she woke when someone shook her by the shoulder. "Cam, we're here."

She stepped out of the van that had been pulled inside the warehouse and the warmth enveloped her. Bishop was a stickler for Cameron handling or supervising the destruction of all physical evidence, with the exception of bodies. He insisted that she consistently switch up the style of the gloves and shoes she used for each job. Bishop never wanted a specific shoe tread or material to be traced back to them. The man had been smart and thorough. She tossed her gloves and shoes into the incinerator.

Another near-death experience, all to either feed people's obsession or increase their net worth. Her team was at the top of the game but all it would take was one mishap and one unexpected element to irrevocably change the course of their lives. She didn't want to think about Bishop's missing file on the team that could send them to prison.

This evening was the reason she had been torn about retiring. These men were the people she spent holidays with, instead of her blood relatives. Thanks to a youthful adventure and one night in jail, she still had minimum contact with her father and brothers. Her father's mistake of choosing his sons over his only daughter still hurt.

She now wanted to ensure Greg and Rob were ready because she understood the cost of not thinking through a plan. Cameron also didn't want her mother to have to identify her remains in the Cook County morgue. Every time they had a close call, anger at her father burst to the surface like lava spewing from a volcano. While she took responsibility for the choices she made, had her father not kicked her out of the house, maybe she'd have the family she wanted. Instead, she was standing in a warehouse burning evidence so she wouldn't become a part of a system meant to make billions off criminals and innocent men alike. A system where good people who made stupid mistakes were pushed into becoming lifetime criminals. Yet, people like Bishop who had no desire to change their lives managed to stay outside those walls.

Unlike Bishop, Cameron was willing to do penance for her past but not behind bars. Her retirement plan had always been to help people who found themselves in unique life and death situations that law enforcement could not invest the time or the manpower to handle. She knew all too well there were individuals willing to use the things people loved. or feared, to get their way. She didn't want them to be forced into a kill or be killed situation. However, getting out of the business proved to be much more difficult for Cameron than getting in. Something always happened causing her to push back the date.

The acrid smell of the scorched material filled the air causing her nose to crinkle. She climbed the wooden stairs to a small room, changed, grabbed her book bag then joined Rob in a dark corner outside a supply room filled with shelves of gloves, license plates, paint and car parts.

"How do you feel?" Rob asked.

She shrugged. "Alive, so I can't complain."

Cameron smiled, studying the worry lines in his toffee-toned face. Rob, with his knack for research, acquiring information, piecing it together, and identifying problems, could have been an FBI intelligence analyst, or with his computer skills, on a corporate IT team.

Across the warehouse, Greg was replacing the license plates on the van which would go into an auto body shop for a paint job tomorrow. He could have been designing and building cars, not just fixing them.

One fateful night had changed the trajectory of her life. Thinking about the broken judicial system her father and brothers had sworn to "serve and protect" had her wanting to body slam someone to the ground. She clenched her fist, taking slow, deep breaths to calm herself. Something that became necessary every time she thought of her so-called family.

Greg walked over minutes later, rubbing his hands on an old rag. "We're good."

She nodded. Mentally and emotionally, she couldn't handle losing anyone else. Six years had passed before she was finally in a good place after missing a chance of creating her own family. She'd almost lost her life, too. The promise to serve and protect the ones she loved on both sides of the law kept her at odds with herself and in a lifestyle she never wanted.

Her fingers stayed crossed that her plan to do both would work out. Cameron's chest tightened and certainty settled over her as JD's dilemma and Jason's warning flashed in her thoughts. More trouble was on the horizon. Whenever that feeling came, her instincts had been spot on.

"Rob, I need you to check up on JD."

One of the few good things to come out of JD's decision to work for Bishop was meeting Greg, Rob and Trenton. She only wished they had been assigned to work with him the night JD's path took a wrong turn changing the course of both their lives.

Rob and Greg exchanged concerned looks. "You know about JD?"

"What's going on?" Cameron questioned, heading toward the exit.

"He's committed to two years." Rob paused, taking a deep breath as he followed her. "With The Warden."

Cameron whipped her head toward Rob. "What?"

"And from what I know about The Warden, there's no breaking in to get JD out," Greg added.

"He's not in any danger." Rob focused on Cameron as she stepped outside.

She loved her cousin, but in every aspect JD was book smart, not street smart. She didn't think he was naïve anymore but he had a knack for being in the wrong place at a bad time. Hence, how he ended up with The Warden. She weighed her options. None of them were efficient, quick, or would minimize retaliation. "Can one of you get into The Warden's organization?"

"Not close enough to get him out." By the lines etched in Rob's face, Cameron understood he didn't consider getting on The Warden's bad side the best idea either. Point taken.

"Only two women are known to have worked in his organization, period. His current girlfriend and a chick named Desiree, who was killed under mysterious circumstances about three or four years ago. Over the past five years, that's been it," Greg announced as they walked the length of the warehouse toward the nook where their vehicles were tucked away.

Rob turned his head toward Cameron. "The most he allows the girlfriend to do is plan parties and entertain guests."

"The only other women who come anywhere near him are the ones his men bring into the compound on the weekends when the fights are held." Greg sighed as he massaged his temples.

"JD's been in four months. He's probably living the life," Rob stated, ignoring the warning look from Greg. "But that could change. We'll need to keep an ear to the ground in case we need to get him out before his term ends."

Cameron halted and looked at Rob. "I'm getting him out."

"Does he actually need rescuing?" Rob rested his hand on the adjacent brick wall and stared into her eyes. "You're supposed to be retiring soon. Let us handle it unless you're postponing your exit from the business, *again*."

She moved around him, continuing to the corner of the building.

Greg quickened his steps and blocked her path as she rounded the corner. "Sis, it's been ages since we've had to save his ass. Let's take this time to figure out how to extract him without making an enemy out of The Warden or getting ourselves killed," he proposed.

Rob nodded as they slowly moved forward toward their vehicles.

Despite what her boys said, her mind was made up. She couldn't sit idle, waiting for them or Jason to figure it out. JD could get caught in the crossfire of someone aiming for The Warden. She found comfort in the fact that her cousin had been issued a sentence, otherwise he'd be missing and assumed dead. Now she wanted the guy who lied on JD and put him in harm's way. Because there was no way that her cousin stole anything from The Warden. JD hadn't lifted any items since his little stay in Cook County.

Cameron glanced at Rob, taking in the stern expression. "Who's the guy that sent him in?"

"I'll dig for more intel." Rob rubbed the back of his neck, a sure sign of his frustration. "Don't make a move until we have a plan."

Unlike her father, she didn't leave people she loved in volatile situations.

"You won't like this suggestion," Greg hedged, "but you might want to contact at least Hawk or Jamie if you don't want to deal with Jason."

"Let's see what we can come up with first," she said, contemplating the earlier exchange with Jason. They were right. She'd rather stab herself in the neck than ask for assistance. "The Warden's network covers a big area but he has a compound in a little hick town downstate, right?"

Greg shifted his focus to the ground. "Yeah. Not far from a bar where his men hang out."

"Stay out of trouble tonight." Rob exhaled and stopped a few feet from her Kawasaki. "We'll meet tomorrow and see what part of the plan we can set in motion to alleviate your need to do something right now."

She would do the same for either of them if there were in trouble. So they would have to accept her decision. "I have plans," Cameron replied.

The two men exchanged a glance that signaled their disbelief. "If you get yourself killed, you can't save JD," Greg reminded her. "We know —"

"Guys let me break it down for you. Every day his chances of dying increases." Cameron slid her book bag onto her back.

People expected danger to be in their face with an obvious sense of urgency that invoked dread and fear. Cameron knew sometimes it was insidious. Evil didn't always lurk in the shadows looking menacing, that it smiled in people's faces and offered to help. Bishop capitalized on making people feel safe in Cameron's presence when her mission was to destroy their world. JD was not in grave danger but that could change in an instant.

Rob grabbed her shoulders as she turned away.

Cameron snapped around.

He lifted his hands in surrender. "I can't ask anyone about the compound layout. The Warden would be on me in a millisecond." His dark-brown eyes pleaded with Greg to back him up.

"Jason was an undercover agent until he got shot a few years ago," Greg said, suggesting their paths may have crossed.

Cameron frowned, knowing what they wanted wouldn't work. "We have to do this without my brother. Besides, he's not going to give us any information."

"I'm going to leave you with this." Greg handed her the helmet he'd taken off the handlebar. "It seems strange that you're willing to die to get JD out, if necessary, but not willing to see your own brother."

They gave her that knowing stare. Past experience over the ten years they'd been connected, told them Cameron couldn't be talked out of this course of action.

Cameron whipped out her cell, sent a text, then hopped on the Kawasaki. By the time she made it to her destination, she would have all the information she needed. Cameron watched them slow drag toward their vehicles before she put on her helmet.

Damn you, Greg.

He did have a point. She would visit Jason, but not tonight. She'd reach out to her contacts first. Hopefully, she wouldn't need her big brother at all.

CHAPTER 5

Jason slid behind the wheel of a Toyota Tacoma. After a final look at his girlfriend's building, he pulled off, deciding against returning to the warmth of her embrace. His mom really liked this one and so did he, but his extensive "traveling" for work would eventually drive her away just like the others.

He sighed as he headed to Rob's spot. This man was the only friend of Cameron's he'd met. After finding out from his mom that she had a day of pampering planned with Cameron, Jason knew without question she was about to make her move. Cameron didn't do "girly stuff" unless a purpose was attached. He had people following her for the last week but she managed to evade a good majority of them.

Jason parked in front of a greystone building, then walked around the corner with umbrella in hand to a storefront office in Bronzeville. Jason shivered as cold rain drops fell from the cloudy afternoon sky.

Through the glass he recognized the man at the desk, even though he now wore a beard.

Jason pulled the heavy, smoked-glass door open and bells chimed as he crossed the threshold.

Rob's head snapped up and his hand slid under the black desk, as he came to his feet. "How may I help you?"

"Talk my sister out of whatever she's planning to do," Jason said, as he approached.

"Did you say crawl through the eye of a needle?" Rob asked, walking to the door, locking it, and pulling the shades. "Because that would be easier than changing Cam's mind."

"Cam may think we don't love her, but we do." Jason leaned the umbrella against the desk and glanced around the space furnished with minimal office but very high-end equipment. "When she goes in, it'll put her on the FBI radar."

"We've tried." Rob perched on the slick edge of the desk, crossing his arms. "She's not budging. Besides she's not going in unless she feels JD's life is on the line."

If history served right, Cameron would first attempt to move near their cousin. Which would put her on The Warden's radar. That wasn't much better. "Can you at least delay her a month or two?"

"You may love her, but don't know your sister very well." Rob chuckled, eyes crinkling in the corners. "The best I can do is provide the support she needs."

"There has to be someone that can get through to her." Jason's phone vibrated. He checked his message and frowned. His people had lost sight of Cameron again.

"Yes, but he's with The Warden and I doubt you want to involve your mom in this." Rob raised his eyes and tightened his lips.

"Fine." Jason glared at Rob as he grabbed his umbrella, realizing how much of Cameron's life he'd missed. He didn't even know if she'd met Rob before Bishop or because of him.

"I'll try again, but the outcome won't be any different." Rob followed him to the door.

Jason froze. "I was afraid of that."

"She's trying to retire." Rob unlocked the door, but didn't open it.

"Seriously?" Jason asked, taken aback by the news.

Rob gave him a half smile. "Yes."

He waited, wanting more details, like when and why now, but Rob gave him a tight-lipped smile indicating that he had said as much as he was willing to say.

"*Retiring.*" Looking Rob in the eyes, Jason asked, "Can you at least tell me when she plans to leave?"

"In a couple of days." Rob pushed the metal bar out, and a spray of rain rushed in.

Jason opened the umbrella. "Thanks."

The cold rain pounded the ground as Jason sprinted to the Tacoma. Maybe with Cameron retiring, he could consider his next career move. Something that didn't require him to lie to his girlfriend about his extended time away. He had stayed at the agency longer than he intended mostly because if Cameron ended up going to prison, it may be the very thing that would destroy the family unit. Their mother was unaware that Cameron was living a double life.

He was struggling to break the cycle of dysfunction between them, but their meetings usually ended in an argument. His girlfriend gave him a hard time about being insensitive to Cameron's situation. She was the only one in the immediate family who was punished for what happened that night. Incurring the wrath of their father was nothing compared to being exiled. Now he understood why his mom was always on him about Cameron. She had Rob and her crew, but not family.

Jason headed to Cameron's brick ranch house on the other side of town and waited outside for hours before she showed up. The heavy rain had become a light drizzle and he'd tired of the repetitive songs on the radio.

She tapped on his window.

He lowered the glass.

"Wondered when you'd make an appearance." Cameron stood, hovering over him in all-black attire, looking more like their father than their mother. Probably due to that stern 'you're three seconds from death' expression that Jake used to scare all his children straight. How she managed to look like the person she hated so much was amazing. "Don't you have a job?"

"I do. One that my baby sister is making twice as hard for me." Jason nodded for her to get in as rain dripped into the truck.

"I haven't seen this much of you since you and your brothers were too afraid to tell mom no." Cameron pushed away from the Tacoma.

Jason raised the window, climbed out of his vehicle, and scrambled to catch up with her.

"Cam, stay out of it, at least for one month. Let me see if I can get JD without causing a stir." Jason stepped in front of her before she reached the concrete stairs.

She pushed him to the side. "Do what you think is best and I'll do the same."

Jason watched her enter the house, knowing he had to get word on the inside. The Warden didn't allow any personal phones, which was why JD hadn't been able to contact anyone who could keep the family updated. Any calls made on the cell phones The Warden issued as well as his land lines were reviewed every thirty minutes before a program alerted the crime boss to any new and unknown number. With The Warden reducing his crew, Jason hated that he couldn't get close to his contact and would have to put a signal in place and let his person come to him.

CHAPTER 6

Life rarely goes as planned but Daron Kincaid never expected that the survival of his family would require him to become the head of a criminal organization. His former wife taught him the hard way the illusion of trust was a dangerous thing. Her betrayal nearly destroyed him and became a catalyst for the descent from successful business man and highly regarded philanthropist to a criminal.

He sat in the back of the limo across from his client liaison. Lex was charismatic, intelligent and an excellent negotiator which made him perfect for the job. Daron reviewed the watch list data on the new people who moved into town within the last three months. He flipped through the five images, stopping at one of Tandria Jenkins. He stared at the screen wondering if she was as captivating in person as her picture depicted. Maybe one of these individuals was behind his latest issues.

In the last few months, there had been more attempts to steal the cargo containers and entry devices than in the last few years. The units were used to ship illegal merchandise as long as it wasn't guns, people, live animals, or drugs. The containers could only be opened by a designated tablet, otherwise the locking mechanism would change every sixty seconds. That feature made him a pretty penny in the streets, especially since the client always had the entry device before the container was shipped.

"Red called," Steve said, and glanced through the lowered partition as they sat at a red light. He was former military and one of few people Daron allowed to guard him. "He's going underground to track a lead on who has Bishop and Kimura's name circulating in the streets."

Daron looked up at the mention of his former mentor and Kimura, one of Bishop's most lethal team members, as Steve returned his attention to the road. "I can give them Bishop's cemetery address. And, I suspect Kimura is in town or will be soon."

Lex tore his eyes away from the entry tablet and focused on Daron. "You sure she'll follow JD here."

"Almost positive." Based on the story Daron heard about Kimura, he was ninety-nine percent sure she'd make an appearance once she knew about JD. He swiped back to the image of Michelle Halston, pulling up her data.

"Since Nicco went to talk to Cole and he had an *accident*." Lex used his finger to make air quotes as he spoke. "I believe you."

When Daron found out JD was working under Cole's street distribution unit, he assigned him to the main office. The warehouse's cameras caught Cole giving JD the new orders that resulted in a stolen shipment after being delivered to wrong address.

"I'm watching his back with the added bonus of knowing Kimura will come make sure he's okay." Daron returned his focus to the screen.

Bishop mentioned in confidence that JD had a photographic memory and was an excellent person to send in when electronic devices were restricted. Cole accusing JD of stealing created an opportunity to throw JD in Daron's second chance program, especially with individuals asking around about Kimura and Bishop.

"Have you considered she might take you out before you're formerly introduced?" Lex asked, pulling a padded box closer.

Daron chuckled. "Based on what I know, unless I physically threatened him. I shouldn't have a problem."

"You're putting her in danger luring her here while you got eyes on you," Steve said, maneuvering out of fundraiser traffic onto a less crowded street.

"Once I can confirm her identity, I'll take care of it." Daron slid the tablet in an inner pocket of his jacket. "So consider JD family."

"But don't let anyone know," Lex added, placing the entry device in the padded box.

"We're here," Steve announced, parking the limo near the brick wall of the corner building in the alley.

Lex glanced at his watch. "Nicco should be arriving with JD soon."

"When this is over, ride up front with Steve." Daron scrolled through his cell taking one last look at the meeting details. "I want to have a private word with JD."

"Nicco's here," Steve announced.

Lex passed his cell to Steve then slid out the limo with the box. Once outside the vehicle, he adjusted the three-thousand-dollar charcoal-grey suit jacket he wore.

"Stay alert," Daron reminded them as the cool breeze carried the scent of garbage in to assault his nose.

Lex joined JD, who wore a black tailored suit with his long hair pulled back into a ponytail. Daron took the notebook like device that Lex passed back to him, sitting it on the leather seat. Nicco pulled off as JD and Lex made their way to a warehouse on the opposite end of the alley to meet with their contact, Gavin.

"I launched the drone." Steve glanced back, frowning. "Did you expect Thad?"

Thad was a hard-core gangster whose name carried a lot of weight in the streets from coast to coast. He was the type of man, you'd rather for him to send an enforcer than handle it personally. The last guy who crossed Thad had received a special visit from him and was rumored to have died a slow painful death, then was shipped back to his second in command.

"Why would he fly in for this?" Daron pulled out his tablet to link to the drone's feed to see the 6'5" muscle-bound man standing outside a

Hummer limousine. "Make sure we don't have shooters up high."

Daron watched the image rise past the warehouse's red brick to the ledge of the building and swing around to all the nearby roof tops. He could see the sun setting but not one sign of a gun man. "Make sure that Thad's shipping container doesn't have guns or drugs."

"I'll put Nicco on it."

Daron didn't want to go to war with Thad, but he couldn't allow him to slide contraband into the shipment. It would set a bad precedent.

"We have a motorcycle about two blocks up in a cross alley." Steve announced.

The bike sped up the alley heading their way as JD and Gavin, who had the box tucked under his arm, stepped outside. The motorcycle stopped short of the warehouse, turning abruptly. The masked passenger hopped off the back of the bike seconds before the cyclist zipped off. Lex and Thad's other associate emerged as the slim man ran past snatching the box. JD grabbed the guy's shirt blocking Lex's shot. Gavin struggled to get the device, causing JD to lose his grip. The thief bolted with the four men on his heels.

Steve was out of his seat. "I don't have a shot." He raced around the front of the vehicle. The guy swiveled to avoid Steve.

Daron stepped out, extended his arm and slammed it against the man's neck. His body hit the asphalt hard.

Thad's Hummer rounded the corner as Daron grabbed the box. "I hope the money was worth it. What comes next will have you regretting this moment for the rest of your life."

The man writhed and moaned on the ground as the group of men hoovered over him.

"You're right," Thad said, pushing past his men. "But I'll be the one making him wish he'd made a different choice." He snatched the thief from the ground like he was a rag doll, then ripped the mask off. The man's ivory skin was bright red and his eyes were bulging.

Daron extended the package. Thad kept his death grip on the back of the thief's neck as he nodded toward the box. Gavin, who had one brown eye and one blue, quickly stepped forward and averted his gaze as he retrieved the package. Daron was immediately suspicious.

Lex and JD leaned against the limo, as Thad escorted the man back to the vehicle with his associates trailing behind. After Thad stuffed the thief in and the other guy slid into the passenger side, Gavin turned back to the limo. Two seconds later, a muffled scream pierced the air.

"Gentleman let's roll." Daron slid in the back of the limo knowing they'd have to retrieve the drone when they were a few blocks away. He also wanted to get out while the limos were still arriving for the fundraiser.

"You're in the back," Lex said, nodded toward the open door as JD went for the passenger seat.

JD's eyes grew twice their size as he followed the instructions.

Steve handed Lex the drone control then raised the divider between the two sections.

"How do you like the art pad?" Daron asked, picking up the sketch book tablet that felt like art paper but the images were stored on a memory card.

JD rubbed his throat and fidgeted with a button on the shirt. "It's excellent for drawing something I know will become digital."

Daron flipped through the images of the clients and the locations. Bishop was right, in addition to having a mind like a computer, he was an extremely talented artist. As far as he knew only four people were aware JD had photographic memory. Bishop didn't want that common knowledge and Daron understood why, especially considering what they did. The organization was only as strong as its weakest link. He couldn't afford for some of JD's shortcomings to become an issue for the organization which is why he had several talks.

"I still need to draw the image of the two men working with Thad." Daron switched out the memory cards and handed the device back to JD.

He needed them to import into his database as reference in case one of them was in on the attempted theft. If either one was associated with the person attempting to interfere with his plans, Daron would have them taken care of, discreetly or at least The Warden would.

♦ ♦ ♦

The essential personnel with Daron's crew were gathered in the spacious office at the compound, waiting to figure out why he'd called this meeting. The space contained a leather couch, love seat, two matching chairs and a bar. Everyone took a seat as Lex and Steve sauntered past and entered through the walnut door behind him. He pulled out the tablet, opened up the watch list document then sat it on a mahogany desk.

"This should be a quick one. Did we cross anybody off our future agenda?" Daron asked, referring to the list of new people who moved into town that they were watching.

"Yes," Steve replied, parking in one of the empty seats. "Three."

"We only have Michelle and Tandria remaining," Lex added, scrolling through his phone.

"I'm waiting on a few things before I remove Michelle," Eric added.

"Updates?" Daron asked, frowning and focusing on Lex. His men had been waiting with bated breath for Tandria to get the green light, but something about her fascinated him, which is why he put Lex on that assignment. She reminded him of someone but he hadn't figured out who.

"We're still digging." Lex's mouth curled into a devilish grin. "Maureen came into the bar soon after I started testing Tandria, so we really didn't have a chance to gauge her reaction."

"I hoped you remembered you were on the clock. If you want to ask her out, you'll have to create an opportunity on your own time," Daron said in a stern tone. "If she's not who she appears to be and she walks in on your arm ... "

"She's my issue to deal with." Lex gave a sly grin, adjusting the jacket of his suit. "Understood."

Daron noted some of the glares shot Lex's way as he turned to Eric. "Anything to report?"

"The dates for Miami are locked in." Eric scrolled through his cell. "The Championship fighters have been contacted."

"Prescott, pushed his arrival back so he won't be flying out with us," Mac added.

"Anything else?" Daron's cell chimed with a reminder. When met with silence, he announced, "Alright. Meeting's over."

He followed the group out of the office. Daron's gaze went to the stairs and settled on the familiar form making her way down.

Tia rocked a revealing red halter dress on her petite, hour-glass figure. His team was surprised Tia finally won him over and he allowed her to move in last month. Everyone knew Tia was chasing money but the relationship was a business decision. At least he recognized exactly what he was getting with her. Tia was always there since she was supposedly related to Mac.

"Hey, Tia, beautiful as always," Lex smiled as she neared them, holding a silver clutch.

Tia slowly spun around, pulling her waist-length black weave over her shoulder. The move showed the dip in the rear of the dress, which displayed a tattoo on her lower back and brought attention to a rear end so large it could have its own area code. She glanced over her shoulder seductively at Daron. "You like?"

Tia sashayed over to Daron and wrapped her arms around him.

"Gorgeous," Daron said, with his hands on her waist.

Steve acknowledge her presence with a nod. "I'll bring the car around."

"Give us a minute and we'll be ready." Daron needed to wrap up one thing before heading out.

Lex threw him a look like good luck then lifted a hand to say bye as he exited.

"Sweetie. You may think this is sudden but I love you," Tia said, stepping back and staring into his eyes. "I really want things to work this ... this relationship .... this moment with us to last."

Daron was surprised at the depth of emotion behind the words and in her eyes. "I wouldn't have invited you to live with me if I didn't believe you wanted this to work."

"Have you thought about retiring?" Tia smiled up at him.

"Are you scared of my lifestyle?" Daron had one of his men escorting her around town as a precaution.

"When I was young and foolish, I didn't appreciate being settled and wanted adventure. Now that I'm older, I recognize the specialness I let slip away." Tia laid her head on his chest. "I found something exquisite with you and I don't want to make the same mistake."

"When we learn from past mistakes, we make better choices and increase our chances of making magic happen next time." He hoped that answer would satisfy her. Things would have to be taken on a day by day basis. Daron hadn't entered this relationship with Tia for love. Besides, the man Tia wanted access to died the day he discovered his wife was cheating on him.

Tia went up on her toes. Daron leaned down to kiss her, catching sight of Mac sliding back around the corner into the hallway.

Is she really having a change of heart or is this a strategy to gain more access to my money?

CHAPTER 7

"Lex Keyes."

The announcement of the name of The Warden's chief liaison snatched Cameron's attention like a fire alarm going off in the middle of the night. Mr. Walsh's gaze lasered in on her as he continued, "This is my new right hand, Tandria Jenkins."

Adrenaline surged through Cameron's body as she smiled up at Lex, who wore a navy tailored suit more fitting for a fashion magazine cover model, instead of with The Warden's squad. "Nice to meet you, Mr. Keyes."

The man, who was gorgeous, sexy and had enough charm to make most women drop it like it's hot, gave her an intense look, extended his light golden-brown hand. "The pleasure's all mine."

"Please make him comfortable while I make a quick call." Mr. Walsh, whose pale face lit up like a little boy opening birthday presents, ambled into his cluttered office, one that spoke to art acquisition he had specialized in for twenty-five years.

"Of course." Cameron stood. "Mr. Keyes, would you like some coffee, water or juice?"

"Call me Lex." This time, he gave her an impish grin as he studied her face, almost as if he was trying to figure out if he knew her. "And coffee would be great."

Cameron felt the heat of his gaze as she grabbed a cup off the shelf in the breakroom and mentally thumbed through the possible reasons that brought one of The Warden's top men directly into The Welshman Project, which didn't have any reflection on the type of dealings that they were into. The Warden's crew was known to put any people moving into town under surveillance. However, they only made actual contact for two reasons; to get laid or when someone had done something to make them suspicious and were flagged.

What did I do that caught their attention? Maybe it was not asking enough questions that made her stand out. Even those avoiding The Warden were curious about the compound.

Within days after that meeting with her men, Cameron moved to this small town just over two hours from Chicago under the alias Tandria. For her own peace of mind, she wanted to be close and prepared to take action if circumstances with JD changed. The reality was, she still might not make it in time, but she couldn't rest if she didn't at least try.

Cameron had only been in town three weeks and was already restless, listless and stir-crazy. Unfortunately, the waiting game had her reviewing her current situation, the past, and the future. This experience felt like she'd arrived at a movie expecting action with a little drama, but landed in a Hallmark production instead. She felt terrible for feeling this way but she'd rather have had to rescue JD. At least she could've come in guns blazing, fists flying, and been done with everything. She was bored and antsy like a kid after the first hour of a sixteen-hour road trip from Chicago to Disney World.

She turned back toward Lex. His eyes dropped to her cleavage. Evidently, the man was living up to his "player" reputation since he couldn't flirt with her while staking out her apartment.

"Mister ... " She paused, smiling. Cameron handed him the mug as she experienced a strange mix of anticipation, excitement, and guilt. "I mean ... Lex. What line of business are you in?"

"I have an entrepreneurial spirit, so I dabble in everything." Lex leaned on the wall near the threshold of Walsh's office, his gaze latched onto her every move.

"What dabbling brings you here?" Cameron reclaimed her chair, crossed one leg over the other, allowing her skirt to ride up higher on her thigh as she logged into the computer.

"Giving your boss a few friendly referrals," Lex replied, and there was a huskiness in his tone that she recognized as a man on the prowl.

Cameron cut her eyes over to him. "And what do you get out of the deal?"

Lex's gaze narrowed as he paused with the mug midway to his lips. "You're an inquisitive little thing, aren't you?"

She returned her focus to her computer. "Merely keeping you entertained."

"Would you like to accompany me to the compound on Friday?" Lex asked in a voice like spun silk, but rubbed her more like scratchy wool.

Cameron let out a sigh, relieved Lex was upholding his reputation. "Is that a night club?" She didn't look away from the contract on the screen. Everyone else she spoke to, only mentioned the place in passing. No reason for him to believe she would know anything more.

"I forgot you haven't been in town long." He strutted over to perch on the edge of her desk as if he owned the joint. "It's a VIP type of spot. Not everyone can get in."

"It's not the best idea for me to go out with Mr. Walsh's associates." She hated to pass on this opportunity, but being on Mr. One-and-Done's arm could ruin her opportunity to get into the fights that could earn her money, but also the only way she'd have consistent access into the compound on a regular basis.

Cameron would rather aim for the low-hanging fruit such as the restaurant owners, the single and shady local politicians or any minor players from The Warden's crew who were invited to every event, than shoot herself in the foot by getting involved with someone at the top. She needed a chance at getting in on multiple occasions.

Lex's eyes widened, his eyebrow lifted as though he couldn't fathom her answer before he gave her a close-lipped smile. "I guess I'll have to forget my referral information."

"Mr. Keyes, save the threats for my boss." Cameron stood, snatching a document from her desk before sliding past him to the copier.

"In that case, I'll call every day until I get you to say yes."

She glanced over her shoulder. Lex had cocked his head to the side to stare at her behind. Cameron replied in the most disinterested tone she could manage, "If you must."

The door to Walsh's office opened, he frowned at the intimate proximity between Lex and Cameron, straightened his expression, then waved their guest inside. "Did you finish the changes on that memo?"

"It's in your inbox."

"How did I ever exist without you?"

"You haven't," she shot back as he smiled and ignored Lex's low appreciative whistle.

Mr. Walsh, a short Irish man, had no clue his new temporary assistant was already knowledgeable about his import/export business. Shortly after enrolling to Loyola University and obtaining a master's degree, she began working for Bishop. He suggested she pick up extra classes to make sure arts and antiques were subjects she was well-versed in. Nothing in the fake resume that Rob had distributed through the proper channels indicated any of those things. Painful, was the only way to describe watching Mr. Walsh underprice items worth far more. For the sake of her cover, she couldn't point it out. She also frequented the local bars, attempting to make new friends; all to validate her cover story and help her stay sane.

Lex stood, gazed into her eyes for a moment. "I'll be talking with you, Tandria."

Cameron debated whether she should accept his offer. She needed to confirm if she'd been red flagged before running into a situation blind. While she'd been able to fool Rob and Greg for a split second, if JD saw her close up and actually recognized her before she had the lay of the land, they'd both be dead.

She rolled the chair back from the desk, looking through the glass window divide into her new boss's office as Lex and Mr. Walsh engaged in conversation. Cameron had temporarily replaced a woman on maternity leave and now worked as an administrative assistant—an easy cover. The town hadn't been as quaint as she'd expected. The Warden and his people lived in a gated community so obscure she couldn't get a decent sighting of the compound. Her drive-bys did result in several sightings of her cousin, who somehow didn't seem any worse for wear.

A solid extraction strategy was in development, one which included a method of keeping her cousin from going missing, to prison, or ending up dead like others who had crossed The Warden. Every attempt to figure out how to breech The Warden's compound led to a dead end. The Warden's multi-layered security system was the reason his enemies always tried to hit him in the streets. If Cameron could get in The Warden's compound during fight nights, then she'd have the layout and an opportunity to record something that would help back The Warden off, if the need arose. Having those two key things and knowing the city increased the odds of her being successful if JD found himself in trouble.

By the time Lex came out of the office, Cameron still held firm to her no. She hoped it wouldn't prevent her from getting another opportunity.

Cameron shot off a text confirming tonight plans with Maureen, an irritatingly-bubbly interior designer she'd met while grabbing lunch at a restaurant near the office.

Her thoughts returned to JD's situation. The information she'd gathered prior to arriving was vital in forming a plan to look out for JD. She was able to link names, Lex, Eric, Steve, and Mac within The Warden's organization with faces. The only people in her file on The Warden who she hadn't seen in person were Prescott, Daron and Daron's girlfriend, Tia. She'd been shocked to see a familiar face in the pictures. His face was fuller but she was fairly sure it was the same Daron she'd met under the alias Autumn years ago. At least things wouldn't be awkward when they crossed paths since he wouldn't recognize her because she looked nothing like she did then.

"Think about the invitation," Lex urged as he swept past her with Mr.

Walsh right behind him.

"I'll see you tomorrow," Mr. Walsh announced, barely glancing her way.

Cameron shut down her computer, then headed toward the restroom, down the hall from the office. She pondered whether she'd have turned down Eric if he'd shown up instead of Lex. Her attraction to Eric was an unexpected distraction. She needed to find a maintenance man whom she felt ambivalent toward and had no connection to The Warden to help take the edge off. Cameron knew the price of being preoccupied and would continue to make every effort to steer clear of Eric. Not being able to participate in her normal evening activities—working the "redistribution" business, the occasional underground fight, among other things—had her searching for trouble to get into. Eric Tillman definitely qualified.

She entered the small restroom and retouched her make-up. JD probably wouldn't recognize her unless he happened to catch her at work with her hair up. Her cousin wasn't always as discreet as she needed him to be. She hoped that wouldn't become an issue. Her hazel eyes were no longer hidden under brown contacts. No one could tell she had dimples courtesy of monthly injections. Bishop had developed a temporary cream and a longer lasting shot because he believed dimples were too distinctive of a trait.

Folding her suit, she slid it in an oversized purse. After stepping into the elevator, she'd taken off the fake glasses and removed some of the pull pins holding her hair in a tight bun. Cameron ran long, manicured nails through her hair, which hung past her shoulders as she made her way out the building.

Minutes later, she shrugged off a light jacket before sliding into the driver's seat of her Camaro. As she drove out heading to Boomerangs, a sports bar The Warden's crew patronized most often, Cameron noticed a dark sedan pulled out behind her.

Dammit. She had been flagged. What other reason existed for them to be tailing her after Lex showed up putting that invite on the table. The coming weeks, without a doubt, would be interesting.

CHAPTER 8

People were under the mistaken impression that Daron's empire was crumbling—being weakened from within. He was well aware of everything that was happening and the efforts of those within trying to weaken the organization. A few surprises might have caught him off guard momentarily, but certain illicit activities of the people in his organization were not one of them. His key team members were drinking and catching up before heading to a reception down the hall.

Mac, who was the shortest of the crew, stood and grabbed everyone's attention. "Let me tell you about Mr. Ladies' Man here." His chubby mocha cheeks vibrated as he chuckled and lifted his glass toward Lex, who glared at him.

Daron slipped out of the room to take a call as Mac began sharing a story, entertaining the guys at Lex's expense. The guys couldn't stop laughing.

"Your timetable has been changed. He will make his move in the next few weeks not in the Fall as originally expected," the deep, gravelly voice on the other end warned. "If you don't have everything in place, you won't like the outcome."

"Be prepared to hold up your end," Daron growled as he walked further into the hallway that separated the two wings of his mansion. "If you don't, you'll be begging for the gates of hell to open up and take you in."

"Are you threatening me?"

"I don't make threats. I make promises." Daron disconnected the call, moving back toward the office's side door.

He hated rushing, but this situation with wrapping up this deal was getting out of his control. He'd always loved spy movies with all their cool high-tech gadgets. That's all he wanted to do when he grew up. Daron glanced in the office, thinking about the series of unfortunate events had set his life off course. His father's unexpected death sent him and his brother, Troy, reeling. Troy dropped out of college and became involved in a number of dirty dealings. Their mother managed to keep Daron on the right path for a while, then he received an offer he couldn't refuse.

Years ago, Daron had the tech business he'd always wanted and a beautiful wife that made him the envy of most men. He had no complaints about any aspect of his life until he was ambushed, attacked, and left to die in a cabin in the mountains by his wife's lover, who also was Daron's business associate. The two conspired to take over his business, cleaned out his bank account, and sold all his belongings before he could fully recover.

They didn't enjoy his riches for long.

Daron slid his phone in his pocket before reentering the room. Eric and Pedro lounged on a plush, black leather couch facing a mahogany desk. Mac was parked in the matching chair while Lex sat on the bar stool.

Eric turned his focus from Lex back to Mac and said, "Tell the story one more time."

"Yeah, we're rolling back from the bar. Lex's telling me about this woman so fine she'd make you stutter." Mac ducked the magazine Lex threw at him, which barely missed his head.

"Which one?" Daron asked, moving near Lex who had one arm

draped on the metal back of the bar stool and his middle finger extended for Mac's benefit.

"Tandria," Eric supplied.

"So we're rolling and he calls this chick." Mac pretended to be driving. "He said about two sentences, then he turns to me with this shell-shocked look and says 'I ... she' then he puts the phone back to his ear and listens."

"'I don't believe she hung up on me,'" Eric and Pedro chimed in, then doubled over with laughter.

"The look on his face!" Mac managed between guffaws. "I had to pull over to the side of the road to stop laughing."

"No, not Lex, the ladies' man," Daron teased, clasping a hand on Lex's shoulder, laughing when he tensed up.

"Yes. Lex, the lover boy." Mac held his side as he looked down. "There's a dent in the car where his chin hit the floor."

"I like the lady already." Daron nudged Lex in the side. "I'd tell you to invite her to the party next weekend but dial tones can't get a yes for an answer."

Lex rose from the leather bar stool and adjusted his jacket. "By next week, she'll be melting in my hands like ice cream in the summer heat."

Mac stared at him with his mouth twisted in disbelief. "I got three thousand that says she won't."

"Fine. Maybe not melting." Lex finished the contents of his glass. "I need another round and to mingle with some of our beautiful female guests."

"It happens to the best of us," Eric teased.

"You should know. Did that Renee chick from the bar ever give you tips on playing pool?" Lex inquired, getting an evil eye from Eric because of another woman who slid through town and swept up Mac's hard-earned cash and Eric's ego.

"He got you on that one," Pedro snickered, trailing them out of the side door.

Daron leaned on the desk. "Eric, wait."

A flash of panic entered Eric's eyes as he complied.

"Have her checked out one more time," Daron whispered into Eric's ear. His focus remained on the corridor where several of them congregated outside the open door. Tia approached wearing a stunning hot-pink dress on her petite frame and gave Mac a quick embrace, but there was a lingering familiarity that put Daron on notice.

Eric nodded. "And if nothing new pops up?"

Daron smiled as she came and stood in the opening, waiting for him to come out. "Then send her boss an invitation to attend with a request for her to be there."

Eric acknowledged Tia's presence with a nod and smile before she moved, leaning on the wall across from the office. "Make sure it's an offer that her boss won't let her refuse," Eric added.

"As always, we're seeing eye to eye. It'll be my entertainment for the evening seeing Lex turned down live and in living color." Daron grinned as he grabbed an envelope off the desk.

"Before you call it a night, get in touch with Prescott. He claims to have a great new contact and I want you to vet him." Daron's gaze went to Tia. "Also confirm when he'll be back in the States."

Eric flipped his wrist up, checking the time. "I'll take care of this before I make it to the reception."

"Last thing." Daron glanced at Tia to see the narrowed eyes staring back at him, tight lips and head cocked to the side as she returned to the open door. "See if you can track down this current Lucifer rumor, make sure it doesn't have any teeth."

Lucifer, evidently, was someone who had it in for Daron and was coming after his organization.

Eric grimaced before he replied, "Will do."

"And if it does, put a million-dollar price tag on the Miami fight tickets in our section and triple that for the seats directly surrounding us." Daron stood, handed him the envelope. "Tell Tia I'll be out in a minute."

Eric stepped outside and gave her the message. Tia pulled her waist-length black weave over her shoulder as she changed directions and followed Eric. She glanced back, but Eric closed the door before she could say anything.

The earlier call had Daron's thoughts on what he'd sacrificed for this moment. He couldn't be this close to finishing what he started, only to have it all slip away.

After Adrian tried to kill him, the road to recovery was brutal. Troy offered him a partnership in a business and a promise to find and destroy his wife and Adrian. Troy almost died trying to track those two down. A close family friend made sure Troy was taken somewhere safe until he healed. Daron found another means to exact revenge that would keep him and his family safe. He had devoted over five years of dealing with evil, risking lives and losing parts of his self that he couldn't get back to make that happen.

The downside of the plan was Daron had to leave himself vulnerable for it to work. He was not only forced to stay in this toxicity that he called a relationship but also pretend to be happy. The last few days she's been acting like a woman in love, not one who merely wanted access to money and power. He didn't trust it but Tia could bury his business if he ended things now. He suspected Kimura, the woman who saved his brother's life, was one of the two woman that had moved into town. Daron needed to protect her from what he knew was coming, but she'd also be his special weapon. No one would suspect she was dangerous and had the skills to assist his team.

Daron pulled up the information on Mickey, the politician who was searching for an organization to hold down his illegal assets while he smiled and played nice with the public. Mickey was a last resort, but Daron's freedom was riding on what happened these next couple of weeks.

CHAPTER 9

Cameron's Saturday morning plans were derailed before she ever opened her eyes. She wondered what emergency had occurred for the trainer, who was the conduit to communicate with her team, requested a weekend session. Carrying a Nike bag, she pulled open the door to the gym, stepped off the concrete and onto the rubber flooring. She cut through the weight machines, which were brightly lit by the sunlight coming through the large front window, to the lockers. Her stomach churned when she laid eyes on her trainer. Oscar stood by the entrance of the women's locker room with a "grab and go" bookbag, packed with her supplies and gear for unexpected trips to handle major issues.

He held out the bag as she approached. "Onyx rises at Midnight."

Damn. Cameron hesitated a moment to absorb the implications. Trepidation filled every fiber of her body and caused her to shiver involuntarily. She scanned the nearly empty gym that smelled like heavy duty disinfectant and had a faint hint of lemon in the air, at least for the time being. The last thing she needed was someone associated with Bishop searching for them at any stage of the game. She nodded and headed into the locker room.

Be grateful for small favors. Had the message been *Onyx lives*, it would have meant she was being flung into the depths of hell that would obliterate the parts of her life that she loved the most. While she was going stir crazy sitting around waiting for something to happen to JD, she didn't need the kind of problems that came from anything associated with her former boss.

During most of the training session, Cameron prioritized her to do list. Tonight, she'd sneak out of town to handle business and try to get back before her shift at Welshman's on Monday.

"I love working out with you," Oscar teased, leaning on the mirrored wall in front of her, bringing her out of her reflection. He held both hands out for her to tap with her toes, an exercise that worked her back, shoulders, arms, and abs. "I get paid to watch you work yourself out and pretend to push you. That's a bonus"

Sweat streamed down her face as she completed the last set of the exercise and she kicked his hand hard.

"No abusing the trainer," he jested, as he snatched a towel off his shoulder, and stepped closer to her.

Her movement halted for a moment before she dropped her body to the ground, then a thought came to mind. Wiping her face with the towel he'd handed her, she asked, "What's up with that Maureen chick?"

"All I know is she appeared on the scene shortly after the compound was completed. She seems to be legit," he insisted in a low voice as they made their way to the machines to work out her lower body.

"I seem legit," she whispered as she passed him. The number of bodies in the gym had increased and the lemony smell caved to the collective body odor and disinfected spray that were being used to wipe down the machines.

Oscar squatted next to the quad machine, adjusting the weight with a few more pounds. "I know someone I can discreetly ask about her."

"Perfect." She slid her body onto the vinyl seat.

"FYI, the rumor is Lucifer is supposedly making his move in the Fall." He stood, resumed the normal level of his voice saying, "Come on. Three sets of twenty-five."

She acknowledged his other comment with a nod. That gave her a few months to do what she needed to get her cousin out safely before Lucifer made his move against The Warden. Every time she passed JD there wasn't a single hint of distress in his expression.

Oscar reached into his pocket, pulling out his cell. "Jay 3 is on the move."

She shook her head. The one thing she knew was that her brother, Jason, couldn't get near her, otherwise he would immediately be on The Warden's radar. She needed to be off The Warden's watch list so she could do some staking out of her own before her brother got in her way. Cameron would feel better once she obtained something incriminating on The Warden.

The energy changed in the room seconds before Oscar tapped her thigh and glanced to his right. Daron and Eric entered in workout clothes, towels thrown over their shoulders, and water bottles in hand. Daron Kincaid, with his smooth terra cotta brown skin, was definitely the man she met years ago at an event in Chicago. He'd picked up a little weight but it looked good on him since it seemed to be all muscle. He topped the six-foot caramel brother next to him by three inches.

The two of them moved across the floor like they owned the place. When they stopped at the chest press machine, people scattered, clearing out the weights area. Daron oozed power, which probably came from working with influential men. Her gaze shifted and roamed Eric's slim but well-built physique. *Mmm. Still sexy.*

"Let's do some cardio," Oscar suggested, grabbing her towel and passing the water bottle her way.

"This is weight day." Cameron took a few sips, then glanced at Daron whose eyes were laser focused on her. "Let's move to the leg press as planned."

As she switched machines, Daron silently commanded her attention. This time, she didn't feel inclined to respond like she had all those years ago. Wrong day. Wrong target.

Cameron didn't know what she was thinking the night she met Daron and let her guard down. She couldn't say she regretted sleeping with him, but that evening helped drive home the fact that she hadn't fully recovered from the traumatic year she'd had. Daron, while attractive, wasn't her type of man. He would have gotten shot down with sniper precision had she been feeling herself.

He turned a heated gaze in her direction. Instead of being the alias Tandria, for a moment Cameron was transported in time and felt like Autumn again. *How did he go from helping someone, who was in town to promote a book, networking at a reception to becoming entangled with The Warden's crew?*

Oscar leaned in close and whispered, "Based on the way they're looking at you, you're their next meal."

Eric's glances were mild, compared to Daron's smoldering looks that threatened to singe her clothes. She understood how she could have been susceptible when she was out of sorts but there was no way it was happening now. Cameron's gaze drifted to Eric as they approached like lions about to take down prey.

"How many sets do you have left?" Daron asked, resting a hand on the top bar of the leg press machine.

"Excuse me?" Cameron asked as she paused between her sets.

Daron stared at her, as if wanting to say she'd heard the question.

"We're done," Oscar admitted.

"We can work in between your sets," Eric suggested, giving her a seductive grin as he dropped down on the machine next to hers.

She extended her legs, pressing the weights up. "I have one set left."

Oscar shot her a warning glare. "She's new in town."

"Clearly." Daron hovered next to her.

"Lucky for you, while you were doing your best impression of a grizzly bear,"—Cameron smiled sweetly, sliding off the machine—"I finished my last set. Enjoy."

She brushed past Daron, glancing back to catch his smirk. Oscar fell in step with her as they went into the cooling-down area to stretch, wrapping up the workout. She pretended not to notice that Daron followed her progress to the locker room.

By the time she showered, changed, and stuffed the "grab and go" bookbag into her gym bag, Eric and Daron were gone. It blew her mind, Daron showed up at the gym today. From what she heard, he had never stepped foot inside before. *So why now?* Cameron didn't like the fact that Daron would have dropped what he was doing to make an appearance. She hadn't even known she would be there until that morning. The last thing she needed was them taking a closer look at her alias especially now that there were issues back home.

CHAPTER 10

Cameron left the gym to run errands, then for the next few hours she set up the apartment. The lights had been programmed to switch on and off at various times. A prior digital taping carried sounds of her opening the refrigerator, cell phone pings, toilet flushing and showers. She was fairly sure not only were they watching her building but also listening. As long as there was no power outage, things would be fine and it would appear as if she'd been home the entire time.

She stretched out on the bed, splaying a hand across the paisley duvet she'd picked up while shopping with her mother, resting until her alarm went off three hours later. She slipped on a black body suit, inserted brown contacts, braided her hair back, then pulled the fitted hood over her head. She finalized the look by snapping a face shield over her nose before sliding on the backpack.

Cameron tipped out of the apartment heading up to the roof. She sprinted to near the edge before jumping onto the roof of the next building. Then, she maneuvered down the fire escape and onto the concrete. Staying close to the wall so no cameras would detect her movement, she dashed to the trail in the park then cut across to the railroad. She had a three-mile run before she hit the motel where her bike was parked and aimed for I-57, leading to Rob's house in Matteson.

As she pulled into Rob's driveway, Greg's Cadillac CT6 sat in the open garage and Rob's Ford Expedition was parked curbside. Any time the Expedition was on the street, they weren't meeting to discuss the situation. She parked next to the CT6 that Rob's slim, muscular physique clad in all black rested on and hopped off her bike. Rob tossed a thin sweat shirt and baseball cap her way. She caught them mid-air.

"We're on the move?" Cameron asked, putting the helmet on the seat but was more focused on studying the worry lines in Rob's toffee face.

He closed the garage door and nodded for her to slide the bookbag off and pull on the sweatshirt and cap. "Trenton said call him, something about you downloading an app."

"I'll call after we make this run."

Rob secured the door and led her to the Expedition, where Greg was waiting in the driver's seat.

"They came to my shop." Greg's bronze face wore a thunderous frown and he smacked the wheel as if he wanted to smash something. He peeled down the street.

His wife and daughter must've been there when it happened. Losing his first spouse to a drive-by shooting made him extremely protective of his current family. Another reason she was concerned about retiring. This was as close as she came to almost leaving the business. Finding out about JD derailed things and now she wasn't sure if she would have gone through with it or delayed it as she'd done in the past. She shook off those thoughts and refocused on the situation at hand.

"What makes you think it's about Bishop?" Cameron asked.

"When I asked what was wrong with his car, he said someone recommended that he speak to me if he wanted to know more about Bishop and Kimura," Greg explained as he gunned toward Governors Highway.

Rob leaned forward, handing Cameron his phone. She studied the picture of the man whose features didn't ring any bells. "He doesn't look familiar."

"You know who I think it is." Rob took back his phone. "The fact is, they showed up at Greg's auto repair shop, not at the office and that falls squarely in the suspicious category."

"I tagged his car." Greg tapped his fingers on the steering wheel as they waited for the red light to change. "It appears he's renting a house in Flossmoor."

Associates of Bishop knew that to reach them, they could make an appointment or leave a message on the office line. "We know Bishop is dead. As far as everyone knows, Kimura is, too," Cameron reminded them.

"Bishop is confirmed. Not everyone believes that Kimura's dead. Red and Ada both know you're alive and kicking." Greg cut his eyes over at her as he slid in and out of the traffic on the street.

Red was the man Bishop considered Kimura's alert system for emergencies in the middle of certain special assignments. He was the ultimate professional, so Cameron utilized his services when necessary. Fortunately, it hadn't been as often as it once was.

"My bet is on Howard," Rob offered.

When Bishop instituted the use of nicknames, he introduced a few clients to Greg as Kimura with only Rob and Howard present. Cameron watched the few times as the meeting took place through a two-way mirror from the security room before Howard and Bishop parted ways. She could see why Rob suspected he was involved, but this reeked of someone else. Something bigger.

"Bishop passed away three years ago and Kimura was supposed to have died two years before that," Cameron said, as if they didn't already know.

"So, who would be looking for Kimura now?" They didn't have the answer to those questions, otherwise Cameron wouldn't have been there.

"Someone could have found Bishop's file," Greg suggested.

She didn't want to think about what would happen if anyone came across that missing file. If it contained anything like the one Bishop gave her before he died, they'd all be spending the rest of their lives in prison.

Cameron realized that she would need to consider getting a burner phone since information on Bishop's missing file couldn't be filtered through Oscar. *One problem at time.* She would deal with how this situation affected being Tandria once she understood what she was dealing with.

Greg drove past the Flossmoor house. The street was pitch black and the lights on the property illuminated the house they were scoping out. At least two guys were walking around inside. Greg doubled back and parked near a row of trees that separated the houses across the street. Cameron glanced back at Rob, who was pointing a device that read heat signatures at the house.

"At least five," Rob announced.

Cameron grabbed his arm. Letting Greg go was like releasing an angry lion into a fine china shop. "You called me in for a reason. It wasn't to storm the castle."

Greg was capable of taking down a few guys. She was called in for a situation that required more than just muscle. Evidently, whatever this was needed to be handled with a little finesse.

"If you go in, he'll be convinced you have the info he needs." Rob waited as Greg closed the door. "He left a business card, right? Call him and I can tell her which one he is."

Cameron pulled off the cap, then put her disguise back in place. She sifted through her bag, grabbing a syringe and few other items.

Greg took out the burner phone and made the call.

"He's in the back bedroom," Rob announced, looking at the device then gesturing to the left side of the house. "Near this end."

"Make sure security cameras are deactivated." Greg glanced over his shoulder as he spoke.

Cameron slid on her gloves, left the truck, ran across the street, then picked the lock, letting herself into the house. She halted as she waited for an armed man to clear the hallway. Then, she raced through the mud room and kitchen to the back, past the figurine display case and the empty chair in the corridor.

The bedroom door opened the moment she reached for the handle.

She pressed her body against the wall, then slammed her arm across the man's chest as he stepped forward.

He stumbled backwards. Quietly closing the door, she jabbed the syringe into his thigh. He grunted when she grabbed him by the shirt, pushing him back to the bed.

"You've been poisoned," she said, in a deep and low voice. "You'll die within two minutes without the antidote."

"What do you want?"

"Why were you sent here? Who are you looking for?" she growled.

"I was sent to find a female associate of Mr. Bishop and Mr. Kimura." His shaky hand pointed to a briefcase.

"Which woman?"

"Miko," he whimpered.

Cameron tried not to react to her alias. Miko, as far as anyone knew was dead, too. During the almost ten years she worked for Bishop, Miko, one of his special projects, was her most consistently used alias. The only two people she'd been allowed to discuss that with were JD and her disguise creator, Ada. Greg, Rob, and Trenton also had special assignments during that time, but Red was assigned to assist them.

The man's eyes rolled back in his head, then closed. He wouldn't remember a thing when he woke. She attached a device between his phone and case to monitor his cell activities before sifting through the contents of the briefcase. Cameron reviewed a "claim" that Miko's grandfather had made her the sole beneficiary of an estate worth millions. She snapped a couple of pictures of the document, wondering who was trying to lure Miko out and why.

Cameron peered into the hallway before stepping out. As she moved away from the door, a man came out of a room down the hall. She reached for her gun and realized she wasn't in her usual gear.

He lifted the Remington. "Don't move."

She inched back toward the window near the wooden display case, eyeing the chair against the wall.

"I will shoot," the man warned.

Cameron leaped behind the display seconds before he pulled the trigger, sending several bullets through the window pane. He cautiously approached as she slid along the wall toward the chair. She grabbed its slotted wood back and slammed it into him several times. He grunted as the wooden legs pummeled his wrist until the weapon clattered to the floor. She whacked the chair across his face. His body hit the floor with a heavy thud. Cameron dropped the chair, grabbed his weapon and sprinted down the hall. Her feet screeched against the polished oak floors as three men blocked her exit.

"You have nowhere to go," the tallest of the them said.

She fired several shots as she ran toward the window. Grabbing the chair, she flung it through the glass before following right behind. Cameron's feet barely hit the grass before bullets flew through the shattered window. Dropping to the lawn, she rolled out of the line of fire and in the direction of the street, then hustled to her feet.

Her heart dropped when two men appeared at the front corner of the building. Cameron glanced back. The four men spilled out of the house. She decided to take her chances with the two blocking her escape and ran toward them.

Both men lifted their weapons.

She exhaled as she came close enough to realize the two men were Greg and Rob.

"You need to haul ass." Greg yelled.

Cameron kicked up a gear knowing her life just got a hell of a lot more complicated.

CHAPTER 11

A sweet pear scent wafted through the bathroom as Daron slipped on his slacks preparing for the Friday evening reception. Tia stepped onto the plush carpet wrapped in a towel. She frowned and sashayed to the walk-in closet where he kept an additional set of extra suits. A few minutes later, she emerged holding his tailored black pinstripe suit, placing it on the damask comforter.

Tia crossed her arms, pouting. "Honey, why do you keep wearing clothes that make you look like you have a dad body?"

He chuckled. She hated when he wore one of the suits with those special pockets for his devices. He couldn't afford for anyone to know he always recorded their interactions. He preferred them to think he was out of shape but it certainly didn't cut down on the number of women who came at him.

"You know that's not true and that's all that matters." He grabbed her hand, resting it on his six pack. "Feels like a fit dad body, doesn't it?"

"Babe, wear one of your tailored suits," she pleaded, then went up on her toes.

He planted a kiss on her lips. "I've got to get to a meeting."

She pouted a bit before grabbing her makeup bag off the bed and stalking to the bathroom.

Oh, she's quite mad but she'll get over it.

He finished dressing and went to the office, leaving Tia to the half hour process of contouring her already beautiful face. When he entered, Lex was sitting in one of the leather chairs directly in front of the desk. Daron took the space across from him and prepared for the next stage of his plan. The following few weeks were critical. His head of security suggested reducing the entire team until everything was wrapped up. Pedro, who was working with the small group of people in the "second chance" program, selected which of those men would be included in that final crew. Daron's screen notified him the moment Tandria checked in.

"Your friend has arrived." Daron grinned, dialing Steve.

Lex chuckled. "You mean, *your* guest has arrived. She's no friend of mine."

Steve laughed. "Oh she's all Lex says she is, and so much more." He relayed how Tandria parked her own car instead of allowing valet to do it, then tried to peek at the guest list.

"She's a character, isn't she?" Daron unlocked a drawer, grabbed his tablet and pulled up the security monitors. When he saw her at the gym, he thought her pictures hadn't done her justice but tonight she looked absolutely amazing.

"I don't think there's a word to describe her," Steve replied, his voice low.

Daron zoomed in closer on her face and frowned, disappointment filling him. "She's not who she says she is."

"Why do you say that?" Steve asked.

"She's wearing my tech," Daron said, shifting the tablet toward Lex. "It seems we have a mutual friend."

Lex leaned over, narrowing his focus on her glasses.

"I'll send Eric to the security room and be there in a minute." Steve disconnected.

Daron had previously owned a company that legally sold the security and tech toys he created to government and private contractors. Until

Jennifer and Adrian had destroyed his life. Now he sold specialized gear, like the glasses Tandria currently sported, to his elite clients. People who worked outside of the law, but had good intentions. With the exception of one person, but that man was now six feet under.

Steve entered the room and locked the door behind him. "Will she be a problem for your plan?"

"Do I need to deliver 'the package' to her place while she's here?" Lex glanced at Tandria on the screen, then focused on Daron.

"No." Daron knew he was taking a risk not sending the technology designed to erase data on flash drives, memory cards, and personal electronics. "We'll do it later."

Steve peered at the image on the tablet, a frown formed on his thin lips. "You're sure?"

Daron nodded. The only way he'd be screwed was if she uploaded any files to the cloud. He didn't expect anything to go down tonight that would be an issue for him. Not knowing what she planned to do with the footage she'd come prepared to record, was the bigger problem. He thought about his clients then wondered if Tandria could be the woman he'd been seeking all this time.

"First, let's see if we can determine why she's here." Daron studied the image on the screen.

Has Kimura found her way to my doorstep?

Daron glided over to his desk, handing Lex an ear plug and a pocket square that had a microphone installed inside. "It's time to greet our guest."

Lex took his pocket square out of his jacket and replaced it with Daron's, sliding the plug in his right ear before walking out the door.

Daron locked it behind him. Steve approached the far-left wall and placed his hand on a panel which opened to reveal a monitor and microphone. Daron handed him a tablet off the desk to display the images on the larger screen.

Steve and Daron paid close attention to the monitor as Lex approached Tandria, who stood in the corner near the buffet table, scanning the people who came a little too close. The jazz music, along with the thrum of chatter as guests milled about, filled their ears. By the time Lex reached her, Tandria had grabbed a Kir Royale from a waiter's serving tray. He tapped on her shoulder. She spun around, her body tense and poised.

"Hello Tandria." Lex picked up a scotch from the other side of the tray.

"We can hear you loud and clear," Daron confirmed.

Lex tilted his head a bit, acknowledging the statement.

A perfectly arched eyebrow lifted and she answered with a cool, "Hello. Mr. Keyes."

Lex's smile transformed to a more serious expression at the ice in her tone and the reason for it. "I wanted to apologize. I was out of line calling like I did."

"Yes, you were." She lifted the rim of her glass to her lips. "I certainly didn't appreciate you dialing me up at an ungodly hour of the morning like a random booty call who had nothing more to do than wait to hear from you."

Lex stepped in closer. "Will you accept my apology?"

The echoes of laughter and a low whistle of appreciation rang in Lex's ear.

She tilted her head to the side, studying him. "Should I? You didn't apologize. You said you wanted to without actually doing so."

"You're not making this easy."

"What? Your change of tactics was well executed and *almost* believable." Tandria finished her drink and placed it on a tray with empty glasses near the bar. "You managed to save yourself from my 'who in the hell do you think you are' speech, so that should be sufficient."

"Ha. Love how she called you out," Daron teased and his gaze shifted to Steve who didn't bother to hide a chuckle.

Lex laughed and lowered his gaze toward the floor. "Okay, I admit defeat." He moved past her, aiming for the exit.

"In that case, I accept your apology," Tandria called after him, the corners of her lush mouth turning upward.

Lex turned to face her, shaking his finger. "You're good."

She laughed and her hazel eyes seemed to sparkle on the monitor.

"I'm the best," she replied in a voice that was pure sensual promise.

"Let's start over." He held out his arm for her. "My name is Lex and I'm your tour guide for the evening."

"Don't think for one minute that you're smooth enough for this tour to end in your bed," she warned as she hooked her arm through his, then allowed him to guide her toward the exit.

Lex took her down a long hallway behind the ballroom that held African artifacts, explaining their history as they went. He opened a huge set of double doors at the end of the hall, revealing a fighting cage in the center of the floor's main level with plush theater seating surrounding the ring. She swept her hair back, lightly touching her glasses.

"We occasionally host fighting events here," Lex explained, studying her spectacles.

"Stop examining her glasses, I think she noticed," Daron instructed.

Tandria slowly slid off her jacket, revealing a black dress that accentuated every curve. Lex glanced up at the nearest camera and gave them the *lord have mercy* look before turning back to face Tandria.

Daron's body tingled with excitement as he moved closer to the screen, taking in the curve of her ass and hips. In that moment he realized something about her reminded him of Autumn. The memories of that night those dark-brown thighs were wrapped around him. The imagine of the brown-eyed woman with locs began to morph to the hazel-eyed woman. His erection pressed against his zipper.

"She noticed and her distraction clearly worked," Steve declared. "Because you're drooling."

Lex wiped his brow and grinned.

Daron knew he wanted to comment, but couldn't.

"Is this all to the tour?" She folded the jacket over her arm. "If it is, you can take me back to the buffet."

"Well," Lex leaned closer to her. "I was hoping for a moment to get to know you without all that noise in the ballroom."

"I might have entertained the idea *if* you had the forethought to bring drinks and food."

He extended his arm, then asked, "Would you like me to check that?"

"I don't plan to stay that long," she explained as she clasped onto his upper arm again, and they walked back down the corridor.

"I hope I can convince you otherwise," he stated in that late-night, slow jam deejay voice.

Tandria stuck her jacket under her arm and played the air violin. "What?"

"How many women swoon when you're trying to make the simplest statement sound sexy?"

Lex chuckled. "You're crazy. You know that?"

She laid a red-manicured hand over her chest. "I'm appalled."

"Mmm, somehow I don't think so." He nodded toward where the party was in full swing. The music levels were higher and the dance floor was packed.

Daron slipped his tablet in the lower inner pocket of the suit. He took a quick peek in the mirror before leaving the office, knowing Steve would keep an eye on things.

Lex's eyes shifted to Daron when he entered the main room. Suddenly the atmosphere became electrified as others took note of his presence. He nodded, acknowledging that he'd lost the ability to communicate with Lex but could still listen in.

Lex leaned in to whisper, "I'll catch up with you later tonight."

"Once I find my boss," Tandria declared, grabbing a flute from the tray of a passing waiter, "I'm heading out."

Lex held up his index finger as a signal to Daron to let him know he'd be over in a minute. "Don't leave without saying goodbye."

"I make no promises." She gestured to her jacket.

Lex shook his head. Daron's focused shifted to Tandria as Lex made his way through the crowd.

She had played the game well. If Daron hadn't noticed those glasses, she could've definitely blindsided them. He found it interesting that she turned Lex's invite down when it was obvious she wanted to be here. Daron was intrigued and curious about who or what Tandria Jenkins really was. He hoped she was Kimura and not someone he'd have to neutralize.

CHAPTER 12

Cameron silently cursed. *Why does Lex keep staring at my glasses?*

She passed a set of royal-blue and white highboys scattered along the right side of the wall as she weaved through the people aiming for the buffet. Even if she got banned from the compound, she'd seen enough of the layout to work on a plan to extract JD. Out of the corners of her eyes, she noticed a bony guy in a lime suit making a beeline in her direction.

She scanned the nearby attendees hoping to see her cousin or her boss, then she spotted a familiar face and maneuvered through the crowd before Mr. Lime Suit reached her. A familiar guest put a halt to things.

"Maureen, I had no idea you'd be here," Cameron exclaimed, genuinely surprised.

"I didn't expect to see you either," Maureen shrieked, as she hugged Cameron, nearly crushing her in the process.

"My boss gave me an ultimatum, either attend or find a new job." She glanced over the room still trying to locate him before returning her focus to the bleached blonde.

Maureen looped her arm under Cameron's and moved her forward toward a group near the buffet. "Let me introduce you to a few of my friends."

They made their way to people who ranged from artists to local business owners, making introductions and small talk. She ran into her boss about an hour later, shortly after JD entered the room. It had been a while since she'd seen her cousin in a tailored black suit, or any suit for that matter. His wavy hair was pulled up in a neat bun at the top of his head with his sides trimmed low. He hated being in suits as much as she did being forced to wear dresses. Didn't seem to keep their mothers from trying.

Angling her hair to cover one side of her face, she waited for the opportune moment to test whether JD would recognize her without a true disguise.

He stepped in line at the bar, and Cameron made her move. Better to do it, than risk him showing up at the office with Lex where he was bound to blow her cover. With trouble brewing, she assumed The Warden's crew would be required to move in twos. She was trying to corner him before he neared the bartender, but she was stopped several times by men trying to engage her in conversation. Her cousin had moved up and a red-haired woman stepped behind him. As Cameron neared, the woman switched to the line next to JD, which seemed to be moving faster.

She lightly touched his arm. "Excuse me. How long do these things usually last?" Cameron asked loud enough for him to hear over the music.

JD turned toward her, glanced at her face and froze. "This is my first one."

Cameron watched as he studied her face, and frowned.

"You remind me of someone." JD stared at her a moment longer. "If I didn't know better, I'd say you were her twin."

Cameron tilted her head, trying to keep her expression neutral. "What's her name?"

"Her name … evades me right now." JD's gaze flickered over the parts of her face that her hair didn't cover.

She was shocked and pleased at how her cousin had matured. Another time JD would've given her away without even thinking of the consequences or the reason she'd come in disguise. He'd been so busy at the transportation company where he worked that they hadn't managed to synchronize their schedules to hang out. When months passed and he had not contacted her, she hadn't been overly concerned because it was the busy season and he was traveling a lot.

The reality that she could have lost JD if The Warden had chosen to make an example out of him, hit her like a power surge; one that temporarily reboots the system. Given he was one of the few members of her family she trusted, it would have been a devasting loss. Suddenly, Cameron's body caved like she was going to faint.

"You okay?" JD grabbed her shoulders, steadying her.

"I guess I had too much to drink." Cameron chuckled, trying to shake off the rush of emotions as he released his hold. If JD recognized her, he knew she had a high tolerance for alcohol and would know the truth.

"Yet you're back in line." JD countered, trying to get her to look him in the eye but also wearing a smile that was all the confirmation she needed.

"Nice meeting you." Cameron veered away from the bar, deciding to stay a while longer. She had to create an opportunity to draw JD away from the party so they could speak. She glanced back and JD slid out of line, trailing her across the room. She changed direction, aiming for the exit instead. Cameron grimaced when Lex left the couple he was with and headed her way. She inhaled and exhaled, then pushed down the emotions that had risen unexpectedly.

"Damn," she muttered as Lex reached her two seconds before JD.

Lex blocked her escape, asking, "You're not trying to sneak out, are you?"

"Sneak out? No. Leave, yes."

He peered over his shoulder, frowned slightly, then nodded at JD. "JD, are you enjoying the party?"

"It's amazing." JD's gaze lowered to the marble.

Lex's gaze flickered between them. "How do you two know each other?"

Cameron was grateful JD took more after his father than his mother because the family resemblance would have given everything away immediately.

"We don't," JD answered.

"We met less than five minutes ago. Hit it off well enough to hold a brief conversation." She grinned, adding. "I didn't even know his name until you came along. So, thank you."

"Well, let me introduce you to a few friends." Lex took her arm, preparing to guide her to the VIP area.

JD's shoulders lowered in defeat as he passed Cameron. She caught him by his arm and asked. "You're bailing on me already?"

"The invitation's for one."

JD glanced at Lex, nodded, and split.

She watched as his slender frame slipped into the crowd and disappeared among the dancers. "I guess he wasn't incorrect with his statement."

"Not at all." Lex took hold of her hand.

Cameron smirked. "Let's go meet these friends of yours."

Lex headed toward a roped off area with a bar. The setup was informal—one long couch in front of a table, loveseat, and chair. Two men occupied the space with the bartender. Once she stepped into the reserved space, a glance beyond showed more seating filled with highboys and round tables with orchid centerpieces.

"Tandria Jenkins, this is Daron Kincaid and Eric Tillman." He gestured toward the two men, who wore designer suits that cost more than four months' pay with Mr. Walsh. "Gentlemen, this is Tandria."

"We've met before." Cameron shook their extended hands. Daron's jacket accentuated a pair of muscular arms but hadn't been tailored to fit his waist, giving the appearance that he was hiding a beer belly.

She knew better, and it made her question why.

"The pleasure's definitely ours," Daron greeted her, holding on to her hands a little longer than necessary. "Why don't you and Lex hang out with us for a few?"

"Unless you can't sit in that outfit," Eric goaded, lifting his drink from the table and taking a sip.

Cameron was caught off guard by the snarky comment which worked well for keeping her attraction to him in check. "The problem isn't whether or not I can sit in this outfit, but whether there's enough room for me and your nasty attitude."

"He's joking," Lex informed her as he glared at Eric, then pointed behind her. "These two joining us, are Mac and Steve."

She shook their hands. They seemed friendly but reserved. Lex led her to the love seat where she laid the jacket over the arm. Cameron skillfully sat in one fluid motion, crossed her legs, tucking the bottom leg underneath her, then smiled at Eric.

Daron took a seat on the couch, put two fingers up and bent them down. The level of the music lowered instantly.

Impressive.

"How long have you lived in town?"

"Less than a month," Cameron answered as surrounding conversations amplified in the background, but everyone's focus seemed to be on her.

"You like it here?" he asked, keeping his eyes trained on hers.

"It's alright."

"Not enough excitement?" Eric questioned, pulling a bar stool between the two couches and sliding on top. "You're looking for a little trouble to get into even though you're trying to behave like a good girl."

Cameron paused, as though trying to gather her thoughts. "Eric, right?"

He nodded.

"Since you seemed to have woken up on the wrong side of the bed this morning, I'm going to refrain from telling you that you're an asshole who can't seem to come out and say what's on his mind."

Mac muttered a smart remark to Steve who chuckled.

"Besides, even good girls behave badly every once in a while," Cameron said with a sly smile.

Lex issued Eric a stern look. "How about you lay off my guest?"

Eric lifted his glass to his lips. "Does your guest always call people she's doesn't know assholes?"

"I'm glad you didn't miss it," she shot back, giving him an ear-to-ear grin. "It would've been a shame for you to be dumb, too. I was officially introduced to Daron, Mac, and Steve here at the same time as you. They seem nice." She motioned toward the other men. "I've been waiting for the Spanish Inquisition to end so I can have an intelligent conversation with someone whose topside doesn't run off like his backside."

"Dayum," Mac said, causing Steve to nudge him into silence.

"That's fine, but I advise you," Eric paused as his focus shifted to Daron, "to shake her down before she leaves."

Daron, Steve and Lex traded looks that Cameron couldn't quite read. "Why, thank you for the compliment," she replied in the sweetest voice she could manage. "I'd have to be an excellent thief to hide anything on me or in this small purse." She lifted her clutch.

"I may not agree with Eric's reasoning but I'm more than willing to give you a pat down," Lex teased and received a sharp elbow to his side from Cameron.

"Tandria, ignore Eric. Heads of security are always a little uptight." Daron gave Eric a warning look. A second later, a petite woman of mixed descent joined the group. Cameron had heard that she'd put in the time and effort trying to be queen to The Warden's kingdom.

"No need to explain," she said, frowning at Eric as Tia gave her the evil eye. "I've met his type before. They always seem more talk than action."

"Lex, is that Mr. McCray?" Daron gestured to a white man wearing an ill-fitting tan suit.

"Yeah, I need to go speak with him for a minute." Lex rose. "If you'll excuse me."

Cameron stood ignoring Tia's jealous glare, grabbing her jacket from the arm of the loveseat.

"Stay," Daron commanded.

She froze and shot a steely gaze at Daron but kept moving.

Lex glanced back at her over his shoulder. "I shouldn't be that long."

"I'm heading out." She extended her purse to Eric. "You want to check this before I go?"

"Not necessary," Eric replied, rising from the bar stool.

"Nice meeting most of you." Cameron gave Eric the evil eye then shifted her attention to the rest of group, gifting them with a warm smile.

Daron blocked her path as she attempted to follow Lex out of the VIP section. "I said stay."

"I don't take orders from you." Cameron brushed past him.

Lex turned and smiled as she grabbed hold of his arm. She didn't bother turning around to gauge Daron's reaction. He wasn't used to someone who didn't jump to obey his command. Although Prescott, one who was considered the most dangerous, wasn't in attendance, she no longer questioned who carried the name "The Warden". She couldn't help but flash back to "Autumn" and Daron having drinks at a bar in Chicago and wondering what happened. Bishop had suspected Daron was mixed up in something more serious than the lighthearted image he portrayed. Whatever plans Bishop had to use Daron never came to fruition. Bishop died before he could execute them.

On her path to the door, Lex and Mr. McCray were speaking near the VIP section. Cameron wondered about Prescott. He was the only one in her file who hadn't made an appearance. While she was convinced Daron was actually The Warden, that left the question of what role Prescott played on the team.

JD reached Cameron as she passed the dance floor. "Heading out?"

She nodded.

"Can I walk with you?" JD fell in step with her.

"Sure."

As they neared the door, someone loudly called JD's name. He gave her a half smile. "Talk to you later. Evidently, Lex is staking his claim and thinks I'm trying to make a move." He disappeared into the sea of people.

"We'll see about that." Cameron stepped aside, searching for Lex in the crowd. But it was Eric barreling her way, giving her the same smoldering look he gave her in the bar the first time they met under the alias Renee while she was doing recon. "For a woman who wasn't interested in coming, you're dressed to catch."

"What concern is it of yours?" Cameron stared at him, inhaling the scent of his cologne —woodsy and masculine despite the hints of lavender and floral notes.

"If you're out to snag bigger fish, he has a woman." Eric motioned toward Daron who had Tia wrapped around him like a python with its next meal.

Daron was handsome but wasn't really her type, which was a good thing. His square jaw line, searing eyes, and imposing stance reminded her too much of the men in her family. The thing between him and "Autumn" was a fluke as a result of having an emotionally challenging year. "She has nothing to worry about."

Eric glanced down, his gaze lingering on her cleavage. "I'll be keeping an eye on you."

"Is it because you're concerned, or you like what you see?" She chuckled then whisked out the door.

The Warden had been the cause of Mr. Walsh's demand for her to attend as she suspected. The next few days would reveal Lex's motives. Would he strictly attempt to get her in bed or would she get another invitation to fight night instead of the after party?

Certain that someone had their eyes on her besides Daron's security team, she dashed down the road to her car. She sensed it like the spring wind blowing against her neck. Cameron caught a glimmer of movement in the shadows across the street beyond the iron gate. The question was, who was it?

Three people came to mind — Jason, Daron's opposition, or maybe the person behind the search for Kimura tracked her there? If it was the latter, JD wouldn't be the only family member in danger.

CHAPTER 13

Jason couldn't afford to have the other FBI agents see whatever landed on his screen. He sat at the end of a u-shaped surveillance workstation in the corner. The team was carefully monitoring who entered Daron's property, since they could never seem to get an overhead image of the compound on the weekends when the guests arrived.

He was currently reviewing the information his contact had left at the drop spot. The informant had to be a member of The Warden's inner circle, based on the nature of the data he'd slipped to them.

"Is that Prescott on the street across from the compound?" One of the agents asked.

Jason hopped up and walked over to Agent Grant's screen. Prescott wasn't supposed to be back in the country yet, but it would make sense because they'd received information from their person today.

"Play it back." Jason focused at the screen. The physical build matched but it wasn't a good enough shot of his face for a definitive confirmation. "Were we notified of his return?"

"I'll check."

"Hey, did we ever figure out who pulled up in the Camaro with that license plate number we couldn't read?" Agent Coney ran his pudgy fingers across several sheets of paper before swiveling around in his chair toward Jason.

Jason looked up from the screen. "The one where the picture of the driver came out crappy too?"

"Yeah."

"No. Why?"

"Just pulled out, but we're having the same problem." Agent Coney turned back to his screen and reached for a coffee mug.

"Send it over to me and I'll see what I can do." Jason moved back to his station, overhearing another agent giving an update over the phone to a superior on the undercover's info drop. There had to be more to this case than they'd been led to believe. He couldn't recall an assignment where the higher ups checked in almost daily.

The Warden's ability to weed out agents and informants was impeccable. Diondre, Jason's undercover agent, finally made it in after several failed attempts to plant a man on The Warden's crew for a span of about five years. Jason was on the team because their superior believed the sloppiness of the man he'd replaced was the reason Daron rejected all previous undercover agents.

Jason was surprised that they kept him on the case after he informed them JD was family. That alone, made him wonder if someone on the team was in Daron's pocket. He couldn't risk being reassigned by asking questions about their motives, especially not now with Cameron inserting herself in the situation. *Baby sis, this is the wrong place and the wrong time.*

Before he reached the laptop, his personal cell vibrated. Jason stepped out of the back room that was being used for surveillance and went to the living room. He lowered himself on a couch before answering.

"I heard JD's former boss has a broken jaw and leg, and a bullet in his shoulder from his own gun," Quinn said.

"Yeah, claimed he fell down the stairs, dropped his gun in the process and it went off." Jason was fairly sure Cameron was responsible. The scenario reminded him of all the conversations he had with people when he was trying to get something solid on Bishop and wanting to get his sister from under the man's thumb.

"Let me know if you need me or even Hawk. We'd rather step in before we get the call from mom," Quinn said his goodbyes then disconnected the line.

Clearly, Bishop had taught Cameron well. She was skilled at not leaving a trace of anything behind. Nothing had come up on the thefts or the body count associated with Kimura's name. Most people believed Kimura was a man. If it hadn't been for one incident, he would have never known his sister was a highly skilled enforcer. Getting caught in this Warden situation would expose the secrets she'd kept well-hidden all these years.

Jason had his work cut for him. He could lose more than his job, and she could lose her life.

♦ ♦ ♦

Oscar had given Cameron an *Onyx rises in New York City* message. One of many lessons Cameron learned under Bishop was that some things needed to be handled personally. She wished she could have sent Greg or Rob to the Big Apple, instead. The fact that Bishop warned her not to review the file in the presence of anyone, other than Ada or JD, scared her. Rob, Greg, and Trenton were her family. If she wasn't here, she would've been at Greg's for his Memorial Day barbecue. She hoped that everything would wrap up by July 4th so she could concentrate on hunting down that file so nothing came back to haunt her. Fingers crossed, Trenton would be back stateside by then.

Cameron weaved through the Saturday morning foot traffic on the sidewalks in Midtown. She headed to Times Square, walking down 7th Avenue. People inquiring about Bishop and Kimura made her cautious. They had searched all the known properties within Bishop's massive estate but came up empty. Trenton tried to run down buildings that could have been purchased under an alias or given as a gift. The search had been on hold when Trenton went overseas due to personal issues and stayed longer than expected.

Honking horns, jack hammers blasting through the concrete, and hammering from a construction site, forced people to talk louder to be heard over the noise. Before the impromptu trip, Cameron had made good progress with Lex. He'd even asked her to go to Florida with them. She turned him down. Daron wasn't acting like a man who was being threatened. Cameron didn't know whether she should be comforted by that or scared. Even at this point, JD was safer with him than back in the street on his own. Right now, she needed to rescue herself.

She received a text saying MEET ME AT BP BE THERE SOON. Cameron replied immediately changed routes, heading to Bryant Park.

If that wasn't bad enough, Ada had notified her that someone had dug up Miko's grave for the second time. The first incident happened shortly after the headstone had been erected. She didn't understand what would make someone do the same thing almost five years later.

Cameron crossed the street to the side.

Ada approached from the opposite end from a line of trees. Her eyes had an Asian slant and her creamy complexion hinted at her Polish and Mexican ancestry. The dark-haired beauty was one of the few people who knew almost every alias or nickname Cameron had ever used. Ada hugged her, then grabbed Cameron's arm and pulled her close, then strolled down the sidewalk.

"Red found something," Ada whispered.

Cameron paused, waiting until an elderly couple ambled past. "He doesn't know the information is for me, does he?"

"No," Ada assured.

Cameron continued walking along the concrete path. "Bishop didn't assign him to the Miko alias for a reason."

"Understood." Ada slid her a folded piece of paper.

"Be careful. Right now, we're assuming that it's about finding me and ... " She went quiet as they weaved through a group of people walking in the opposite direction. "But it could be about tracking down Bishop's elite team."

Ada frowned, and there was a hint of fear in her eyes.

"Miko was the only known associate of both Bishop and Kimura." Cameron raised her eyebrow.

"I'll have Red—"

"No," Cameron said. "Red is holding my file that Bishop gave to him and he's supposed to pass along to an unidentified associate *if* he asks."

"If?" Ada's eyebrow shot up.

"Exactly." She scanned the crowd. "He won't tell me who it is or why Bishop, even in death, is determined for this person to have it."

"Wow." Ada crinkled up her pert nose. "I didn't know."

"Red has never given me a reason not to trust him," Cameron brought their stroll to a halt and turned toward her. "But we shouldn't involve him in this."

Ada gave her a quick embrace then walked toward a car. Cameron kept her eyes on her until she was safely in her vehicle and drove down the street. Cameron strolled the concrete path as if taking in the greenery, but she was mostly observing various people and their activities, making sure she hadn't missed anyone suspicious. When she finished, she made the trek to the office in Chelsea which was about fifteen minutes away.

Staying near the curb, she kept her dark-blue hair hanging over her face to minimize how much of her image could be captured by ATM and security cameras. She flipped open Ada's note that contained a company name and DC address. How this visit went would determine where she was heading next. When she pushed the door open of the dingy white brick building and entered the lobby, she was shocked there wasn't more security.

The elevator banks and display board listing the floors of each company were the only things that greeted her. She pressed for the elevator to come, and the black doors squeaked as they parted. The odd thing was this Red Lightning Research company had no internet presence, which meant she had no idea what they actually did. Her fingers were crossed that they didn't work weekends. She could let herself in and search the place without initiating contact with anyone.

Cameron stepped out on the white tile, noting the door leading to the stairs on the other side. She continued down the hallway until a modern office came into view. She approached a woman with milky skin and dark-brown hair pulled into a tight bun, who sat behind a long, white reception desk. "Hello, I'm here to speak with Mr. Drucker."

"Do you have an appointment?" The woman inquired with a snippy tone as she stared at the fake scar that ran down Cameron's cheek.

"No, I was told he was looking for information on a friend. I thought I could help." She smiled as she laid the business card the man had given Greg on the desk and then walked away.

"Wait. Wait," the woman called out.

Cameron faced her, tucking a strand of hair behind her right ear.

"Drucker is the head of Research and Development. We're the administrative department within the group."

"Well, I guess some things aren't meant to be." Cameron retraced her steps, heading down the hallway to the door which lead to the stairwell.

She caught a flurry of movement out the corners of her eyes, then swiveled and grabbed the syringe seconds before the blonde man could plunge it into her neck. Her heart slammed against her chest as they struggled on the landing.

He flung her against the wall, knocking the wind out of her upon contact. The door banged shut. Her arm trembled under his weight as she fought to keep the needle from plunging into her skin. She released one hand and jammed the heel of it into his chin then rammed her knee into his crotch. The man grunted in pain and moved back, losing his footing. He grabbed for her arm then the banister. The syringe dropped to the floor.

Cameron's back slammed against the banister as he yanked her down the stairs with him. She groaned and held on to him, using his body to cushion the impact. She slid off him and her shoulder banged into the landing below. The stairwell door above them opened. *Damn.* A man in a black suit stepped in, lifted a Beretta and fired. The bullet barely missed her leg as Cameron rolled to her right, bashing her ankle on the tread below. She ran down the stairs to the street level, pushing the door open. Cameron squinted as the sun hit her eyes.

As her feet hit the concrete sidewalk and her body slid in between the pedestrians milling about, two large men were on her tail before one of the men from the stairwell rushed out the door. Her shoulder, back, and ankle throbbed as she zigzagged through the crowd, heading to the intersection. When she rounded the corner, she pulled the hood over her hair.

Cameron dipped into a convenience store taking long strides to the back. She peered over the aisle's shelving to see the men pushing through the pedestrians. One of them doubled back and peered through glass. She ducked behind the shelves of hair product pretending to examine an item on the bottom. After a few minutes, she slipped on a pair of sunglasses then moved closer to the exit. When a crowd of people walked near the door, she filtered out among them. Cameron's heart was still pumping at an accelerated rate as she crossed the street, then hailed a cab to the airport.

She purchased a ticket to DC. When she landed at National Regan, she changed her blue hair to jet black and cabbed it to China Town. The streets of DC seemed quiet compared to the chaotic symphony of New York as she entered through a smoked glass door. She'd realized why the address Ada had given her seemed so familiar. An ex, Nathan, used to have an office in the place. Her heart hurt like someone had slammed it with a sledgehammer. The universe must be messing with her. All these bittersweet memories.

You're here to find Howard, not take a trip down memory lane.

Ignoring the ache in her body, she quickly maneuvered to the building directory as Howard entered the lobby wearing a tight brown suit, talking on his cell. His Louis Vuitton shoes clicked against the tile. His olive complexion seemed flushed. She pulled her black hair over the fake scar.

"What do you mean a woman stopped by the office?" he asked, shooting by her without so much as a glance.

Cameron followed him out the door.

"Hey, I'm heading to Florida to get a lead on Kimura through one of Ship's clients. Pressure Greg to find out more about this Miko person."

She texted Rob. HOWARD'S GOING TO FLORIDA. FIND OUT WHEN AND WHERE. Accepting Lex's offer to go to Miami was now top priority and served two purposes. The perfect position to watch over JD and also be near her team as they hunted for Howard and Bishop's old contact. Things were about to heat up.

CHAPTER 14

"One day you'll have to make the decision to save yourself first."

Bishop's voice echoed in Cameron's head. She spent most of the work week at Welshman's trying to recall Bishop's Florida contacts and hoping she wouldn't have to choose between retrieving the file and extracting her cousin. Her emotions were like quicksand that had her side stepping one after another to stay focused on giving herself and JD a chance for a better future.

Cameron picked up the case with the laced business cards and slid on the specialized bracelets with the oblong beads. Each bead released a needle upon contact, injecting a dose of the knockout drug. The likelihood she needed her tools tonight were slim, but Cameron didn't want to take chances. She donned a sundress that hugged her curves and paired it with strappy sandals before she headed back out to meet Lex. His determination to have her fall under his charm was working in her favor. She now had a solid extraction plan. The only thing left was getting leverage against Daron.

A black Sonata trailed her to the Italian restaurant, Tuscan Nirvana. Once Lex arrived, as usual, it would disappear. She thought they would have stopped watching by now. Clearly, she hadn't been crossed off the list.

The parking lot was full for a Thursday evening. She pulled into a spot not far from the take-out door. As always, she arrived a few minutes earlier than expected and surveyed the area for exit routes. With camera phones and social media, she could never be absolutely sure that someone hadn't captured something that could lead the wrong people to her. She walked around the front of the building, stood under the red awning, and waited near the entrance. A handsome man with flawless espresso skin, wearing a white linen outfit that clung to his muscles, held the door open. She shook her head.

"If your date doesn't show, I'll happily treat you to dinner." He gave her a megawatt grin before crossing the threshold.

Lex pulled up in a Jaguar F-Pace and valet parked near the entrance. "Hey, sorry I'm late." He kissed her on the cheek, eying the guy who'd just disappeared into the restaurant. "Almost too late, eh?"

She smiled, because Lex, who was always dressed to impress, wore a tan, tailored suit. What does his dressed-down gear look like? "You're on time. I got here a little early."

"I don't understand why you insist on driving." He opened the glass door, allowing her to move past. "I'd love to pick you up and take you out for once."

"We're not dating, Lex. It's easier for me to meet you," she explained as they entered the dimly-lit room. The tables were covered with white linen with a votive candle flickering in the center.

They approached the hostess and were directed to a cozy table deep inside the restaurant. Lex pulled out her chair. "I understand. We're developing a friendship. Picking you up doesn't change that."

"And not picking me up doesn't change anything, either."

Lex angled his chair for an unobstructed view of the entrance.

Since he laid off that playboy swagger that came so naturally to him, she found she actually enjoyed his company. A pleasant surprise, especially since she missed hanging out with her crew.

The scent of fresh tomato and basil had her stomach rumbling. Her busy day didn't afford any time for a real meal. "How about you pick me up tomorrow to play some basketball?"

He eyed her with open curiosity. "Basketball?"

"I haven't played since I got here," she said, relishing his expression. "I can't have my skills getting rusty." Shaking up his image of her as a "girly girl" would be a good thing if she wanted a chance to get into the fights.

"Watching you play should be a real treat." Lex opened the menu. "I'm glad you agreed to go on the trip. You're still coming, aren't you?"

"Yes," she answered, giving her empty stomach a pat. "Now can we order some food?"

He grinned.

While she scanned the specials, Lex's phone vibrated and he slid it in his lap to check the screen.

"I hope it's not a problem, but we're leaving for Florida Thursday instead of next Friday and we'll be there for a little over a week."

"It looks like you'd better call up your Plan B." Cameron gave him the side eye and smirked. "But make sure she's gone when I get there."

"I'll be spending most of this evening and tomorrow convincing you to make it happen."

Lex's focus returned to the cell in his lap.

A group of businessmen approached the hostess stand, and the hairs on the back of Cameron's neck stood on end. Trouble had arrived.

The newcomers maneuvered through the tables, as if they were on the hunt.

She didn't know who was the intended target and wasn't trying to find out. The weapons she had on her wouldn't create a win. She was good, but she wasn't bullet proof.

Cameron tapped Lex on the thigh and nodded toward the men. "We need to leave."

Recognition flickered on his face. He quickly rose as the men split up and combed through the restaurant.

She followed Lex as he melted into the nearest wall. He guided her through the kitchen, then the carryout area, until they made it to the back-parking lot.

"I'm sorry," she said, prepared to let loose with the story of hiding from an abusive boyfriend, if necessary. "I'm overreacting. Where I come from, men coming in that way are looking to wreak havoc. Once they find their target, nothing else matters."

"Don't apologize. Being cautious is not always a bad thing." Lex raced across the parking lot and pulled her to the front of the building. Then he froze, pushing her back around the corner, growling, "Shit."

"What?" Cameron peered around Lex's body. "What in the hell is going on?"

Five suits blocked the front door. Lex's truck was hemmed in the valet parking area by two black Durangos. She could breathe a little better because they weren't there for her.

"Whatever it is," Lex reached under his jacket. "We don't need to be a part of it."

She gripped his arm to stop him from going for what she assumed was a firearm. "Can we take my car and come back for yours later?"

Lex studied the men before focusing on her. "Sounds like a plan."

She jerked her thumb in the opposite direction.

They changed directions, but as they passed the carryout door, the suits pushed their way outside.

"Lex, we need to speak with you," one of them said.

Her head snapped toward Lex.

"I don't have time right now." He grabbed her and pushed her in front of him, whispering, "If I tell you to move out, don't ask questions."

"Not a problem." She auto started the Camaro that sat several feet from them.

The men advanced, their eyes intent on Lex. "We didn't mean that as a question."

"Move."

Lex and Cameron raced across the parking lot with the men on their tails.

"Where are your keys?" Lex yelled.

"I'm driving." Cameron snatched open the door. "Get in."

Lex didn't have time to argue. As soon as he was halfway into the passenger seat, she took off. Cameron hit the side street. Seconds later, several black trucks rounded the corner.

"I'd buckle up if I were you."

She gunned the engine, heading up County Road.

Lex pulled out his cell and speed dialed a number. "Hey, I've got a little trouble. Jackson, Inc. interrupted my dinner. My truck's still at the restaurant." He gave their current location then paused, glanced out the rear window and added, "Two deep."

He must have increased the volume on his end because she heard Eric ask, "Any shots fired?"

"Not yet," Lex answered, fixing his eyes on Cameron and holding on tight to the handle above him.

"Head to the highway. We'll meet you there," Eric instructed. "I'll send somebody to the restaurant for your truck."

Despite the head start, one of their pursuers stayed on her tail. With the growing traffic, he was closing in on her, almost kissing her bumper. He went to ram her but she slid onto the soft shoulder. Tires screeched as the truck braked to avoid hitting the car that had been in front of her. She weaved in and out of traffic to get ahead of them.

"Damn," she muttered, when she got stuck behind a slow car in the fast lane that had yet to pass the vehicle next to it. The lead Durango would catch up if she didn't get around.

The second truck slowed and shifted to the shoulder.

Cameron used that small gap and gunned it.

By the time the Durango followed, she had put some breathing distance between them.

"Head to the highway," Lex growled.

"That damn girl is driving?" Eric yelled. "What the hell were you thinking?"

"Eric. Not now." Lex kept glancing out the side mirror.

"How far are you away from the spot?" Eric asked at the top of his voice.

Cameron slid a glance at Lex.

"Five minutes." Lex disconnected as the first spray of bullets hit the car.

As soon as she made it to the open road, Cameron pushed the pedal closer to the floor. A check in the rearview mirror told her she'd put enough space between them. She didn't want to have to explain why she had bullet-proof windows. When she passed a gas station and a half mile remained before the exit, two Hummers appeared and blocked the road behind them. Tires squealed as they came to a halt.

"You can slow down," Lex advised as his phone vibrated. He answered on speaker, "Hey, thanks."

"No problem, but we need to have a meeting," Eric stated.

"When? Tonight?"

"You weren't the only one visited by those Jackson goons. Just one of the lucky ones," Eric informed him.

"I'll have Tandria drop me off at the bar. Pick me up there." He tucked the phone in his pocket.

Cameron took the next exit, returning to town. The adrenaline was still coursing through her veins because her actions tonight hadn't helped the cover story she invented. Hopefully, it would help her get into the fights.

"You're never quiet," Lex stated.

She slowed even more as they entered city limits. "I know better than to ask questions."

"Take this in case you can't reach me." Lex handed her a card with Eric's name and number. "If anything goes down, call."

She flipped the card and placed it on the dashboard. "I can take care of myself, trust me."

"I'm not going to argue with you," he shot back as she pulled up to Boomerangs. "Not right now."

"Try not to have another incident tonight," Cameron teased, as Lex opened the door.

Lex chuckled, stepping out of the car. "I'll see you tomorrow on the courts."

"If you can't make it, text me," she suggested with a smile, but the challenge was out there for him to accept or not.

Lex nodded and surveyed the area before he entered Boomerangs.

Tonight, the first shots had been fired. JD was no longer in the middle of an oncoming war.

The war had started.

CHAPTER 15

Jason hadn't been surprised when Diondre informed him that Tia had been going through Daron's things. Diondre couldn't say anything since they were both in areas where they weren't supposed to be. The image of his sister playing basketball with Lex that came across his screen was what floored him. He didn't expect her to get that close, that quickly. Now, he waited in her apartment as she dropped a duffle bag on the floor and closed the door behind her.

Switching on the light, she proceeded across the wood floor as he stood in the hallway near the kitchen. He stepped out, encountered the flick of her wrist and quickly moved back. Something breezed past him and lodged in the cabinet. Cameron froze before she launched a second item.

With arms crossed, he moved in front of her. "What did you throw at me?" He looked back at the card stuck in the wood panel.

She released a long, slow breath, sliding something into her waistband. "What in the hell are you doing here?"

"You couldn't stay out of it for a couple of months like I told you to," Jason fumed.

"Who are you and what do you want?" She pulled out her cell. "I'm calling the police."

"Cut the act. My guy's the one watching tonight," he explained, as she moved closer to the opening. "I'm so angry with you right now."

"You tracked me down to give me a lecture?" She brushed past him and stormed into the kitchen. "Un-freakin-believable."

"Do you know how many lives you're endangering? I'd haul your butt out of here right now," he threatened, as he trailed behind her, "if it didn't look suspicious for you to suddenly disappear."

She grabbed a bottle of Dasani out of the fridge. "I'm seeing this thing through. I'm not giving you an opportunity to bail out on JD."

"JD is not as bad off as you think. My man's keeping an eye on him." He leaned on the back of a kitchen chair. "He'll make sure nothing happens to him."

"Your man's got bigger problems to deal with. He won't have time to be watching JD's back." She glared at him. "If the power's split, your guy will be watching his own back."

"Cameron ... Dammit! Stay out of it." Jason thrust his finger at her.

"I can't." Her nostrils flared as she gave him the evil eye, then guzzled down her water. "I won't leave JD's life to chance."

Jason blocked her path, as she tried to exit the kitchen. "Is this about JD's safety or your issues with Dad?"

She shoved him back into the hallway, maneuvered around him, and made tracks to the living room. "I'm not in denial about my motivation or what it stems from. I accept that JD's matured but —"

"JD. Mature?"

"He actually thinks before he speaks," she defended, snatching the remote off a crimson couch.

"I understand that you've gone through this whole metamorphosis trying to make sure he's okay, but you need to step back," Jason demanded, as she switched on the news.

She stood facing the television with her back to him. "If I thought you'd keep me in the loop, I would. But I've devoted—"

"JD's fine. The only warning he's gotten was from Lex about you." He snatched the remote and switched off the telecast. "Are you really helping him? Lex could've made his life a living hell."

Cameron put a finger to her cheek as if thinking about what he'd said. "Okay after this trip with Lex, I'll back off."

"Do it now," Jason insisted, swiveling her to face him.

"I've already agreed to go." She knocked his arms away. "It'll raise suspicions if I'm M.I.A."

Jason locked a steely glare on her for a few seconds. He could feel a vein throbbing at his temple.

"Who is your inside man?" she asked. "Does he know who I am?"

"I can't tell you that, and not yet." Jason grabbed an orange out of the crystal bowl on the kitchen table and then a Dasani from her fridge, knowing it would piss her off. She never did like sharing her food, or people rummaging through her things without permission. He peeled the orange and tossed the outer layer in the trash. "I'm serious. Stay out of it."

"Stay out of what, brother dear?" She smirked and then glared at him. "I have a *respectable* job now, isn't that what you wanted?"

He willed himself to relax as he gripped her shoulder. "Leave it alone."

"Fine." Cameron brushed his hand away. "*After* the trip."

"Keep your word on that, or I'm going to arrest you my damn self." Jason gritted his teeth and stormed toward the door. He paused, turned slowly around, and gave her a mischievous grin. "Mom mentioned you were on a project. I guess I'll tell her I saw you and that she'll see you on her birthday after all."

She charged over to him, pushing him in the chest. "Don't you dare."

He chuckled. "Dare, what, sister dear?" he asked, sounding all innocent as he swept out of her place.

Jason left out of the rear entrance, moving to his car near the park across from her apartment, then leaned on the trunk of the black Sonata eating the orange he'd taken. One thing he knew was, his sister was good at stealth mode. She was always sneaking out of her room, going to the kitchen, or Dad's "nobody better touch" stash for snacks and would somehow return before their parents discovered what she'd done.

He and his brothers always got in trouble for it until Dad came home late one night and caught her on a lawn chair in the backyard chowing down on a plate of snickerdoodles. He called her the Cookie Monster and the name stuck. She might be wily, but Jason needed to make sure no one saw her. The goal was to get her completely out of the way, not bring trouble to his parents' house.

He'd banked on Cameron not wanting all her brothers showing up at her doorstep. Especially now. Last time she went a month without contacting their mom, a family meeting was called. Their mom demanded that they find Cameron.

It took them over three months. To say she was surprised to see them, was an understatement. Their mom had been right to be concerned. According to JD, she'd almost died and had been recovering at a friend's place in DC. Whatever happened had messed her up to the point she actually let them help.

His mind was still trying process that it was his mother's decision for Cameron to stay with Aunt Renee, and that led to Cameron being estranged from their father. While he was unsure of the reason, he knew Caroline was the tether that kept Cameron connected to them. If that link was severed, then his sister would have no ties to the immediate family. *Is that why Mom was pushing me to reach out to Cameron to create another connection so she could come clean?* Maybe a visit from Cameron would help the birthday dinner not be so awkward since it would be the first time everyone had gotten together since Jason asked the estrangement question.

The weather was beautiful, not too hot and not to cool. Jason gazed up at the moon in the midnight sky. A sudden movement caught his eye. The shadow jumped between the roofs of the two six-story buildings. Fifteen minutes passed, and no other motion on the street. If it was indeed Cameron, she'd made a quiet exit. Diondre's shift was ending and Jason didn't want to be there when his replacement arrived.

He slid behind the wheel as he dialed his mother. The instant Cameron made an appearance at the house, his mom would text him. Maybe it was time to reach out to the others. Once she was in Florida it would be harder to help her without coordinating with the local offices down there.

Jason put the phone to his ear and sighed. *How many rules I have to break to keep her safe?*

CHAPTER 16

Jason had forced her hand. Cameron had to sneak out last night so she could take her mom to a birthday breakfast at a local diner. This would be interesting given she had to be back in time for Lex to pick her up. The family home loomed as she approached the concrete stairs. She attempted to call her mother from the car but Caroline Stone was intentionally not answering. Cameron would bet money on it. This would be the first time she'd come over, knowing her dad was home. *Damn you, Jason.* She tugged on the sides of the denim dress her mother had selected, then took a deep breath before ringing the bell. Nerves were jittery like it was her first day at a new school. A minute later, her dad peered out of the window. Then, the door opened.

"Cookie Monster," her dad said in a soft voice, as if he didn't believe it. His hazel eyes widened and gave her a once over. "You look great."

She was thrown off by the way he said her nickname. Her heart thumped loudly in her ears. An image of him coming in and tickling her after another box of cookies came up missing, entered her mind. She didn't know how much time passed before she managed to speak. "Ummm ... is Mom ready?"

He stepped back, but Cameron couldn't get her feet to move forward. "She's looking for the earrings you sent her."

"Well, I … uh … Tell her. I'm … Ummm."

"Cookie," he whispered, reaching for her.

"I'm in the car waiting," she said, moving out of range.

Jake's eyes held a sorrowful glint.

She realized one bad memory had completely wiped out her ability to remember any good times.

"Not necessary, dear. I'm here." Caroline went up on tip toe, and Jake leaned down to kiss her. "See you in a couple of hours."

"Enjoy yourselves." He stood, staring at Cameron a moment longer before pushing the oak door forward.

Cameron proceeded down the steps at her mother's side. "Baby girl, too much time has passed for you to still be holding on to being angry at him, especially since you haven't been willing to talk to him."

"Mom, I have every reason to feel that way. What could he say that could change?"

"A lot of details that you weren't privy to as a child." Silence was palpable until her mother broke the tension with, "You look gorgeous in that dress. I'm going to get a son-in-law yet."

"Ma!" She shot her mom a "give me a break" look.

Caroline hooked her arm under Cameron's. "You'd rather talk about seeing your dad?"

"What were you saying about a son-in-law?" Cameron laughed, unlocking the Charger.

"I thought so." Her mother smiled as she slid into the passenger seat.

Cameron pulled off, heading to a nearby restaurant instead of the Black-owned restaurant her mom liked that was up north. Time constraints dictated a change in plans.

"I'm sorry your brother ruined your surprise." Caroline turned the radio to a channel playing old school R&B. Mom loved anything Luther Vandross.

Cameron scanned the area as she pulled into a parking spot. Her worst fear was that all the bad things she'd done for Bishop would come back on her family and she wouldn't be able to save them.

They stepped into the small eatery and the scent of bacon and coffee greeted them. Her mom frowned as they stood behind the couple near the host stand. Cameron smiled, realizing she must not have responded to something her mom had said.

"You have a beautiful smile," said a tall, chocolate man with a goatee.

Cameron looked to her left, giving him the side eye as she muttered, "Thanks."

Her mother nudged her in the side, signaling her to behave. She'd rather endure that than have her notice that her dimples weren't present when she smiled. Cameron nodded toward the host. Her mom stepped up and gave their names. The wait was fifteen minutes. She knew she was in trouble when her mother went to stand next to a group of men that included the one who complimented her.

"Which one of you is the oldest sister?" the man from earlier asked.

"You're so adorable. This is my daughter, Cameron." She reached out a hand and yanked Cameron closer.

The hostess called out a name behind them. The man motioned for his friends to go without him. "Nice to meet you. Do you have a minute?"

"We wouldn't want to keep you from your people," Cameron said, as her mom tugged her arm in a warning gesture.

He grinned, pulled out his wallet, and handed a business card to Cameron. "My cell number is on the bottom. Hopefully, you'll give me a call."

She took the card, planning to toss it at the first chance she got.

"Have a wonderful breakfast, ladies."

"Cameron Jordan Stone." Caroline rested her hands on her hips. "Stop being rude."

"I'm not being rude." Cameron was glad to hear their name being called. Not that her mom was going to leave it alone. Caroline snatched the man's card from her hand as they made it to the table.

"Nathan Elliott." Caroline mused, before glancing down the row of tables at him and his friends.

Her head snapped toward her mother. If she only knew how close she'd come to having a son-in-law named Nathan. Nathan King. But that was a lifetime ago. The man had made her believe she was lovable and as deserving of a family of her own as anyone else. She placed her hand on her stomach, saddened by the fact that fate didn't agree. Strangely enough, the only man who'd come close to making her feel that again was an anomaly due to everything that happened with her ex. Thankfully that one night with Daron forced her to face the truth that she wasn't okay and she started the healing process.

"Sweetie, are you okay?" Caroline put down her menu.

Cameron pulled herself together, focusing on her mother's concerned expression. "Yeah, this latest project is intense. But enough about that, we're here to celebrate your birthday. What's the rest of the family got planned?"

The waitress walked up before her mom could answer. After the brunette woman took their orders of blueberry pancakes, hash browns and scrambled eggs, her mother clasped her hands over Cameron's, then leaned forward. "What about Rob? Is he single?"

"Ma, we're talking about your *other* birthday plans." Cameron tilted her head, silently pleading with her mother to stop her frustrating matchmaking attempts.

"That boy's in love with you. Why won't you give him a chance?" Caroline shifted back on the vinyl bench, grabbing her coffee to sip, disappointment in her brown eyes.

"You've met him *one* time. How do you know?" Cameron smiled and thanked the waitress as she set a glass of orange juice in front of her.

Her mother met Rob when she had insisted on visiting her at work, which was why Rob still worked out of the Bronzeville office unless they were expecting someone in their South Loop office.

Caroline peered over her mug. "A mother knows these things. That man wants you."

"Yet you're trying to push me off on that Nathan dude?"

"Increasing the odds of success," Caroline replied, unapologetically.

"What about those birthday plans of yours?" she asked as the waitress returned with their food, then spent the next forty-five minutes talking about her mom's schedule for the day. Her brothers were doing a big dinner party for their mother.

"Will you be in town for Father's Day?" Caroline asked, as they headed to the parking lot.

Cameron's phone vibrated and she silently cursed when the message came through. Lex was picking her up an hour earlier than expected. "I'll still be in the thick of things. I'm heading back much sooner than even I anticipated."

She couldn't catch a break. First Jason, her dad, now her mom stirring up memories of her ex. As she pulled up to her brick ranch house in Flossmoor, she noticed Quinn's Terrain Denali out front. Jason wasn't planning to make it easy for her to get back in time for her flight.

Quinn approached as she exited her vehicle. "Cammy, whose heart you trying to break."

She pursed her lips. "Let's cut to the chase. Jason sent you." Glancing at the time, she reminded herself to get rid of him and fast. She had two and a half hours before Lex arrived.

"I need a female point of view on something." Quinn grabbed her wrist as she tried to walk away. "I'm serious."

"Running late for an appointment. We'll have to chat another time." Cameron trotted toward the black, steel screen door. She needed to be in Florida to track down Howard's meeting and the name of his client. Howard's apartment and office would be searched for any clues the moment he was in the air.

Glancing back, she was shocked he didn't push.

Quinn slid back in his Denali. She went into her bedroom, threw on a pair of jogging pants, tucking her denim dress into the waistband then she grabbed a light jacket and her backpack. When she reached the threshold, Quinn's and another vehicle had now blocked her in. She headed to the back, stepping out onto the deck, then rounded the corner. Hawk's Pathfinder was waiting on the side street.

She pulled out her cell. "Rob, meet me on the trail and pull out the device that stops cameras from recording."

"What happened?" he asked.

Cameron headed to the entertainment room. She pressed the button on the armoire to reveal the hidden hallway that connected to a series of dimly-lit tunnels. Bishop insisted on her having a panic room and escape tunnels built in. Considering what she did for him, she didn't argue. Cameron never imagined she'd need them to sneak away from her own family. "My brothers are trying to delay my departure. Plus, I've got less time than expected to get back."

"Say no more. I'll see you there," Rob responded.

When she reached the end of the tunnel, she climbed up the ladder between two bushes. Closing the latch, she grabbed the motorcycle hidden amongst the greenery. At this rate, she was sure she'd be sneaking in the back of her building at the same time as Lex was pulling up.

She walked her bike to the next street, noticed a police car sitting near the left corner and cursed. Cameron slid her helmet on and took off to the right. As she reached the intersection, she saw Hawk sitting on a motorcycle a few feet away. She pulled over near the cars parked on the street, not wanting to risk leading him to Rob and her storage facility.

She flipped up the visor on her helmet. "Hey Hawk."

"Jason figured you'd manage to get out." He gave her a knowing smirk.

Dammit. Nicely done, Jason. Cameron wouldn't be able to shake Hawk without endangering their lives. "Is that why your truck is parked on the side street?"

She pulled out her cell and texted both Lex and Rob that something came up and she wouldn't be able to make it. Good thing Trenton had her download the hidden app on her smartphone. When needed, she activated it to contact her team. Otherwise, she would've had to post on social media and hope Rob could figure out her message.

"So I'm going with you, or are you coming with me?" Hawk grabbed his helmet.

Cameron ignored the curious look from the blonde man walking a dog on the sideway. "I'm coming with you." She slid her visor down, knowing that at the first opportunity to leave safely, she would.

When she rounded the corner and two more motorcycles came into view, she realized Jason was in rare form. She followed Hawk to the northern suburb of Chicago to a house in Lake Bluff. Jason was making sure that even if she slipped out, she couldn't grab her luggage and make it in time for the flight.

"So how long will this place be my prison?" Cameron swung her leg off the bike, trailing him to the door of a gray brick two-story house.

"Just a couple of hours." Hawk said, before answering a ringing smartphone.

She glanced back to Quinn. "What did you want a female opinion on?"

"Oh, so now you want to talk," Quinn teased, his broad shoulder bumped her as Hawk crossed the threshold.

"It's seems I've got time." Cameron entered the contemporary living room. "But first I have a question for you since Hawk is on the phone."

"I'm listening."

"When did babysitting your sister become a favorite pastime?"

"Cam, you have a call." Hawk handed her the cell before Quinn could answer.

"What the hell did you do?" Jason's voice seethed frustration.

"Not what I planned to do." Cameron's hand tightened on the phone. "Otherwise, I wouldn't be here talking to you."

"Lex and the crew are not leaving without you."

Cameron snickered. "Really?" She checked her messages. "So, the only way you can guarantee they're on that plane is to let me go."

"Everything within me is screaming to keep you locked safely away, but having them look for you may be worse," Jason was silent for a moment. "Forty-eight hours, Cam. Then make a valid excuse for leaving. Family emergency. Get into a fight with Lex. I don't care but get out of there. If you don't, I'll pull you out. And it won't be pretty."

"Yes, sir," Cameron said, smiling as she handed the phone back to Hawk.

Her brothers shook their heads as she gave them each a consoling pat on the back trying not to smirk too much, then grabbed her helmet. Cameron couldn't give Jason a chance to make good on that threat. More than JD's life could be riding on what happened in Florida.

CHAPTER 17

Under Miami's setting sun, Daron was feeling the heat in more ways than one. He looked out at the large pool where Tia and Mac played a game of volleyball against Eric and Tandria. His attraction to her was getting harder to hide. When Tandria entered the airport with that damn denim material gripping her breasts as if it wasn't going to contain them and clinging to the curves of her hips like a second skin, he literally stopped in his tracks. Tia had to tug his arm. The timing unfortunately wasn't right. He had to deal with his situation with Tia first, and he couldn't end things with her yet. Though they hadn't been intimate for months.

His current plans jeopardized the lives of the men closest to him, but it was the only way to end this deadly game he'd gotten sucked into. Losing Desiree was hard. She was the person who watched for new faces, listened for rumors, and discreetly passed information along to the team. Desiree refused to play nice with Prescott and wouldn't leave when Daron tried to send her away. Now he had to make sure his developing feelings for someone else didn't become the death of him or her.

Daron's focus shifted to Tandria as she jumped out of the water, spiking the ball toward Tia who quickly moved out of the way.

"Aww, come on. This ain't dodge ball," Mac yelled as Tia lost the game for them.

Tia bounced over to the stairs leading out of the pool. "Whatever."

Eric laughed and gave Tandria a high five, then waded to the net to take it down. Tandria dove under the water and glided to the edge. She stood, pushing her wet, silky hair out of her face. She wore a sexy, knitted swimsuit that accentuated her small waist and had Daron wishing he wasn't in such a complicated situation. He couldn't lie and say that he didn't want to explore every inch of Tandria's curvaceous body. Something about Tandria was familiar, he'd seen flickers of Autumn in the way she looked at him even though the women didn't look alike. Autumn was dark brown with locs and brown eyes, and had beautiful artwork tatted on her body. She and Tandria were built the same but Autumn had been a lot thicker.

Eric stood next to Tandria as she leaned on the pool's interior wall. Based on the evil glare she gave him, he must have made a snarky remark.

Daron peered at Lex, who sat on the chair next to him, nodding toward the spot where Eric and Tandria were going at it again. "The sparks flying off them are ludicrous. They're either going to kill each other or—"

"Let's not go there," Lex scoffed, slicing his eyes toward him. "Besides, the man I have to worry about is sitting *right* next to me."

"My girl's drying off on the other side of the pool." Daron tilted his head toward Tia but kept his eyes on Tandria. He was convinced Tandria wasn't sent by Lucifer to harm him. She'd had several opportunities to take him out if she wanted. However, Red was unreachable which meant he couldn't confirm that she was indeed Kimura.

"I can't tell you how long it's been since I've seen that glint in your eye." Lex stood, then leaned over and whispered, "After all you've been through … *if* I *have to* give her up and accept defeat at the hands of another man, I'd rather it be you than Eric."

Daron detected a slight attitude in his statement. He glanced at Lex but said nothing. Mac had settled in one of the patio chairs with a Coors Light in hand.

Tia sashayed over to them.

Daron inhaled deeply as Lex straightened and Tia quickly claimed the spot Lex had vacated.

"That was fun." Tia placed her hand possessively on Daron's thigh, something that irritated him, especially today.

"Want anything to drink?" He removed her hand and stood. "I'll grab it on the way back."

"A diet coke please," she replied in a sultry voice that did nothing for him.

Daron leaned in and kissed her on the cheek. "You need Lex to pick anything up for the week?"

"I have everything covered." Tia smiled up at them. "As long as Mac picks up Prescott in time for the festivities, we're all set."

Tia had motives for staying with him. Trust only went so far.

His steps were in tandem with Lex's. Neither one said anything until they cleared the building and reached Lex's Rolls Royce. Since Daron had people watching his every move, Lex had to handle several private runs to confirm everything was in place for the next step of their plan.

"I'll pick up the package and leave it in the secured room for you." Lex pressed the key to unlock the car doors. His phone rang as he slid behind the wheel. Daron waited a moment before returning to the house.

"The pick-up timing was moved back." Lex was out of the car in a flash.

"Do I need to push back the yacht's departure tonight? I plan to make sure Tandria is there."

"No," Lex's tone was curt as he trudged back toward the mansion. "Let's get back to the ladies."

Daron caught him by the arm. "Is there an issue?"

Lex snatched away. "What problem could we possibly have?"

"Don't tell me you've fallen for her." Daron watched as Lex moved toward the door. "I selected you for a reason."

Lex pivoted around, his eyes flashing fire. "I was your safe choice as a place holder while you got your shit together with Tia."

"Oh, you really want me to end my relationship with Tia now?" Daron glanced at the door to make sure no one came out. "If I did that, we'd all be in prison, and Tandria would be on to the next man."

"If a woman like Tandria wanted to be with me, I'd give settling down a try." Lex advanced toward Daron. "So understand this, if she changes her mind about me while you're still not in a position to make your intentions known, you're screwed."

Lex marched toward the door.

"Damn," Daron muttered as he took long strides to catch up with him.

He'd always appreciated Lex's bluntness, but this wasn't one of those moments. Daron had only felt an intense and powerful pull like he experienced with Tandria with one other woman, Autumn. Unfortunately, the timing wasn't right to explore the connection with her back then. He was navigating a field of landmines, bringing her along for the ride would have put her life at risk. Daron refused to be responsible for extinguishing her light too soon. Despite his current situation, Daron was not letting this second chance go without doing everything within his power to explore the possibilities with Tandria, short of being sent to prison. Lex wouldn't get a chance to make that statement of being in a relationship with her a reality. Daron was already thinking of counter moves to ensure he was in a position to make Tandria his woman.

CHAPTER 18

Eric became aware of several things. Daron had selected a room for Tandria near the terrace, which was known as his "thinking" spot. He rarely put people there unless they had a full house.

He didn't miss Daron's eyes roaming over Tandria like she was his woman instead of Tia, as well as a hint of venom in his eyes as he moved away from Tia. Fleeting, but there. He doubted Tia noticed it.

Tandria had.

He had yet to figure Tandria's angle but she kept her focus on Daron and Lex while playing volleyball. Eric was fascinated by her. While he teased her about Daron, he'd never caught her flirting with him like some of the women Lex had brought into their circle.

Eric moved in the water until he blocked Tandria's view. "Do you have a thing for the boss? Is that why Lex doesn't stand a chance?"

Tandria lifted herself out the pool, dried off, then wrapped a long sarong around her body. "For a man who doesn't like me, you're always in my face about something. And I doubt it's Lex or Daron who you're asking for."

Eric stayed in the pool taking a moment to compose himself, otherwise his attraction would be obvious. After a few minutes, he hopped out and grabbed a towel from the small square patio table. "It's interesting you're the only woman here besides Tia."

"Ask Lex," she said, as she settled on the lounge chair and slid her sunglasses on. "I'm only here to find out if there are really fights that can earn people quite a bit of money. I could use a little extra cash."

"You fight?" Eric laughed as he looked in the direction Tandria was staring. Daron and Lex had returned, shooting silent daggers at each other and making Eric wonder what happened in such a short time. Those two were pretty tight. "That's hilarious."

She smirked and waved him off. "Whatever. Don't make me kick your ass to prove my point."

"Hey guys," Eric yelled, attracting everyone's attention. "We've been used."

"What?" Lex asked as he followed Daron across the deck toward Tia.

"Tandria's hoping to get into a fight night." He laughed again, this time slapping his knee to show how ludicrous that sounded.

Daron handed Tia a soda. "How did you hear about those?"

"Let's say a few friends didn't think it was wise for me to be hanging with Lex." Tandria shifted on her seat.

Eric's gaze landed on her thighs, the thickness of them was more enticing than he original surmised.

"Someone warned you about me? I'm shocked," Lex joked as his eyes widened to the size of saucers, and his jaw dropped in mock surprise.

Daron raised an eyebrow, but his gaze narrowed on Tandria. "You really want to fight?"

"Does it have the potential to earn a person thirty thou?" She swung her feet to the deck and stood, forcing Eric to lean back on the lounger to avoid being knocked back.

"Yeah," Lex responded, his wary gaze on Daron, but his stony expression told him how he really felt. He didn't want her anywhere near that kind of action.

Daron stared at Lex then Eric. Mac belly laughed at the end of the pool. Tia grimaced and gave Tandria a look that could've made a grown man tremble in his boots.

She shot Mac an evil glare before smiling and said, "Then I want to fight."

"Okay, if you pass the test then you're in." Daron gave her a once-over and shrugged.

Tia stared up at Daron as if to say *you're really going to let her do this?*

"Don't patronize me." Tandria shot Daron a glare. "I expect that from Eric."

"I'm sorry. It's hard to imagine you in the ring," Daron explained, trying but failing to keep a straight face.

Eric laughed again. She flicked her towel and popped him on the leg. He yelped, rubbing the tender spot and Mac nearly slid back into the deep end.

Tandria turned to Daron. "What's the test?"

"Fight one of our best men and last at least two rounds." Daron crossed his arms then grinned at Lex, who frowned.

Lex lifted his hands as if to say it was Daron's call, but the tense set of his shoulders indicated he wouldn't be able happy about anyone selected.

"Give me ten minutes to get ready." Tandria grabbed the rest of her stuff off the lounge chair.

Several of them exchanged shocked expressions. Daron's head snapped toward Lex. "She's serious, I take it. Since none of our newbies are here, it has to be one of you."

Lex's eyes wandered to Tandria's body as though sizing her up. "It has to be Mac."

Eric was a little surprised Daron was even entertaining the possibility. While he had back-up fighters on deck, in case someone didn't make it, he'd have to eliminate someone who qualified to allow Tandria to fight.

Tandria moved quickly across the deck to Daron and Lex as they continued to debate who would have the honor of challenging her.

Mac dropped down and stayed rooted to the patio chair. "Where is this supposed to take place?"

"The gym," Daron responded, but he didn't sound sure.

All eyes were on Tandria, who took long strides exiting the pool area. Eric stood.

"You sure about this?" Mac asked as he rose.

"Go get changed," Daron commanded.

Eric went to rinse off the chlorine, then changed his clothes and ambled into the gym.

Tandria showed up a few minutes later, dressed in form-fitting black workout pants and a matching tank.

Daron led her past the treadmills and the weight machines to the boxing ring near the silver stadium seats right before the fight room. The moment Mac entered the ring with his jersey shorts and graphic t-shirt, Tandria started laughing so hard, Eric thought she would burst into tears.

"I'm sorry," she said, trying to contain herself. "Sometimes I forget y'all don't know me."

Mac was a wheel man. His strength was driving, not kicking ass. Mac was stocky and slow compared to most of Daron's other crew. Probably the reason Daron chose him to fight against her. The fact that she found the situation so funny was alarming.

"Alright, remember. Two rounds," Daron reiterated after the boxing gloves were on.

"I wouldn't sit if I were you," she said to Daron, stopping him before he made it to the seats situated around the practice ring. "This isn't going to take long."

When the bell rang, Tandria came out looking like she was ready for a runway walk instead of a fight.

Eric knew this fight wouldn't last long. After a couple of punches from Mac, Daron would end things.

"Are you guys really sure about this?" Mac stepped back as Tandria swung wildly, dodging a blow.

"Tandria, if that's all you got, I'll go get my pop-up punching bag for you," Eric teased from the sidelines, causing a round of laughter to echo in the space.

Soon as Mac dropped his guard, she threw several fiery punches that landed in Mac's gut, chest, and face. All the men came to their feet, gaping. Mac dropped to the canvas stretched flat on his back. "No need Eric," she shot back. "You're so full of hot air I can use you."

Mac rolled to his knees and tried to stand but staggered backward and hit the ropes. He shook his head and blinked several times.

"You're so wrong for that," Lex announced, but his smile was pure admiration.

"What?" Tandria asked, grinning as she bounced on her toes, ready for the next round.

Daron's cheeks and lips tightened as he elaborated on Lex's comment, "Using the fact that we thought you were too feminine to fight."

"Me," Tandria gave them an innocent look, complete with a petulant pout then leaned on the rope with a seductively playful smirk.

"That doesn't count." Daron glanced at Eric. "Are you ready?"

"Always." Eric's smile widened.

Daron leaned in, whispering, "Don't hurt her, but make her sore as hell."

A glint of mischief lit her eyes even though her expression remained the same. *Did she hear what Daron said?*

Lex leaned over saying something in Daron's ear that Eric couldn't catch. Daron chuckled and it didn't sit well with Eric.

Eric entered the ring and slid on his gloves in a matter of minutes. Easy was not the word Eric would use to describe fighting her. He bobbed and weaved as she threw one-two combos.

Tandria blocked his jab and hit him with an upper cut to the chin. Eric's head snapped back. He tuned out the heckling coming from the sidelines and took their sparring match a little more seriously. First, he thought to humor her a bit. Then trying to keep her punches from connecting with his body became the goal. Eric was dripping with sweat by the time the second bell rang.

"Tandria you're in," Daron announced, before discussing with Lex how he enjoyed the fight.

"Next time I won't hold back," Tandria threatened as she sashayed to the other side of the ring.

Eric stripped off his gloves, tossed them to the mat, and stepped out of the ring. Lex tipped over, imitating Eric dodging punches. "Eric, I *loved* your imitation of one of those pop-up punching bags."

"We'll see you around." Daron waved at Tandria as he trailed Lex toward the exit.

Eric was on their heels. He was surprised Tia had been so quiet but she had no love for Tandria to begin with. She was probably saving the angry words all for Daron later tonight. Eric glanced back to Mac and Tia lagging behind, walking a little too close to each other.

Tandria waved as they left. Something weird was going on but he couldn't tell if it was Tandria's success in the ring, the threat to Daron's organization, or something else causing the disruption. Daron paused at the threshold, then turned to face them. "Tia, you and Tandria will join us on the yacht."

"You're serious?" Tia squealed with delight, pushing past Mac, Eric, and Lex who stepped back as she wrapped her arms around Daron's waist.

"Eric, let Tandria know."

Dismissed as though he was nothing more than an errand boy, he headed in Tandria's direction. She had wandered to the other end of the room where the main fights occurred. Two fighting cages stood on each side. The walls were lined with plush theater seating. During the fights, air walls separated the gym from the arena and more seats were added.

Eric trotted over. "Hey, Daron would like you to join us tonight on the boat."

"I'm hanging out with Tia tonight, remember?" Tandria spun around, crossing her arms over her breasts.

Lex went through gorgeous women the way he changed his designer suits, what was different about this one?

Eric had found a few attractive, but he'd never been drawn to them like he was to Tandria. This woman had come in and dusted them all in her Black Girl Magic. "Her plans have changed too."

"Is this your doing?" She stepped forward and poked him in the chest.

His gaze dropped from her mesmerizing eyes to those kissable lips. He gently lifted her finger from his chest. "Listen, this invite comes straight from Daron." Eric smiled, knowing the only reason Daron let Tia accompany them was to ensure Tandria's presence.

Her hazel orbs narrowed as she gave him the evil eye. "I'd better go get cleaned up." She brushed past Eric.

He wasn't sure it was a smart move on Daron's part to bring her here with so much going on. No doubt when Prescott arrived, he'd be all over her. Prescott, with his arrogance, rudeness, and tendency to play big shot, was not Lex's favorite person. Eric's either. If nothing else, it was going to be an interesting week. An explosive one if Daron couldn't manage the animosity between them. Then again, that could work in Eric's favor.

CHAPTER 19

Cameron's body cut through the water in the second pool tucked between a small, white brick house with black-trimmed windows and the main mansion. She didn't want to raise suspicion by suddenly switching from the main pool when she made her attempt to connect with JD. The invitation to the yacht was nothing more than a ploy to keep an eye on her but at least it gave her another view of the property.

She flipped, pushing off the interior wall. Her read on people was pretty good but too many individuals in this scenario were acting as though they had something to hide. Was Eric trying to redirect the sexual energy flowing between them? She couldn't lie. She took pleasure in getting a little payback when she snatched a hole in his ego yesterday.

Although Eric was the head of security, she had the distinct feeling Lex was Daron's right-hand man. Daron himself was somewhat of an anomaly. His actions didn't match her expectations of a sinister crime lord or his rumored behavior of being hard, calculating, and cunning. She wondered if Jason's inside man and Daron's traitor was one and the same.

After swimming laps for about thirty minutes to exercise, Cameron then took the long route back to her room. She wanted a better idea of how this mansion was laid out, where the cameras were placed, and an alternate route to get to the second pool where she expected JD and the others to spend their time.

Steve, who was security transportation coordinator, stepped into the corridor between the two living spaces and waved as she reached the black wood-and-glass door to the main house.

She gave him a half grin, knowing her chance of talking to her cousin or sneaking off premises would increase exponentially if Steve wasn't in the surveillance room when she made the attempt. He was always alert, even when he appeared otherwise occupied. The steel door further up the hall quietly shut as Steve reentered that room.

When she stepped in the back-interior hallway, Lex dressed in a leisure outfit, was typing into his phone and moving toward her, but looked up to say. "Hey beautiful. Weren't you going to the spa with Tia?"

"On my way to change now." Cameron shifted the bag on her shoulder.

Lex slid the phone into his pocket. "Why were you swimming in the other pool?"

"I noticed it last night coming back from the yacht and figured I'd check it out." She gestured at the stairs and moved toward them.

Lex changed direction and walked by her side. "When Prescott gets here, do me a favor? Try your best to keep your distance."

"A little difficult if we're in the same house," Cameron shot back as she stopped with a foot on the first step.

He leaned on the black metal banister and his gaze narrowed. "If your skill at fighting and evading questions are any indication, then you'll do fine."

"Whatever." She playfully shoved him further against the handrail.

She didn't want to be bothered with Prescott either. Her main goals were to speak with JD, find a route to sneak out, and create a plausible excuse for doing so—if she got caught. She didn't want to consider what would happen if she needed to leave during one of their scheduled outings. Too many eyes would be working to prevent an easy escape.

"Did you remember to bring your passport?" Lex inquired, as his phone chimed.

"Of course," Cameron replied, cringing inwardly knowing she didn't have a passport under Tandria Jenkins. Thanks to Rob she could have it by the end of the day. The tricky part was that she'd need to get to him to retrieve it.

◆ ◆ ◆

Cameron froze momentarily the minute she saw Eric waiting by the car. At least it wasn't Steve. With the events they had planned, this time with Tia might be her only opportunity to handle that personal business. He opened the doors of the Phantom for them. Tia chattered about the different spa treatments she enjoyed for the entire ride. Cameron was sure she'd covered every one listed in the brochure they'd looked at the previous day. *Does she have interest outside of Daron and maintaining her beauty routines?*

"We're here." Eric pulled in front of a light-grey building that housed the Radiance spa.

Eric helped Tia out as Cameron slid from the backseat. He trotted around to hold Cameron's door, standing a little too close for comfort.

"How do you feel about Lex?" Tia asked, twisting a brand-new diamond ring around her finger as she waited on the sidewalk.

A loaded question, since Tia probably wanted to know if Cameron had designs on Daron.

Eric's eyes locked onto her as though he was curious about her answer. She put some distance between them and the car before saying, "He's cool to hang with, but that's about it."

"Lex knows this?" Tia caught the silver door handle as someone with her penciled eyebrows drawn in badly exited the building.

"It's not a question of whether Lex knows," Cameron stated as she entered the quaint reception area that had more spa products than seating. "But if he accepts it."

"It's something about you that Daron trusts, which is rare for him. Especially with females. It took me over two years of proving myself before ... " Tia shrugged as she moved toward the counter. "It's not important."

"I'm not trying to get attached to these guys." Cameron simmered inwardly, wondering what Tia's end game was. She was clearly not in love with Daron, otherwise his distant behavior would bother her. Too many secrets were floating around the mansion.

"Someone will be with you momentarily," the brunette spa attendant said, then returned the headset to her ear.

Tia smiled at the brunette, then turned to Cameron and said, "Honey, I don't know if you realize it, but they're already attached to you. All of them."

"Don't worry. This extended vacation is my last time hanging out with them." Cameron hadn't expected to get this close to the inner circle. She wasn't trying to make an enemy out of them, unless it was her last resort. Being too familiar could cause issues.

"Oh, I'm not worried at all." A huge grin spread across her face. "Does Lex know?"

"I plan to tell him before I leave."

Tia let out a sigh. "Lex is a good guy. You're the first woman I've seen more than once. The only one that ever got invited to stay in the *main house*."

"When I get back, I need to concentrate on finding another job." Cameron tried to reassure her that she wasn't a threat, but the set of Tia's small shoulders said otherwise.

Tia leaned toward her. "I want to be more involved in Daron's business."

"Really?" Cameron couldn't imagine what Tia wanted to do in his organization and didn't care. Her conversation didn't lead one to believe she could be taken seriously.

"Yes, I want to ... oh." Tia noticed the brunette waving her over to the desk and left Cameron's side.

The young black woman motioned for Cameron as a client walked away and Tia was being led toward the back area. Cameron had changed her treatments to access the whirlpool and sauna only, instead of the fifty-minute body wrap and fifty-minute massage, but Tia didn't need to know that.

Tia headed into the wait area as Cameron was being shown to the lockers. "Meet me back at the lockers after you're done," Tia directed as she entered a room with white curtains. The sounds of a rainforest played softly in the background and seeped into the hallway.

The attendant gave Cameron a locker key then showed her the showers and the whirlpool-sauna area. At times like this, she hated being the only girl on the team. Otherwise, she could have had someone meet her here. She wished she'd thought to reach out to Kathleen Frost, one of the few women she trusted in the field.

She changed into a black jogging suit, putting in fake teeth that gave her an overbite, then cotton balls in her cheeks to give her face a fuller appearance. With a long black wig and a pair of oversized glasses, she walked to a silver door that had been propped open. She assumed it was for the smokers who worked there.

As Cameron crossed over the threshold, Tia slid into the passenger side of a burgundy car with Mac waiting at the wheel. Cameron stayed back until they disappeared from that block before she left to meet the guys down the street. She thanked her good fortune that she'd caught sight of Tia's move. Cameron couldn't afford to be sneaking back in at the same time.

She rounded the corner and found Rob standing near the curb. She approached him, lowering her sunglasses.

He grinned, shook his head, escorted her around to the van, then tapped on the side. The door slid open. Greg extended a hand to help her in, giving her a gun then the passport as the door closed.

"Greg, it's nice to see you, but you handing me a weapon first is not a good sign."

Cameron had requested an ankle holster. Her jogging pants couldn't sustain the weight of the gun and her pockets weren't deep enough.

"Howard had our decoy followed," Greg explained as Rob climbed into the passenger side, then picked up the laptop between the seats and held it out to her. "They approached him in Tampa when he left the hotel room."

She glanced at the screen. "He's heading this way."

Rob nodded. "That Tampa flight was a distraction. He's in Fort Lauderdale."

"A two-man team is tracking him, trying to find out the time of the meeting." Greg moved into the driver's seat. She hoped both situations would be wrapped up by the time she left Florida so that she could enjoy the fourth of July with some of her favorite people.

"Rob, hack into the spa's system and figure out how to put me in for a treatment in case someone asks." She passed the laptop back to him.

"The intel suggested Lucifer plans to strike before Daron leaves Florida."

"It looks like I'm here to the end after all." She scanned her new passport. Lex had mentioned that JD would leave out for Illinois on the Sunday before they left. The original plan was to leave before the fights, if she had the opportunity to speak to JD.

Greg started the van. "JD needs to survive whatever Lucifer has planned for Daron this week. If he does, he'll be alright."

She gave instructions of two properties to rent depending on the picture she posted then reviewed their plan for dealing with Howard.

"I'd better get going." Cameron slid out of the van, aiming to make it back before Tia. Her heart raced when she noticed that Eric stood where she needed to turn to get to the rear entrance of the spa. She jammed her hands in her pocket and kept her head down until she cleared the way past him.

He looked up, dismissed her, and focused on his cell.

She swept inside and hurried to a stall to undress. Cameron wrapped the Ruger in the jogging gear and stashed it in the locker. A couple of minutes later, she was sitting on a wood bench, wrapped in a white towel along with a blonde and brunette who were stretched out with their eyes closed.

Tia poked her head into the sauna, pulling a fluffy white robe tight around her. "If you're ready to go, Eric can take you back. I'm … having another treatment."

"I can stay and relax until you're ready." Cameron grinned, ignoring the evil daggers the two women across the room shot their way for holding a conversation in the quiet area.

Tia grimaced and her hand went into her hair, smoothing it from her face. "Honey, it's no problem. Daron already knows. You should leave."

Cameron let Tia off the hook but it meant she'd be alone with Eric for the first time.

Cameron didn't believe Eric being stuck on a call the entire ride back was a coincidence. When they arrived at the mansion, she went into the kitchen to grab some water and a piece of fruit from a silver three-tiered display on the island. As she left with the fruit in her bag, Daron and Lex entered the entertainment room with a guy she recognized but couldn't place. He appeared Caucasian from a distance but the closer she came, she realized he was of mixed heritage. Prescott. In the picture she had of him, his hair wasn't as long. Now it was hanging over his face as though he was using it to hide his features, just as she was. Even from a distance, he rubbed her the wrong way.

With so many men in the place, it was hard to be absolutely sure who "Jason's eyes" were on the inside. But she was convinced it wasn't Prescott, unless he was using his position to aid a takeover. She had seen a few corrupt agents try. This man didn't have his agent on ex-military vibe anywhere on him.

Since his negative energy had hit her from across the room, she stepped out of the doorway—to avoid meeting him—until she thought they cleared the space. Cameron moved quickly toward the stairs until she realized she'd left the water and doubled back.

Daron and company entered the foyer from the entertainment room. She stopped when she reached them, kicking herself in the ass for backtracking.

"Tandria, this is Prescott my second-in-command," Daron said, gesturing to a man who was a few inches shorter. "Prescott, Tandria, a multifaceted diamond that we're still trying to figure out whether she's in the rough or polished."

She took his extended hand, and his thumb caressed her skin. Cameron didn't miss the spatter of blood on his cuff. "Prescott is an interesting first name."

He gave her a lengthy once-over as he stated, "It's actually my last."

"How long have you worked with Daron?" Cameron tugged her hand from his grasp, which he seemed reluctant to release. She found it fascinating that while she knew about him, no one but Tia ever mentioned him by name. The only time Lex had spoken of Prescott was to warn her to avoid him. Lex and Eric silently moved toward her and each flanked her side as though she needed protection.

"For years."

"Interesting," Cameron mused, as she frowned, hoping to get a reaction.

Prescott cut his eyes toward Daron then to her. "Why are you frowning?"

Cameron gave him a slow smile. "I'm surprised I haven't met you before today. All the important people are present and accounted for."

His gray eyes devoured her as though she was his next meal. "I mostly handle Daron's *foreign* accounts. I'd love to take you to dinner and tell you more about it."

Both Lex and Eric stiffened.

She almost laughed.

Daron put his palm up to halt Lex's movement.

"That sounds interesting, but no thanks," Cameron replied. Prescott without a doubt was the bad seed in the bunch. "Enjoy your evening, gentlemen."

She made a break for it before anyone could say otherwise. She felt their gazes boring a hole in her back. Lex was instantly by her side. "How was the spa?"

"Good," Cameron replied. Her feet moved over the stonewashed oak planks until she reached the stainless-steel refrigerator. She grabbed two bottles of Glaceau Smartwater.

Lex's lower back rested against the marble counter. "Are you planning to take another swim tonight?"

"No." She extended a bottle to him. He shook his head and she tucked both in her arms.

"Good," Lex replied. "I'd hate to go blow for blow with Prescott his first night in."

Cameron smiled as Lex shadow boxed for several seconds.

Prescott reeked of evil. Lex didn't have to worry. She could practically smell the body count on him.

During her time as Kimura, she'd met enough men like him that she'd happily annihilate, given the opportunity. The next few days might prove her wrong, but she doubted it. She gave Lex's back a gentle pat.

He extended his arm before escorting her upstairs. He pressed his lips to her cheek, nodded, then made his way to the opposite end of the corridor. She didn't think the nod was for her. Steve must have been on security, which meant no exploring the grounds tonight.

CHAPTER 20

The next evening, Daron fumed as he watched the recording of Tia sneaking back into the mansion. She thought her moves were undetected because the main camera was shifted out of position but Tia was unaware of the secondary system. Daron locked the tablet in the safe and left the office expecting everyone with exception of Tia, to be assembled in the foyer. Lex stood near the threshold in a slate-blue tailored suit, scrolling through his cell.

Daron sauntered up next to Lex. "We'll be taking the Executive tonight."

The instant Tandria arrived wearing a one-shoulder jumpsuit that complimented her curves, she had his complete attention. The seductive sway of her hips as she made a slow runway model strut toward Lex, was hypnotizing. She was well aware of her power.

Eric entered from the kitchen, avoiding eye contact with Tandria.

What happened when he'd gone to notify Tandria they were almost ready to leave?

Lex shifted his gaze to see what had made Eric change direction, then kissed her on the cheek. "Hey, Beautiful."

Daron's gaze swept over her body again, then came back to her eyes, which earned him a searing glare from Lex. "No glasses tonight?"

"I decided to give my face a break." Tandria slipped her hands into her pockets as if she was disturbed that he'd honed in on the glasses.

"Where's Tia?" Daron glanced at Eric, ignoring the vibrating cell in his pocket.

Eric checked his watch. "I gave her the ten-minute warning."

"Tandria, go see what's taking her so long." Daron pulled out the cell and replied to the text about pushing the meeting time back.

"Whoa." Tandria crossed her arms and glared at him. "When did you put me on the payroll?"

Daron's head snapped up from the phone. "What?"

"I'm not paid to take orders from you." She turned toward Lex before returning her focus to him. "Now if Lex *asks* me to do it, I will."

"You want to be *paid* to take orders, 'cause I got cash," Daron shot back, reaching for his wallet.

"Beautiful," Lex's gaze shifted between the two of them. "Would you mind—"

"Not necessary," Steve came from the back hallway wearing a charcoal suit with a white collarless shirt. "Tia needs another thirty minutes. Prescott said he and Mac will meet us at the reception."

"Eric, Steve," Daron ordered in an authoritative voice. "Stay here and take the truck."

"Mac and Prescott have the Phantom," Eric reminded him.

"Lex." Daron nodded toward the kitchen.

He frowned as his arm dropped from Tandria's waist. "See you in a few."

Lex snatched a set of keys off the rack on the wall.

"We'll meet you outside," Daron informed Lex, then turned to Steve. "If she's not ready in thirty minutes, leave her and have Pedro and JD come up to the house to keep watch."

"She's not going to be happy," Steve stated, angling toward the stairs to the upper level.

"Then she should've been down here like the rest of us." Daron opened the door. "I don't want to be there all night."

Daron didn't miss the *someone's fed up* look Tandria shot at Steve and Eric.

Steve's gaze shifted to the Rolex on his wrist.

Daron stormed out, calling, "Tandria, come on."

Tandria seemed to compose herself before following him outside. "Mr. Bossy, you're going to have to work on your tone and your manners."

"Do you have a problem with me?" Daron stepped closer, becoming intoxicated by the sensual scent of her perfume with notes of plum, mandarin, and blackberry. That hint of blackberry brought Autumn to the forefront of his mind but back then it was mixed with a vanilla scent.

"Not as long as you don't think I'm one of your men." Tandria moved toward him leaving mere inches between them, kissing distance. "I'm not afraid of you. They are."

Daron gave her an intense stare down, trying not to glance at her full breasts which were inches from his chest. "Maybe you should be."

Tandria smirked, unfazed. "But I'm not."

Lex pulled up out front in a slick black Porsche Panamera whose exterior gleamed under the moonlight.

Daron stepped back. "I'll work on it. Now get in the car." The corners of Daron's mouth curved into a smile as he opened the passenger door for her.

She didn't miss a beat as she walked back toward the house seconds later. He enjoyed the view a moment before saying, "Would you please get in?"

Tandria returned, hitting him with her purse then gracefully lowering herself into the passenger seat.

Daron rounded the car to slide in behind Lex. The drive through the neighborhood and over the bridge was quiet. Daron knew Lex was not happy that he was driving instead of Steve. Daron was days from being free to pursue Tandria and figure out what was next for him but he also needed to focus on the business that had him in Miami. Concentrating on work was easier when he kept Lex's alone time with Tandria to a minimum. Since Daron couldn't actively seek opportunities to know Tandria better, spending time with her and Lex was as good as it got.

The number of times Lex checked the mirrors and changed lanes was concerning. Daron swiped the back of the seat where he'd affixed a thin clear tablet that blended into the material. He pulled up the cameras that had been installed and found a Ford Fusion moving lane for lane with them on the expressway.

"Which one of you do I have to thank for my extended vacation?" Tandria glanced over her shoulder but she seemed to be looking out the rear window.

"Why do you think we're involved?" Daron asked.

"I requested two days off and I got over a week," she said, shifting her gaze to between Lex and him then looked out the glass behind Daron.

Daron returned his focus on the screen. The Fusion was right behind them when Lex whipped toward the off-ramp.

Lex shared a quick glance with Daron. "Clearly, your boss likes you."

"Mmm hmm," she mused.

The Fusion zipped past them.

Tandria's shoulder dropped as she settled back into the passenger seat. Daron figured she'd spotted the car trailing them and was discreetly trying to check it for herself. The more he was around her, the more he was convinced that she was Kimura. She had a right to be concerned. Someone, either the infamous "Lucifer" or one of his elite clients, wanted to prevent him from pulling the last of the secured storage containers out of circulation.

The second turn Lex made led them down a dark two-lane street. On the right was the highway wall. Other streets ran to their left, but Daron could barely read the signs. That was cause for alarm. If someone came after them, the Porsche was trapped.

Lex checked his rearview mirror again. "We should pass on this event."

This area felt a little seedy but Daron and the team had attended an event at the hotel before. Not his favorite place because of how the area looked at night. However, he needed to meet with his contact face to face. Daron didn't want to leave any digital footprints. He'd just have to reschedule.

Daron peered through the glass, then pulled out his phone. "I'll text Steve and let him know."

Their vehicle rolled over something that felt like a speed bump before they made it into a well-lit area. Lex paused at one of the buildings that had a small garage with only one way in and out. He pushed forward, possibly searching for somewhere to pull over. On the right, lay a path with palm trees in front of a fence and a concrete wall. Not the best place to examine the Panamera.

"That's the hotel at the end of the block," Lex said.

Daron's cell rang, and he answered. He inhaled sharply, as he was informed someone had intentionally misdirected him and was given the correct address.

"I'll see if I can make it within the hour." Daron sat his phone next to him.

He reached under the seat and passed Lex a weapon. "The email invite had the wrong address due to a glitch. The host thought everyone was contacted about the mistake," Daron explained even though he knew it wasn't the entire truth.

As they neared the end of the street, a food truck drove in front of them and blocked their path. Lex slammed on the brakes. Tandria and Daron jerked forward, but the seatbelts kept them secure.

Lex put the Porsche in reverse, heading back in the direction of that eerie darkness.

Another truck came from the opposite direction, blocking them in. The doors of the food truck opened.

Lex hit the brakes again, threw the car into drive, and picked up speed as the men who emerged from the truck lifted assault rifles, aimed, and fired.

He swerved into the park at the end the block; one tire in the grass, one on the sidewalk.

Daron grabbed hold of the driver's seat and Tandria held on to the door handle and the dashboard as Lex barely braked to make a right turn onto the street. The Panamera fishtailed and they barely missed hitting a passing Chrysler. Lex straightened, then sped around the Pacifica they'd nearly hit. He took another right to avoid getting stopped by a red light.

"Find somewhere safe to pull over," Daron ordered as he keyed the code into his phone to unlock an app that detected foreign objects on a vehicle. He unbuckled the seat belt and shined the flashlight from his phone to scan all over the back seat. The phone light changed from bright white to red, confirming his suspicions, something was attached to the Panamera. Lex pulled into a garage and followed the ramp several levels up and parked on an upper, less populated, level. Daron snatched off his suit jacket.

"It's on," Lex announced referring to the inhibitor device that blacked out the security cameras on three levels as the trunk popped open.

Tandria shot them an *are you crazy* stare as he and Lex stepped out of the car. "Is stopping a good idea, gentlemen?"

Daron laid his jacket on the backseat, hoping that it was only a tracking device and not something more explosive. "Don't have a choice," Daron stated, closing the door.

Whoever was coming for the device was the bigger threat. The Panamera didn't carry the firepower that the other vehicles did since they didn't use it as often. Unfortunately, it meant they would be outgunned.

CHAPTER 21

Cameron climbed out, shocked that Daron and Lex openly carried their weapons in a parking lot full of cameras. Daron tossed a blanket on the concrete behind the Porsche and pulled a little box from the trunk. He rolled up his sleeves, stuck a Beretta in his front waistband, and stretched out on his back.

Lex stepped in front of him to protect him as Daron worked under the car. She peered over his shoulder at Daron.

"How long do we have?" Lex asked, focused on the ramp leading to their location.

"Maybe five or ten minutes, based on traffic, lights … plus they have to make it through the lower floors of the garage," Daron responded, sticking his head under the Panamera.

Cameron turned her back to the trunk, glancing down at Lex's Glock. "I'm first-rate with a gun too."

"If I had another one, I'd happily hand it to you." Lex looked at Daron, who grimaced.

She stared at Daron's Beretta but didn't comment. If the roles were reversed, she doubted she'd have given up hers either, but they needed more fire power than this.

The screech of tires made them all snap to attention.

Lex nodded toward the Panamera. "Get in."

"How much time do you need?" She scurried to the passenger side.

"Five minutes at least," Daron replied.

Cameron grabbed her purse and pulled out what appeared to be a nail file case. She sprinted down the ramp.

"Where you going?" Lex called after her, sounding worried.

"To buy a couple of minutes," she said, but didn't break her stride.

Daron called out to Lex. "The device only takes out cameras on three floors."

"I heard you," Cameron called out.

She sprinted to the bottom of the level below them. A Chevrolet Malibu was inching up the concrete. She squatted between the last car and the wall, allowing the Malibu to move past without seeing her. Still at a safe distance, she tipped up, aimed the file case at the right back tire and pressed the button to send blades flying, then repeated on the left. Staying low, she moved up the incline to the front of the parked cars. Cameron glanced at her watch as she crept along the wall to the top of the ramp. Daron should almost be done detaching the device from the Porsche. The back tires blew out before their unwanted guests reached the level where Daron and Lex were situated.

All four doors of the Chevrolet flew open. Bodies whipped out right after.

Cameron cursed. The way the men were positioned, she couldn't take all four out fast enough.

"You're outnumbered," the driver snarled at Lex as the other three inched away. "I suggest you throw down your gun."

Lex held his ground, and replied, "I can't do that."

She pulled out the business card holder, removed four of them, then slid two in each palm. Cameron crept up behind the men. "Sorry about your tires."

"Tandria. No," Lex yelled.

Three of them spun around to face her. She flung the cards; hit two targets square in the chest and one in the back as he turned to make it into the Malibu. The driver ducked as the bodies dropped, but she managed to put one in his shoulder. He yanked out the card and threw it to the concrete. His fingers probably felt singed since it was designed with a heating mechanism to remove fingerprints after use.

Lex raised his gun.

The driver dived into the car seconds before the bullets hit his side, shattering the window. Cameron cursed as she inched up the incline to the right of the Malibu. The driver still had his gun. The drug on that card would take a little longer to kick in since he pulled it out so fast. She studied the angle of the door. The man didn't have a clear shot.

As she neared the Malibu, the driver remained in place.

"Tandria, move," Daron yelled, throwing items in the trunk then slamming it shut. He pulled out a Beretta, glanced at Lex, then motioned toward the driver's side.

Lex moved as directed, opening Daron's door before sliding behind the wheel.

As Cameron ran up the incline, the passenger side popped open. She hopped in. Her heart raced as she snapped the seat belt in place. Daron backed up, his gun aimed at the parking ramp until he reached the opening then climbed in.

"Well, damn girl," Lex said as he peeled away. "You can back me up any time."

"There's at least one more car below us." Cameron ignored his statement and the quick side eye he gave.

The Panamera raced down the ramp until it reached the next level. Lex glanced up at the rearview mirror. "Are we still going to the reception?"

Daron unrolled his sleeves, growling, "No."

Cameron reached into her purse, pulled out a wet wipe and handed it over. She had no doubt they would bring up tonight at a later time.

Daron swiped the cloth over his hands, eased into his jacket then began typing into his cell.

Neither Lex nor Daron seemed astonished by her actions. *This incident may change tomorrow's plans to go to Key West.* A good thing. She'd hated the idea of Rob or Greg driving that distance only to replenish her supplies and give her an update on Howard. She hoped to be able to slip away from the group long enough for some verbal and detailed information on Howard's moves to find Bishop's old contact. She wanted to know if the search of Howard's office and home had given any clue to the identity of his client.

Lex's head snapped in her direction as they came to a stop light. "Again, what is it that you do for a living?"

"I'm an *administrative assistant*," she answered, working hard to keep a straight face.

Daron broke into laughter that echoed through the interior. "I've been saying I needed to hire an administrative assistant. Didn't realize they came with enough skills to take down four armed men."

"Funny," she said, dryly. "How about you two concentrate on getting us back to where we're staying without any more incidents?"

The remainder of the ride was uneventful as Lex took an extended route back. She was glad to see the mansion, and the security crew walking the grounds, come into view. Cameron slid out of her heels the moment they crossed the threshold. Her bare feet moved quickly over the wooden floor after she bid them all goodnight. Instead of going to her bedroom, she detoured to the terrace. She placed her high-heels next to her chair and replayed the evening's events.

Five minutes later, Cameron heard voices underneath her. "You can't put her life at risk like that," Lex's words were filled with anger.

"As you see, Tandria is fully capable of handling herself," Daron shot back. "Is this really about me putting her in danger or you wanting her for ... "

Their words trailed off. She didn't think anything of the silence until she heard her name.

"Tandria."

She was on her feet in an instant. Daron and Lex stood by the poolside waving up at her. *Now how did they know I was up here?* She frowned as she waved and reclaimed her seat. *Steve must be doing security tonight.*

The bit of conversation between Daron and Lex clued her in to the strain between the two that she occasionally felt. She hadn't expected to be at the root of their issue.

Several minutes later, Lex stepped onto the terrace. "Don't stay up too late. We're still doing Key West tomorrow."

They are crazy. She stared at him like he'd lost his mind. He grinned and closed the terrace doors. Tomorrow, she had to create an opportunity to connect with her men and replenish her supplies. She didn't want to give her brother a chance to keep his promise to put her behind bars. Cameron glanced at her phone, tempted to use the app Trenton had her install but it was too risky to use in the mansion because Daron's use of tech nearly mirrored her own. The app, when activated, allowed her to contact her team instead of leaving a message via a post on social media. Trenton warned her against using it near The Warden's team unless it was an emergency, she wasn't in the mood to find out why.

Upon entering her bedroom, a folded piece of paper caught her eye. Someone must have slipped it under her door. She picked it up. The note read, *Your forty-eight hours will be up soon.*

She sighed, whispering, "Jason."

CHAPTER 22

Cameron still couldn't believe they were still traveling to Key West. She flung her bag on her shoulder, crossed the threshold wondering about the real reason behind the almost four-hour drive. She hated that she had to stick close to the group until it was time to meet her team so that Jason couldn't intercept and put her out of play.

Mac waved as she passed the Range Rover, heading for Lex who stood next to a Phantom.

Tia pouted with arms locked over her chest, standing near the trunk having an intense conversation with Daron.

"I prefer the truck for longer trips," Tia whined, her voice grating on Cameron's nerves.

"Steve, you ride with us. Tia, ride in the truck," Daron ordered, then slid into the back seat.

Tia smiled as she shot by Cameron, who glanced back to see Mac sliding behind the wheel. Daron's eyebrow shot upward as he clocked that move and how elated Tia seemed to be about the arrangement. Prescott switched seats so Tia could ride shotgun. Eric secured the house then hopped in the Range Rover. No one but Daron seemed to pick up on the fact that Tia constantly maneuvered to be with Mac. Cameron shook her head. Tia and Mac couldn't be more obvious.

Steve caught up with Cameron, then leaned in to whisper, "This is going to be a good trip after all."

She chuckled before she opened the passenger door, knowing that Tia would be talking nonstop about fashion, reality shows, and celebrity gossip. Steve smiled as he slid into the backseat.

On the ride to Key West, all three men were relaxed, talking, laughing about the past. She rarely heard Steve speak, since he was usually in the security room. These two weren't only Daron's employees, they were his friends.

"Ms. Tandria, now that we have you in a position where you can't run. What is it that you really do?" Daron asked.

Cameron wondered when this conversation would come around again. They let her slip off to bed with no mention of anything. "I currently work—"

"Wait." Lex laughed. "Please don't say at Walsh's company."

"It's where I work." She glared at Lex. He glared back, then chuckled.

Steve placed his hands on her seat and tilted forward. "We're not talking about your *cover* job."

"Okay. Okay. I'll tell you what I do … " Cameron pivoted back to Daron with a taunting stare. "Once you share what it is that *you* do."

She smirked, hoping this would be enough to stop the questions.

"I'm in real estate investments," Daron answered.

Cameron snickered. "I mean, your *real* job, not your *cover* job."

All three men laughed. Daron pulled out his vibrating cell, stared at the screen a moment then said, "She sure knows how to shut down a conversation."

"Mmm hmm," Steve chimed in, but his gaze narrowed on Cameron and it put her on notice. "Let's talk about something simple. Some of the favorite places you've visited."

"Does Florida count?" Cameron replied, knowing this wasn't a simple question. They were hunting, trying to either track down or confirm something. They named a few areas, asking if she'd been before. Most of the ones they mentioned were places where she'd been using the street name Kimura.

She refused to fall into a trap. Already Daron was showing signs that he could be linking her to Autumn. She realized she was in trouble, no one could share a night like that and walk away untouched especially since he woke up alone.

Once they arrived, everyone except Prescott, Mac, and Eric joined a trolley tour. They got off at the Southernmost Point to take pictures in front of a red, black, white and yellow concrete buoy. She half listened as they talked about the spot being approximately ninety miles from Cuba. Her mind kept creeping into the past, thinking about her ex. Nathan, had brought her here once. That time, all the love, laughter and joy were blown away leaving only the sounds of beeping medical equipment as the paramedics rushed her to the hospital trying to save her life. She woke to find Nathan had left her side. He never returned. *Cam, don't go there.* Tears formed in her eyes.

Sweat ran down her back as she stepped away, needing to distance herself from the group. Her heart stopped momentarily as she caught a glimpse of a familiar tawny brown face in the crowd. Jason tilted the sunglasses down slightly and winked at her before blending with the other tourists. Cameron quickly backtracked to rejoin the group. Jason would, without a doubt, snatch her off the streets and have his inside person supply Lex with excuses for her absence. She scanned the crew and by the time the trolley arrived for them to hop back on, Steve had mysteriously reappeared. Tia snuggled into Daron. Steve gave Daron a nod then he lowered himself on to the bench.

Another stop allowed them to visit the Ernest Hemmingway house and museum. Daron walked ahead with Tia attached to his side.

Cameron quickly toured the area, bumping into Daron and Tia several times but not Lex or Steve. If the pattern held true, Steve and Lex would reappear right before the trolley returned in thirty minutes.

She stepped outside, worried something came up and her team either couldn't make the drive or that they hadn't seen what she posted on social media. Cameron went back on the first level and was about to open the communication app, seconds before Rob entered. Crossing the threshold, she maneuvered through the house until reaching a more crowded room. Cameron unzipped her purse and slowly squeezed in between two couples to look at a case with displays of books. Rob dropped the package into her oversized bag, then left the way he came. She moved toward an old typewriter on a table.

Cameron had just the made it over to the wooden desk moments before Daron poked his head in the room and tapped his watch. She followed Tia and Daron outside. A few minutes later, Lex and Steve came bounding out of the house. Cameron gave Lex a knowing look to say she knew he'd left the premises as they boarded the trolley again. He nudged Steve then winked at Cameron before closing the distance between them, interlocking his arm with hers and smiling as though nothing was amiss. The Mallory Square area was the next point where they were supposed to meet the rest of the group.

"It's hot and humid," Tia whined.

Daron glared as if to say *everybody knows*.

She turned and flounced toward the nearby mist machines.

After a few minutes of waiting, Daron suggested, "Let's get some drinks and appetizers."

As the group walked to the restaurant, Cameron noticed that Lex's bag was fuller than when they'd first left. About twenty minutes later, they finished eating and Eric entered the restaurant. He tapped Daron on the shoulder and headed back out.

Daron waved for the bill.

Tia nearly knocked the fellow behind her over getting out of her chair as she raced to depart.

The three men looked at each other as Daron pulled out his wallet. Cameron had yet to break the code on their silent exchanges. Steve walked toward the exit with Lex right behind him.

Cameron attempted to follow but a lady at the table next to them stood right as Cameron made a move and blocked her way.

Daron stood on the other side handing the cash to their waitress. He stepped back to let Cameron go first, then held her shoulder gently tugging her back to him.

"When you're ready to be honest with us," Daron whispered in her ear. "We're ready to be honest with you."

Something radiated through Cameron's body in that moment that she didn't quite understand. A flash of emotion hit her but she quickly discounted the feeling as being nostalgic, tired, and stressed. Special times with Nathan flipped through her mind but she shook them off.

Cameron realize there was a large list of similarities between the two men, but there were differences that made the distinctions between their personalities relevant. Nathan was in your face while Daron was more laid back. Nathan was more of a workaholic, while Daron seemed to make time to laugh and have a little fun in the midst of it all.

She reminded herself being in an emotional state was how Cameron ended up getting entangled with Daron all those years ago. The last thing she needed was to be distracted by the past in the middle of this situation.

Daron held on to her moments longer than necessary then released her and maneuvered through the crowd. Lex waited at the door, holding it open for her. They probably would only be honest in the fact that they'd tell her what they assumed she already knew.

She was glad to be heading out of Key West.

Daron's cell rang while they were in the Phantom. He answered and managed to hold an hour-long conversation with one-word responses. Once he ended the call, the three of them talked sports and exchanged funny stories while grilling Cameron on the sly.

She didn't give them an inkling whether they were on the right path or not.

Two hours later, they piled out of the vehicles in front of the mansion. She declined the offer to play pool. Mac or Eric could remember her as Renee from Boomerangs. She hated that, because this would be the first time they were in the entertainment room. Cameron had yet to explore that space. She'd only seen enough to know there was a half-glass, half-concrete wall that separated the gaming tables from the nightclub-like lounge area. With everyone gathered there, at least she could slip away and talk to JD without any issues.

Prescott blocked her path as she moved toward the stairs. "I hate that we didn't have more time to spend with each other today."

"I don't," Lex uttered, scowling at Prescott as he walked up behind him. With a hand to her elbow, Lex escorted Cameron to the upper level and moved down the corridor to her room. "Sorry about that. I know you can handle yourself."

"But?" Cameron leaned on the wall next to her door.

"His behavior is out of line," Lex growled.

Lightly shoving his shoulder, she said, "Don't let him push your buttons."

Lex nodded and walked away, but the set of his shoulder said that Prescott was in for a come to Jesus meeting.

Cameron unlocked her door, placed her things on the bed, and was back out the door again and across the hall. She stepped onto the terrace.

JD was on the grounds near the other pool, a perfect opportunity.

She darted across the hall to her room to change into a swimsuit. This might be her only chance to warn him that things were about to go south and she didn't mean of the border.

CHAPTER 23

Cameron's team found a good lead on the location of Howard's meeting but still nothing on his client. She didn't bother to shine the special light against the blank paper to see the words on the note Rob had slipped into her bag along with the supplies she needed. Howard sending men to search for "Greg" in Fort Lauderdale was not a good thing. The fact the Red Lightning Research Company cleared out the office in New York also didn't sit well with her.

Right now, JD needed to be her focus. The situation with the file wasn't going anywhere and she'd handle it later. She locked everything in the hidden compartment of the suitcase and turned on some music before heading to the pool. He was swimming laps when she arrived. JD emerged from the water as she crossed the slate-grey deck.

"Hi," she acknowledged him in a casual manner as she placed her bag on the lounger.

Instead of responding, JD dived underneath the water and swam a few laps. Cameron turned on the device to disrupt Daron's security team's ability to hear what was being said. They would be listening to music streaming from the bedroom instead.

"I was wondering what the hell happened that you'd make such a drastic change without visiting Ada," JD said as he stepped out of the pool.

She frowned; it was a shame that looking like a more feminine version of herself was considered a 'drastic change'. "If you'd check in with a sister every now and then, I wouldn't have to go to extreme measures," Cameron teased, knowing his lack of contact had to do his landing under The Warden's watchful eye and not for lack of wanting to keep in touch.

"I don't need to be rescued or for you to go into Killer Cam mode." He dried off with a striped towel a few feet away from her. "This was one time being the fall guy worked in my favor. When I'm done here, I'll tell you everything."

Cameron wondered how Daron taught JD to be more discreet. "I kind of can see why. But keep your eyes open or I may be coming back for you sooner than you think."

"For what?" JD reached for a t-shirt.

"The Warden's looking for a traitor within the ranks." She slid off her glasses and laid a business card next it. "Whoever it is, will make his move soon."

Resting his hand on top of the card on the table, JD peeked at it before sliding it into his pocket, then slipped on his flip flops. "I'll tread lightly."

Cameron peeled off her sarong, laying it on the lounger, then pulled her hair into a ponytail as JD walked away.

"Christina?" he asked.

"I'd rather they think you're picking up girls, than think you're up to something," Cameron stated, sitting a water bottle near the edge. "If things change and you decide you need me, call." After hearing JD's okay, she launched her body into the water.

Over the years, she'd watched him be a chameleon trying to fit in. Whatever his latest group of friends were into, he was into as well. Now she was seeing a more mature and confident version of her cousin, Cameron was grateful the situation hadn't required immediate action. Now she could put out the other fires. In the past, the only times he seemed poised was in the presence of people he was comfortable with or when he was on assignment with Bishop's elite team. As her body sliced through the cool water, she could only hope JD had finally stopped trying to be someone he wasn't.

After Daron's and his crew's clever grilling techniques today on the Key West trip, Cameron was glad the drive to Fort Lauderdale tomorrow wouldn't give them as much time to interrogate her. Her plan was to ditch Tia and follow the guys.

With things escalating, Cameron needed to record something worthy of forcing Daron not to retaliate if she left with JD. She was planning for the worst-case scenario because if things changed, she was getting her cousin out and not looking back. Cameron wasn't fooled by Daron's laid-back demeanor, people who crossed him had a tendency to disappear or end up dead. She was not taking any chances.

Cameron swam a few more laps then moved to the edge, wrapping her fingers around the Smartwater and taking a sip.

Prescott walked onto the patio in his swim gear, taking purposeful strides to the pool.

"I didn't expect to see you here," Prescott claimed.

She slicked her wet hair back. "Then you won't miss me when I leave." Cameron rose to her full height and walked to the stairs.

"Oh, but I will." He grabbed her hand and yanked her toward him.

"I suggest you let me go." Cameron's eyes went from his face to her wrist.

Prescott complied. "I want to offer you a job."

"I already have one." She maneuvered around him and climbed up the steps.

He stayed on the stairs but placed his back on the pool's handrail. "From what I hear, not for long."

Cameron smiled as Daron and Lex doubled back on the path heading her way. "My winnings will keep me afloat." She picked up the water bottle, and his gaze followed every move.

"How do you plan to explain all that money and no job?" Prescott crept up the stairs toward her.

"Not your concern." Cameron leaned on the rail. "Enjoy your swim."

Prescott gave her a wicked grin, seizing her arm, "Think about working for me."

"Doing what? You're not the man with power."

"Don't underestimate me." Prescott snatched her toward him and growled, "I hate to see something bad happen to someone as stunning as you."

"Do we have a problem here?" Daron's voice boomed. His gaze locked on to Prescott, threatening bodily harm as he advanced toward them.

Prescott snarled, tighten his grip on her arm as Daron and Lex flanked her side. Cameron pretended to attempt to lift Prescott's fingers from her arm.

"You're going have to skip the swim tonight Prescott," Lex said, removing Prescott's hand from her arm.

"We got work to do." Daron slid his jacket back, revealing the Beretta in his waistband. "Now."

"Until next time, gorgeous." Prescott stalked up the stairs.

Daron put a vise grip on Prescott's forearm leading him toward the mansion.

Cameron would have love to eavesdrop on the conversation between them because based on the snarl on Daron's face, his laid-back side had left the building. In its place was the man that people feared on the streets.

CHAPTER 24

On the mansion's terrace unwinding from the trip to Bimini, Bahamas, Daron lounged on a patio chair reflecting on the elaborate lie he was living. The strategy of keeping things fluid was more taxing than expected. No one was ready when he'd announced at the crack of dawn that they were going to Bimini instead of Fort Lauderdale. Well, except Tandria. She was always ready and down for whatever.

The image of Eric leaning forward trying to kiss Tandria in Bimini flashed in Daron's mind. Daron had wanted so badly to snatch Eric by the neck and slam his head against that nearby wooden hut. He'd always known Lex was not his only competition. Daron had been doing his best to keep Eric and Tandria apart but Prescott's insistence on going to the beach with the ladies left him no choice but to send Eric. Lex's presence was needed at a business meeting. Daron was buying time until he ended things with Tia, which was so close.

He put his hand on the Beretta when he felt her enter although he didn't hear any other sound except the cell vibrating on the table.

"Should I be concerned?" Daron moved his hand on the patio table in front of the weapon. His eyes took in the cream swimsuit that accentuated the curve of her breasts and the diamond-shaped cutout, showcasing a flat stomach.

Tandria lowered herself on a white patio chair then sat a bottle of Glaceau Smartwater and a bag on the floor between them. "Not unless you have a problem with honesty."

He shifted his chair where he could see the doors, then signaled for Steve to keep the area restricted so no one else in security could see them on their screens. His focus returned to the beauty that he'd begun to crave more and more with each encounter. "It depends on the question."

"Why are you with Tia? It's obvious that it's not a good match." she asked.

He sighed, knowing he couldn't answer as truthfully as she wanted. "It's complicated."

She leaned over and whispered, "She'll eventually catch you mean-mugging her on the down low."

Daron stared at her lush lips wanting to feel them on his, then said, "She knows I'm under a lot of pressure."

"Mmm hmm," Tandria scoffed. "People who are miserably in love fascinate me."

"Who says it's love?" Daron fired back as Tandria reached for the Glaceau.

"Love is usually the number one reason for staying in bad situations." She adjusted the peach sarong and settled in. "Unless love was never the issue in the first place."

His eyes roamed over her toned, tanned legs, appreciating the sight. "I have my reasons."

"I'm not judging. Some people prefer to be miserably in love to being ultimately alone. If that's you," she said, before taking a sip of water. "I can respect your decision, though I don't understand it."

"Question for you." He inched closer. His body, aching with raging desire, had him fighting the urge to make physical contact. "Why do you care?"

Tandria gave a sly grin, tilting her head slightly. "I'm curious what would make a man in your position sleep with a woman next to him every night that he doesn't seem to like and obviously doesn't trust."

"What makes a woman spend time with a man she's not willing to give a real shot at a committed relationship?" Daron knew she had an ulterior motive for hanging with Lex just as he had one for allowing certain people in his inner circle. Tia served a purpose. They all did.

"My situation with Lex isn't the same." She took a sip, set the bottle in her bag then leaned back in the chair. "We're friends. If he's willing to continue to fill that role hoping to change my mind, that's on him. I was honest about that from day one."

Glancing at the doors behind him, Daron gave himself a moment to settle the sensations coursing through him. "No chance of him getting out of friendship hell?"

Tandria uncrossed her legs, sat up, and gave him a stern look. "I don't do playboys. I like men with a lot more ... substance."

"Lex is different with you." Daron was curious if Tandria was attracted to any of his people or whether they were all pawns in her game. He preferred the latter only because it meant Lex didn't stand a chance. But where did that leave him?

"Seeing that he hasn't flirted with a woman since bringing me here. I believe you." She stood, walking to the banister and looking out at the pool before turning back to face him. "Change doesn't come easy. I can't be the woman he uses to work out the kinks."

"Interesting." Daron was happy she'd sought him out. He'd been hoping for some time alone with her but considering his circumstances, he had to give the appearance of being unaffected. Now that they were alone, he realized he was in trouble. She ignited a fire in him that only she could extinguish. He wanted to know what it would feel like to have her trembling underneath him.

"Besides, Lex and Steve are the only ones you actually trust in your crew. I hate to leave you one man short because I took him out due to his indiscretions." She leaned on the banister her hazel eyes focused on him. Her sarong slid open giving a delicious peek at the rest of her swimsuit.

"You roll like that?" Daron chuckled as he tore his eyes away from the textured cream pattern at the juncture of her thighs only to find himself appreciating the curve of her hip.

She lifted an eyebrow. "You know I do."

"Why does that feel more like a warning?" Daron rose to his feet, picking up the Beretta off the table next to him, and sliding it into his waistband.

"I don't mince words." She gave him an intense stare. "If I wanted to threaten you, I would."

He closed the distance between them, inhaling her seductive and sensual scent; jasmine with hints of vanilla and lavender. "Do you have a man?"

"For someone who already has a woman, you're very curious about *my* love life." She grabbed her belongings, gave him a wicked smile over her shoulder, then swept across the threshold.

He couldn't say anything. She was right. Tia had interrogated him the other night about Tandria. Trying to figure out what it was about her that drew his men's attention. The two women had their own level of physically beauty but what excited him about Tandria was her intelligence, quick wit and keen sense of observation. What Tia really wanted to know was how Tandria managed to get past his distrustful nature and why he had invited her into the inner circle so quickly. He damn sure wasn't going to tell her he was attracted to Tandria or that he was ninety percent sure she was Kimura, Bishop's former lethal weapon. *Could she also be Autumn?*

A splash below caught his attention. Tandria's smooth strokes cut through the water as she swam the length of the pool. The last woman people were aware he trusted was Desiree. Sadly, she was expendable in the eyes of the people attempting to take his life. No one knew he had another woman quietly working in his organization. To keep her safe, he made sure the individuals paid for what they did to Desiree. For his plan to work, he needed to stay away from Tandria and keep playing ignorant to things going on around him.

Daron's gaze locked in on Tandria, whose eyes had given a silent signal of come hither rather than stay away when she exited.

A bad idea, but I'm in the mood for a swim.

CHAPTER 25

The drive to Fort Lauderdale was quicker than Key West or Bimini, especially since her thoughts were somewhere else. Cameron's mind was reeling last night at the pool and the sudden desire to have Daron's lips on her. She fought to block out images of their previous sexual encounter that had her moist in all the wrong places. The conversation from the previous evening replayed in her head.

Daron moved closer to her. "What drives you?"

In the moment, with barely an inch between them as her eyes took in the true state of his body as it glistened from the pool water. "I'm not sure how to answer that."

"You have to be living a similar lifestyle to mine," he said with such confidence as if he had no doubt it was the truth. "What drove you there?"

She leaned against the edge of the pool and thought about it for a minute. "Anger and stupidity."

"You're an intelligent woman." He rested his arm on the ledge next to her.

Cameron resisted the urge to pull him toward her by rotating her neck, then shifting a bit so that she could lift herself out of the water.

"Yes, but I recently realized I've been reacting to life instead using my intellect to live my best life."

Daron rotated his body toward her, grazing her leg in the process.

"When I get home," she said. "I'll implement the plan that I should've been smart enough to put in place years ago. If I'd done it long ago, the woman before you would be extremely different."

If she had done what she was attempting to do, their paths probably would have never crossed.

"I've no issue with the woman who's in front of me." The corners of Daron's mouth curved up.

She couldn't deny he had a beautiful smile when it was genuine. Cameron gazed out at the water as the man next to her was throwing off her equilibrium and causing her pulse to race. Her eyes went from his chest to his abs. Both were chiseled to perfection. She could feel the heat of desire building in her center as her eyes dropped lower and ...

Cameron shook off the memories from last night. *Remember why you are here.* Becoming the "other woman" was not part of the strategy. Even though she was fairly certain that Tia hadn't been "his" woman for quite some time. Today was going to be pure torture for her since she was spending the entire day on Las Olas Boulevard with Prescott, Tia, and Mac. On second thought, it would be a good thing. She wouldn't have been able to slip away from Steve, Lex, and Daron so easily as she waited for Greg and Rob to pick her up from a nearby coffee bar.

When a black Impala pulled up in front of her, she scanned the area to make sure she didn't see any familiar faces before sliding into the back seat.

"Where are we heading?" Cameron asked, as they drove away.

Greg maneuvered the Impala through the crowded streets. "Howard's meeting."

Daylight made it harder to become invisible in an area that would most likely give them a great vantage point. She dragged her sundress over her head, plaited her hair, took off her sandals, and pulled on her gym shoes. Rob handed her a lightweight jacket after she adjusted her spandex capris.

Twenty minutes later, they drew near a dingy, two-story building with a silver rolling door near the entrance.

Cameron inhaled deeply trying to center her thoughts. She didn't even want to consider the possibility of not getting back to Fort Lauderdale in time or bumping into Daron or any of his people. She didn't want to awaken the beast that hid behind his laid-back personality. Greg slowed the Impala as they passed two men sitting in chairs positioned to the right and left of the large silver door.

"Is Howard already in there?" Cameron surveyed the area. The block attached to the building seemed abandoned, but the next one had an active strip mall.

Greg pulled over to the curb. "I assume so."

"How are we doing this?" Rob asked.

With Greg's height and dreads, he would be too recognizable. She'd handle this with Rob. "Rob, get into their security system and confirm Howard is actually inside before we do this."

"He isn't, but he will be." Greg turned, looking out the rear window.

She turned back to see a Lincoln slowly driving into the building. "Do you have equipment to listen?"

"Yes." Rob paused, "but it's not the one you can hear from a distance."

"Have you handled the cameras?" Cameron asked, putting on a baseball cap and sunglasses while Rob did the same. "Remember, I can't come back bloody and bruised."

They got out, speed-walking toward Howard, who was in the Lincoln. The information wouldn't do them any good if they weren't in the room when it was given. Cameron listened to Rob describe what he saw inside. Right before she reached the men who sat near the doorway, she bent down to tie her shoe. Rob kept walking.

"Keep it moving," the man closest to Cameron growled, getting to his feet.

Cameron flung two cards; one hit his chest, the other lodged in his partner's shoulder. She rushed forward, catching his body and lowering him into the chair positioning them as if they were napping on the job. Rob did the same to his partner. She peeked inside the building before running low for the nearest cover behind a pile of boxes.

"Why the sudden interest in Bishop and Kimura?" An older, chubby man in a beige linen suit, asked.

Howard's olive complexion was darker than the last time Cameron had seen him. He sat his briefcase down on a metal table. His polo shirt lifted from his slacks revealing the butt of a gun. "Is Greg Kimura?"

She inched forward, trying to get a better angle to see what was in the briefcase. Howard clicked it open. His two bodyguards blocked her view. When they shifted, there were stacks of money piled inside the case between them. "My client is looking for a lady associate of theirs."

Rob was positioned slightly behind her with a cell out to snap a picture. Mr. Beige Suit closed the case. "Are you searching for his daughter?"

"He doesn't have a daughter," Howard stated.

"Bishop warned me you were that kind of trouble that should be handled if you ever darkened my doorstep." He pulled out a Glock and put a bullet in Howard before the man understood what was happening.

Howard's bodyguard returned fire as they backed up toward the Lincoln.

Both Cameron and Rob reared back. Her heart thumped rapidly in her chest as she broke for the door, staying low with Rob on her heels. Once they were outside, they ran full-speed down the block.

The Impala slammed into reverse heading their way. Cameron hopped in seconds before Rob closed the door.

Greg floored the accelerator.

The Lincoln came careening down the street and gunned past them as Greg turned into the strip mall.

"Besides getting the tail off us," Cameron said, grabbing her sundress with the adrenalin pumping through her veins at an increased level. "Howard will no longer be a problem." She should have been relieved, but his death left unanswered questions. Biggest one, who hired him.

"His clients will have to regroup and find someone else," Rob said, sounding reassured.

"Which will buy some time for us to find the file," Greg added as he pulled out of the strip mall's parking lot.

"I might have a lead," Cameron announced as she took a few calming breaths. "I'm going to reach out to a few people. Hopefully, by the time we get JD safely back home, I'll have answers." She stared out the window and gasped, swearing a familiar face flashed in a passing car but that was impossible. Her father was probably at work ordering people around. No way Jake Stone could be in Ft. Lauderdale. Her demons were tapping on her shoulder and she didn't know how long she could keep them at bay.

Rob glanced back at her. "Cam, are you okay?"

She nodded. She would be soon. "You two should retire when I do."

Rob scoffed and pinned his eyes on Greg who'd given Rob a guarded glance. "We'll think about it."

She might actually be able to enjoy retiring once Bishop's file was in hand and no one would try to end her life long before she was ready. The moment Bishop's associate mentioned "his daughter", she realized where the file was located. Bishop's dying words were *tell my daughter to visit home*. At the time, everyone was puzzled, the same as Howard. Bishop didn't have a daughter. Now she, with an inward laugh, realized he was talking about *her*. The file must be at the Chicago house they used when she pretended to be his daughter for a period of time. As soon as she was back in the Windy City, she'd retrieve it.

Until she actually laid eyes on the contents and knew what she was dealing with, she wouldn't share all the details with her team. She planned to ingest the pertinent information, then incinerate it. Cameron couldn't have Bishop's life coming back to sink its teeth in her, without the ability to bite back.

CHAPTER 26

Eric kept his gaze on the monitors. On screen, people milled around waiting for the fights to start.

Mac, Prescott, and Lex entered the security room. Each one heading down a different row of stations with screens fixed on a different area of the mansion.

Eric's station had monitors for all the areas with one massive screen in the middle. In the front of the room, Steve stood checking the largest one of five huge LED surveillance displays, then left to make the final preparations so they could watch the fights before doing their security shift.

Prescott reviewed the guest list to see who'd checked in. Mac did the same with the fighter list.

Eric switched the feed to the grounds to make sure all the guards were in place. He was surprised to see Tandria poolside, relaxing as though she wouldn't be stepping into the ring. She stood, left the area, and bumped into JD in the corridor leading back to the house.

Eric looked up from the monitor over at Lex. "What's with Tandria and JD?"

Lex hit a few buttons and listened to their conversation. "From the sounds of it, not much. Why are you singling out Tandria?" Lex picked up the security rotation list. "She's more of a distraction to you than she has ever been to me."

Eric observed as she parted ways with JD. "I admit, I'm not immune to Tandria's charms."

"As if I didn't know," Lex shot back, then pulled out a tablet comparing the information to the paper.

"What's this?" Eric switched to a screen where two of the fighters were arguing.

Lex tapped Eric's shoulder. "Put monitor eleven on the center screen and on speaker."

"Listen, if you keep your mouth shut, we'll be gone before anything goes down." The man grabbed her arm and pulled the woman close.

"You shouldn't have … " She crossed her arms over her slight bosom. "We shouldn't get involved in this. If The Warden finds out we're working with Lucifer … "

"I lied about our destination," he replied. "But honey, we could make almost a hundred grand a piece."

She pushed him away. "No good to me if I'm dead."

Eric used his handset to radio Pedro to detain the couple. His head tilted toward the dim control board. Someone had intentionally disconnected the lines so the couple could get away. The nearest two-way radio was on the other side of the aisle since Steve had taken one with him. Eric pulled out his cell and snapped a picture then called Pedro. "A couple in sector two, if you see them, detain them." Eric texted their image over, then put the phone back to his face. "I'll be down in a minute."

Seven guys in the room, including himself. One of them was Lucifer or worked for him. He studied each person's face, but none showed any sign they were involved. He exchanged concerned looks with Lex and Mac, then focused on the screen again. Eric couldn't remember if Prescott was there when he shifted the action to the center monitor.

Mac and Lex departed. The fights had begun. Most people were seated in the arena. Once Steve returned with six other men, Eric gave

Steve an update then peered at the monitor to see if Daron was already in the stadium. He wasn't.

Eric went in search of Daron and found him in the office leaning on a white oak desk swishing brandy around in his glass as though millions weren't riding on tonight's outcome. He informed Daron of what transpired.

Finishing off the last of the brown liquid, Daron stated, "Anyone who isn't already here or on the list tomorrow does not enter."

"What about the caterers?" Eric was astounded he didn't cancel the party altogether. That amount of people flowing into the mansion increased the odds that whatever Lucifer was planning would be successful.

They spent the next few minutes working out the details of the new arrangement. "You and Tandria pick up the food. Lex and Tia will pick up the linen and centerpieces. And send Prescott and Mac for the liquor. No one who hasn't worked the parties before are allowed inside."

Many evenings after most of them had turned in, Lex disappeared from the property. The assumption had been he was off seeing other women since Tandria wasn't sharing his bed. Now Eric wasn't so sure. "Do you trust Lex enough to—"

"Whether Lex is the traitor, who knows." Daron grabbed his phone off the desk, giving him a steely look. "Besides, you were one of the seven men in the room. Can I trust you?"

Eric put up one finger, relieved he didn't have to answer that question as he listened to what was being said in his earpiece. The team had spotted the girl. "Put someone on her. Don't approach unless you can do so without making a scene."

Daron glanced down at his Versace watch. "Let's go," he said, setting the glass down near a rich purple cabinet that housed the limited-edition liquors. "We're beyond the halfway mark."

Eric followed him out. When they arrived at the arena, Prescott, Tia, and Lex were already there. Mac slid in a few minutes later. Daron took his seat and scowled through the fights.

"Warden," a balding man with emerald eyes turned toward their seats.

"Could I have a few minutes of your time to discuss a joint venture?"

"Of course," Prescott responded before Daron could say a word.

Eric shook his head. Prescott loved playing big shot as a cover but anyone paying attention would know who was running things. Eric noticed that Daron was allowing Prescott to do more initial intake for local business. Eric would bet money Daron was using Prescott's need to be seen to his advantage.

Daron flicked his finger to the side signaling Prescott to take the conversation to the back. Prescott motioned for the man to follow as he left the stands.

By the time Prescott returned to his seat, only four fighters remained. Eric had missed Tandria's first two fights. She'd clearly won because she was back in the ring with a black tank and shorts, fighting Cher, who had won last year championship match. From the grimace on Cher's face, she had no intention of letting Tandria win. The win could add fifty thousand-dollars to the thirty thousand she'd already banked.

The bell rung to start the bout. Cher came out blazing; jab, hook, and cross combinations but Tandria blocked most of them. Every once in a while, Cher got in a solid punch.

Eric leaned over to Daron. "Cher's probably still stinging from the first blow Tandria landed."

"You would know." Daron laughed as the referee separated them.

"Lex, your new friend is a bad ass woman," Prescott raved, appreciation and lust in his gaze.

"Yeah and off limits to you," Lex shot back at him.

Eric was hoping that Lex and Prescott wouldn't become the main attraction. Tandria being there had reignited Lex's dislike of Prescott. Daron had been managing the personality conflicts, but Prescott hitting on Tandria could be the breaking point. What was it about her that brought out the beast in them?

Cher came out the next round and hit Tandria with a one-two combination, followed by a knee to the gut and then a hip throw.

"Aww," the crowd moaned, rising to their feet as Tandria's body hit the canvas with Cher putting her in the head lock. Then, she tried for an arm isolation. If Cher could secure it, she would win.

Eric glanced at Daron as Tandria pummeled Cher's side with her free hand, then switched to the top.

The crowd roared. The bell rang signaling the end of the round.

"Your girl had me worried for a minute," Prescott said, lowering himself into the plush chair along with the rest of the people who settled around them.

Next round, Cher threw a few jabs followed by a side kick to the shoulder.

Tandria landed a series of punches, backing Cher into the cage. She landed on Cher, ramming a knee into her torso several more times before delivering numerous jabs. The area above Cher's right eye swelled as she directed a kick to Tandria's shoulder.

Tandria grabbed Cher's leg, lifted her from the floor and slammed her to the ground, then followed the woman down to the mat, fist flying in rapid succession.

"Damn," Eric rose to his feet, not expecting that move.

Cher struggled with Tandria to keep from being put into a submission hold, but eventually had no other choice and tapped out.

The last two male fighters stepped into the cage. Tandria got to her feet, pulled off her gloves and attempted to make her way to where they were seated. She wore a mask of indifference as she walked the aisle. People filed out of their seats and blocked her path, congratulating her. Eric shifted his legs to let Lex go past as she neared.

"Great fight, but I have a feeling you held back," Lex said as he pulled her sweaty body into an embrace, then extended a bottled water.

Eric stared at her bright-red torso. "Do you need to be checked out?"

"I'm good." Tandria's reddened fingers curled around the Smartwater.

He swore Daron was about to snatch Prescott backwards after he pushed through the aisle, tripping over Eric's legs to get to her. Lex wedged himself between Tandria and Prescott, daring the man to try him.

Prescott maneuvered around Lex. "You're fierce and very skilled. How long have you been fighting?"

Daron stood, tapping Eric on the shoulder before stepping down to the floor next to their seat to join the group. "Let's move to the back, so our guests can enjoy the final fight."

"Not necessary. I'm about to get cleaned up." Tandria tossed back the bottle of water.

Eric joined the group and noticed Tia giving Daron an evil stare as she sat with her arms crossed and lips tightly squeezed together, looking more like a petulant teenager.

"We'll walk you out," Daron insisted as he walked away from the seats.

Tia rolled her eyes and turned her attention back to the current fight. Eric was right behind them.

Daron held the security door open to the back hallway leading to the house. "Tandria, would you mind helping us with party prep tomorrow?"

"Not at all." She rolled her shoulders back before executing a few moves to loosen up. "Alright. Carry on. I know my way back."

"You're foregoing your swim?" Lex asked, keeping an intense gaze on Tandria.

"Maybe," she replied as he gently maneuvered her away from Prescott, who'd placed himself directly in her path. "If I don't get some rest, I'll be barely functioning tomorrow."

Eric glanced back to see Mac slip out of the arena, heading in the opposite direction. He wondered if there was a reason Mac had become the invisible man lately.

Daron, Lex, and Prescott rejoined Tia. Eric followed Steve to the security room so they could monitor departures, which went smoothly except for those too drunk to drive and were giving security a hard time. Eric stepped out, intending to make his rounds.

Eric patrolled the remainder of the grounds, checked in with Pedro, then headed back to the security room. Steve's eyes locked on him when he entered. His face was grim as he moved closer to the screen while reaching for the radio.

"What is it?" Eric rushed over to the screen to see Prescott creeping up the hall near the terrace. *Dammit! The only reason Prescott had to be in that particular section of the house was Tandria.* No one went near the terrace unless they were looking for Daron. Since Tandria had been on property, Daron hadn't been out there as much.

Steve pointed to the door. "Go now."

Eric bolted toward Tandria's room with his heart racing. His breath quickened as he took the stairs two at time up to the corridor leading to the terrace. The light spilled through her open door into the hallway. He pulled his gun and burst in to find Prescott on the floor, balled up in a fetal position. Tandria gripped a red lace negligee in her hand and a cell phone in the other.

"What in the hell were you thinking?" Tandria threw it on Prescott.

Prescott lifted his hand. "It was only a gift."

"Men don't usually break into women's room to give unboxed gifts. Psycho." Tandria's nose flared as she raised her gaze to Eric.

He put the safety back on his gun and slipped it in his waist band. As he advanced toward Prescott, Tandria's phone flashed.

Tia rushed in behind him. "What's going on?" she gasped, her eyes widening as if they were going to burst from the sockets. She watched Prescott getting off the floor, holding the flimsy material. "Has every man in this house lost their damn mind over this chick?"

She stomped out of the room, yelling for Daron all down the hallway.

Eric's heart rate returned to normal as he grabbed Prescott by the arm. "You need to sleep off those drinks, man."

He glanced back at Tandria, who smirked. Both of them knew Prescott was not that drunk. No doubt about it. Prescott's days with this crew were numbered.

CHAPTER 27

Cameron inhaled the aroma of Cuban coffee as her gaze skimmed the patron filled bistro tables. She shot another glance toward the glass doors, knowing she couldn't wait any longer. She'd polished off most of her coffee, trying to kill time for Greg to arrive. Exhaling, she picked up her bag and left the café in search of Eric.

She'd taken a few steps when, out of the corners of her eyes, she noticed a man approaching her. She reached for her wand, then relaxed recognizing the familiar face.

Eric stood across the street in the parking lot, leaning on the hood of the Phantom, his expression impatient as he scrolled through his cell.

"Come with me." Greg pushed her toward a white cargo van parked close to the coffee shop.

Cameron pretended to struggle a bit when she noticed that Eric had spotted them. Greg handed her the keys to the condo she'd instructed them to rent near Biscayne Bay and an envelope. She slid the items in her purse. "What the hell?"

"Sorry I was late, but I got caught up," he whispered as he ushered her behind the van.

She looked up as two big men advanced on them. "Are they with you?"

"No," Greg said, reaching for his gun.

Cameron put her hand over it. "Have everybody ready to go, but wait until I get there or post the picture."

The signals were clear. If she posted a rainbow, everything was fine. Rain or landscaping, meant she needed them.

She extracted the weapon from his waistband then pretended to slam him against the panel of the van. She tried not to smile as Greg's hand pounded the metal panel for effect. His body slid down to the concrete then she spun and pointed the gun at the two men.

They held up their hands and nodded toward Greg. "We only want to talk to him."

Eric appeared behind her, and the two men quickly retreated. She figured it had more to do with Eric's appearance than the weapon making her point. Cameron stepped over Greg to get to Eric, pushing him in the opposite direction. "Let's get out of here."

"What the hell happened?" Eric resisted a moment before turning around and grabbing her arm.

She placed the Remington in her purse. "Can we talk in the car?"

"Sure," he replied, giving her a once-over. "You okay? Why are you looking at me like that?"

Cameron wrinkled her nose and turned up her lips as they hurried across the street. "Don't start being nice to me. It's not Eric-like," she teased.

Eric swiftly moved toward the Phantom, scanning the area. "What, Tandria? Can't I change my mind about you?"

Eric being genuinely concerned threw her off, fueling her curiosity about what his real personality was like once the mask was pulled back. She slid into the passenger side, then said, "I'm not convinced. You're being too nice."

"In that case, did you and Prescott have a good conversation at the pool?" Eric glanced in the direction of the white van.

"As a matter of fact, we did." She smirked, hoping to keep him distracted as Greg made a hasty exit. She hated the fact that she had his gun, especially with those two men on his tail.

"What happened out there?" Eric pulled out of the lot.

"Why was I assigned to go with you instead of Lex?"

Eric frowned. "I didn't do the assigning."

What were the three amigos up to this time?

Eric glanced in the rear-view mirror. "You can answer my question now."

"The guy tried to steal my purse, but clearly he had his own problems." Her phone flashed. Angling her phone away from Eric, she discreetly pulled up the camera feed in her room to see the maid bringing in more towels. She caught a glimpse of Daron entering right behind the housekeeper. She locked the phone, knowing it was time for her to get out.

◆ ◆ ◆

Eric drove to a diner a few minutes out. She followed him past the deli counter to a red leather booth in the back. He slid into the side on the wall. Cameron went to the opposite end, but angled her body with her back toward the window so that she could see the front door.

He peered at a single cream sheet, which served as a menu. "Cameron, did Lex say what time he'd be back?"

She didn't say a word to indicate she heard him call her government name and not her alias, instead she checked out the food choices.

"I'll take that as a no. Oh, I spoke to Jay today." Eric smiled, then tapped on the table. "Hey, I'm talking to you."

Tilting her head up, she smiled. "Oh, I thought you were on your phone. What were you saying?"

Why'd he select now to let me know he's working with my brother?

"I know who you are." Eric stopped talking as the waitress approached. After they ordered, Eric tried to get back to the conversation. "I agree with your brother. You need to let us handle this. Don't put yourself in the crossfire of what's brewing."

"What's up with Prescott?" Opening her purse, she pulled out a clip, twisted her hair up and fastened it to the top of her head.

Eric's leg brushed against hers under the table. "Are you attracted to him?"

"Don't answer a question with a question. I need to know on a scale from one to ten, will I have to break any of his arms if he keeps invading my personal space?"

"You may have won the fight night, but Prescott is a contender on a whole 'nother level." Eric checked his phone.

"Is he as good as you?" she teased.

Eric chuckled. "Well, I wouldn't say—"

"Fine." She gave him a devilish smirk. "I almost took you out and I didn't even come with all I had."

"I was being gentle with you … " Eric zoned out for a second. She tossed a napkin at him, snapping him out of his pondering.

"Gentle, my behind. You were trying to put me in my place." She leaned back, giving him a dirty glare.

Their waitress approached with their food, bringing their conversation to a temporary end. Midway through their meal and debate, Eric's phone rang. The order for the party was ready. "We'll grab everything once we finish up here."

"I'm ready when you are." She took one last bite.

When the check came, she stood. Eric reached for her arm. "Hold up. You can afford your half of the meal."

"I can, but when a man invites me to lunch for the purpose of trying to pump me for information, the event is no longer Dutch." She hoisted her purse over her shoulder and sauntered away.

"Oh, you're full of it." He dropped the money on the table and followed her through the door. "Where did you get that faulty logic?"

"Does it matter? In the end you still paid." She slipped into the passenger seat of the Phantom.

Eric started the engine and drove off, chuckling. "You're a mess."

"Is that a bad thing?" She grabbed her sunglasses, sliding them on her face.

Stopping at a light, he glanced at her. "You've got all these men mesmerized by you, even Daron. That's not normal."

Cameron flipped down the visor and applied a bronze gloss to her lips. "I can't control that."

"You can and you do very well," Eric said as he moved closer to their destination.

She flipped the visor up. "Bull."

Eric pulled in front of the entrance of La Calle restaurant. "Is your wardrobe selected to seduce or do you just make everything you wear seem sexy?"

"Would you shut up? Get out and get the food so we can get back," Cameron commanded.

He popped open the trunk and exited the car.

When Eric walked inside La Calle, she got out and leaned on the side of the car. She could feel someone watching them while casually surveying her surroundings. She was partially responsible for that poorly-executed incident earlier. The appearance of the two men looking for Greg let her know that her crew needed to be prepared for anything and everything tonight. Nothing suspicious stood out in the area. Cameron's attention shifted to Eric, who came out carrying three heavy chafing pans.

"I should have taken the truck." He stopped as she approached him.

"I'm not coming with you, if you have to make a second trip." Cameron took one of the pans from him and headed to the trunk, using the opportunity to check out the activity across the street. She still didn't see anything out of place.

Eric repeated the trip, putting more items inside the vehicle.

"Hey, I'm going in this time. We'll take forever doing it this way." Cameron didn't know if her brother was watching Eric's back or not. She didn't want to find out the hard way.

"Like you could carry more," Eric challenged.

"Let me put it this way. I'll get more out to the car than you could." She reached in and grabbed her purse, then unclipped her hair.

"Alright, I'll wait here." Eric stood near the Phantom with an expression that clearly showed his doubt. "Ask for food for the Winthrop party."

Cameron sashayed inside where a couple of guys wearing white uniforms loaded the food on the counter. She approached the men. With a seductive smile that she'd perfected recently, she asked, "Is this the food for the Winthrop party?"

"Yes," the taller, lanky guy answered, pausing as he glanced at her face, then slid a gaze down her body.

She slung her purse across her chest, then grabbed a pan. "Thanks."

The lanky guy rushed to her side, extracting the pan from her hands. "Here, let me help you."

"It goes to the Phantom out front," Cameron said as he and the other man with him grabbed a few trays each. A third guy came from the back of the restaurant and grabbed several more.

As they headed for the door, she grabbed the last tray off the counter and followed them out. After being reprimand by one of the men for not being a gentleman, Eric grabbed the tray from Cameron. The trunk and the boxes in the back seat were filled with food. She tried to tip the men, but they wouldn't accept.

"Well done, Tandria." Eric clapped when they sat in the car.

"Learned early on, some men are suckers for a pretty face and nice body." Cameron smiled.

Eric rolled down the street slowly. "We aren't that shallow."

"Yeah, right, if I was mugly and out of shape." She glanced at the back seat full of food. "I seriously doubt I'd have gotten help like that."

"All men—"

"Whatever."

Cameron wasn't concerned about whether or not men were shallow. She was more disturbed by the fact that Daron pawned her off on Eric instead of Lex, but he also visited her room. What was he looking for?

CHAPTER 28

The house was quiet as Daron wrapped up his meeting with Maureen. He ushered her out the back way to avoid bumping into anyone. The team was due to arrive back from their assignments soon. Daron was in a precarious position, which made him anxious. His cell vibrated, jarring him out of his thoughts.

"I checked in with Nicco and the other team," Steve said, referring to the rest of the security personnel he'd flown into Miami.

Daron returned to his office, grabbed Tandria's luggage and locked it up. "Anything suspicious or out of the ordinary happened while handling the tasks?"

"Tandria had an incident, but she handled the situation before Eric reached her. No one else had any complications," Steve relayed, then updated him on the particulars.

"Make sure everyone is on point. You know what's riding on this." Daron disconnected the call.

He left his office a half hour later to hear Eric and Tandria going at it in the hallway.

"Don't tell me what the role of the woman is," Tandria argued.

"I'm not saying you should stay barefoot and pregnant. It's not your place to be the head of the house," Eric defended.

"When I'm working full-time just like him, don't expect me to be the only one coming home cooking and cleaning," Tandria volleyed back.

"You two make nice," Daron said, chuckling at Eric's frustrated expression. "I assume the food is in the kitchen."

"Yeah. I've gone over the restaurant's instructions with Rosa," Eric explained.

"Check over the staff and guest lists, then get the security system up and running." Steve had probably already done this, but a second pair of eyes never hurt.

"I'm on it." Eric's gaze lingered on Tandria before aiming for the surveillance room.

"Tandria." Daron called to her as she began walking away. "Let's talk for a second."

He guided her to take a seat on the plum couch in his office. "The housekeeping told me ... " he paused as he poured himself some scotch and took a sip. "You already packed your suitcase and had it at your door."

"I'm out of here tomorrow." Tandria placed her sunglasses on the end table.

"I thought you were leaving with us on Monday." Daron didn't miss the way she'd placed the sunglasses, facing his desk. Now he could give her the information on an upcoming meeting without being obvious or raising suspicion.

"I didn't expect to be summoned until after I told Lex. Let's just say, I'm getting too attached to you guys." She leaned on the couch's arm, her body angled, seductively. "I'll be leaving town in a couple of months."

"No plans to stay in touch?" Daron set his drink down to lock the office door.

She shifted her purse from the couch to her lap. "I'm not good with stuff like that."

"I don't have to tell you you're gorgeous with a fabulous shape and a beautiful mind." Daron advanced on her. "You're full of surprise and mystery that draw men like moths to a flame."

"So, my personality sucks," Tandria teased as he stopped within a few feet of her.

"That's not it. You have a good sense of humor and a great personality," he added, grinning down at her. "And you're no stranger to danger."

"I never took you as someone who doesn't say exactly what he means." She stood, then took several steps away from him, but her eyes locked on to his.

He laughed. "The point is, you know who I am."

"Okay." She adjusted the purse over her shoulder.

Daron held down the button on the device in his pocket to prevent her glasses from recording. He settled a serious gaze on her and stepped in. "Tandria, stop playing and pretending with me. You know my nickname and my true line of business."

Tandria tilted her head and gave him a tight-lipped smile. "I admit, I've heard rumors."

"Tandria," His tone was husky and he stood close enough to kiss her. "What are you really after?"

She stared into his eyes but didn't step back. "A fun time and a little excitement."

"If I wasn't and circumstances were different … " He paused, reminding himself of what was at stake but his gaze lingered on her lips. "I'd give you more excitement than you could handle."

"A man who honors a woman who doesn't honor him, I admire that." Tandria sidestepped his innuendo.

He loved the fact that she refused to show any weakness, fear, or other emotion. Daron inched closer to her lips, pausing right before they touched. He smiled, turned away and went back to his desk. "You, my dear, are straight from the never-back-down street. You may look, talk, walk, and act like a lady ninety percent of the time, but you fight and hold your ground like a straight up thug."

"Don't know what to say to that." She lowered herself to the cushion, crossing her legs. "Now that you've tested me. Why did you really call me here?"

"I make no qualms about it. I'm attracted to you, but since it's not possible to become more … involved, I'd love for you to become Eric's right hand. I liked how you had Lex's back in several recent incidents." The true intent behind his comment was more for a reaction than him wanting her with Eric.

She raised one eyebrow. "But … "

"Let this be a warning. If you're a Fed or trying to betray me to anyone, be it a cop or another organization, you won't like what happens next." Daron sat his Beretta on the desk. She didn't flinch or attempt to unzip her bag to get the weapon stashed in her purse.

Tandria walked to his desk, leaned over, and rested her weight on her hands. "You know as well as I do, I'm not the one you're looking for. A person is only considered a traitor if they've been on the inside."

"Mmm." He laughed. "You're either crazy as hell or have balls of steel."

"I honestly came here for one thing and one thing only," she admitted, then held up a hand to ward off his questions. "No, I'm not crazy enough to say what it is. When I got here, I discovered my mission was null and void. Now it's time to make an exit," she stated bluntly.

Daron moved his Beretta out of her reach and tucked it in his waistband. He wasn't crazy either. He'd seen her in action. "Since I'm going to let that suffice as an answer for now. I've one thing to ask of you."

She straightened up and issued him a suspicious glare. "I'm listening."

"Be my eyes and ears tonight." The earlier sweep of her room wasn't planned. He was heading to the terrace and noticed the luggage by the door when the housekeeper went in.

It had been a while since he'd had this much trouble tracking down information on a person. He had his suspicions about her identity but wanted confirmation before saying anything. Red, the only person who could verify she was Kimura, had gone underground and couldn't be contacted.

She stared at him as if he'd lost his mind. "They're not going to have a conversation of any magnitude in front of me."

Daron rounded the desk and stood close to her. "But they may make reference to joining a new team, mention the name Lucifer, or anything of that nature—"

"I'll keep my eyes and ears open."

Daron reached into his pocket and pulled out a card. "This is my private line. Call and let me know who I should be checking out."

"Why do you trust me to do this?"

Daron smiled. "My instincts say I can."

"Yet, your instinct can't—"

"They can't positively confirm my traitors' identity." Daron wasn't willing to give her too much information. A ten percent chance of being wrong about her at this point posed too much of a risk.

"Or you know and don't want to say." She flipped the business cards through her fingers.

He stepped back. "Conversation is over."

"Fair enough." Tandria headed for the door.

"Oh, by the way." Daron flashed a devilish grin, and she turned at the sound of his voice. "I confiscated your luggage to make sure you don't slip out without saying bye."

"I figured as much." She glanced at the business card, handed it back to him, and left.

His phone vibrated in his pocket, sliding out to find out Red had finally resurfaced. He'd sent several pictures down to him, hoping he'd confirm Kimura's identity for him tonight. He'd consistently requested info, but had been too distracted by other things to follow up. He didn't want the woman who saved his brother's life to become another casualty of his war with Lucifer.

CHAPTER 29

Why didn't they increase security tonight?

Standing on the terrace wearing a red dress with sheer lace accentuating her waist, Cameron didn't see much activity on the back lawn. Pedro, and one other guy, roamed the grounds out back. She needed to find out what shift JD was working. The late shift meant it was going to be a long night. The party started hours ago, but Cameron had been waiting for the opportunity to retrieve the sunglasses she'd intentionally left behind in Daron's office.

She heard it. The distinct sound of the security room door opening and closing, then silence. Steve was the only person who came out without making a sound. She left the terrace, striding down the hallway to the stairs. The more distance from the terrace, the louder the music grew. She caught Steve as he headed into the kitchen.

"Hey," Cameron called out, causing him to halt his movement. "Is Daron in his office? I left my sunglasses in there earlier."

She hoped Daron was already at the party. The encounter in the office had shaken her a bit. Daron shared the traits that made her fall in love with Nathan even though their personalities were distinctively different.

The last thing she needed right now was a reminder of the past and a painful trip down memory lane. She was grateful that she'd be soon putting distance between the person silently demanding the awakening of desires she buried long ago.

A weird glint lit in Steve's eye. "I'll get them."

Cameron watched him, feeling as though she was being set up, but for what? Daron didn't even question when she gave him back the card. Now Steve was giving her strange looks.

Steve returned a few minutes later with the glasses. Cameron thanked him then took them up to her room and returned them to their case. Before heading back down, she stepped out to the terrace one last time. Now that she knew for sure that Eric was Jason's inside man, she was going for the obvious choice as the traitor since Prescott acted like a man that wanted more power. Why hasn't Daron shut him down?

Her head snapped toward the sound of knocking. Steve pulled the terrace door open. "You do realize the party is the other way."

"I'm going."

Steve stepped back so she could pass him. The heat in his gaze didn't miss Cameron. She hesitated in the hallway that separated the main house from the entertaining space. Downstairs, the music was pumping and folks dressed like movie stars were engaged in lively conversations. Cameron felt like she'd had arrived at the party of the year. She couldn't even see the buffet due to the sea of people with drinks in hand.

Lex and Eric stared at her with a hint of longing in their eyes, but she wasn't ready to go into the lion's den. Lex moved her way, but an older woman stopped him.

Cameron sighed and continued surveying the room. Her mind was still fighting to keep her from dwelling on the past. This isn't the time to be having a moment, Cameron. Get it together.

Mac mingled with a group of women on the opposite end near the buffet. She was surprised that Daron and Tia weren't present. Prescott was on the couch of the VIP area with Maureen cozily tucked at his side. Were they dating or was this first round flirting? Checking into Maureen's background kept getting pushed to bottom of the pile, but now it would be a priority. Her presence in Miami had Cameron convinced she was a low-key player in the game but those were the ones who could be planted to catch people off guard.

After grabbing a martini from the bar, she fought her way to the buffet. She mingled with the guests waiting to taste the assortment of food. Maureen blocked her path demanding a conversation as Cameron snacked on the appetizers. Cameron excused herself from the small talk when Daron and Tia entered the room. She greeted them, then made her way toward Lex and Eric.

Before she could reach Lex, Prescott cut her off.

"Hey beautiful. You want to dance?" he asked, licking his lips as his eyes roamed her body.

She plastered on a smile as she said, "No."

Prescott grabbed her arm. Her eyes sliced back at him almost forgetting where she was.

"You don't want to go there," she warned through her teeth, challenging him to do something else out of line so she'd have a reason to make a scene.

"Maybe I do." He stroked his fingers over one of her breasts.

Cameron grabbed his fingers quickly, causing her silver bangle to slide down her arm. "What in the hell is wrong with you? I should break them as a reminder for you not to touch a woman without her consent." She bent them back as far as they'd go.

If they weren't in a room full of people, she would have taken one of the beads off her other bracelet and put him out for a couple of hours.

He seemed oblivious to pain. "Are you trying to turn me on?" he questioned in a sultry tone, eyelids low and a devilish smirk on his lips as she applied more pressure before releasing his hand. With a last predatory look, he sauntered away from her.

Prescott had melted into the crowd by the time Lex made it to her.

Cameron shook her head. Bishop was right. The right mix of lady and roughneck was intriguing. Maybe it was too intriguing because Prescott was clowning and she was ready to put him in check.

Lex watched Prescott retreating, eyes shooting daggers. "What did Prescott do?"

"I'm not going to give you a reason to get into it with him tonight." She adjusted her glasses and sighed.

Lex embraced her. "Girl, you look good enough to … " He gave her a wicked grin, staring at her dress. "What perfume are you wearing?"

"I'd tell you, but I don't want you to have your gold diggers all up in my scent." She tapped him playfully on his upper arm.

He took her hand and guided her through throngs of people to the less crowded area where he and Eric had been standing. Eric nodded as they approached.

"Hello Eric," she said dryly.

Eric gave her the once-over. "Fashionably late, I see."

Lex chuckled. "She was probably avoiding you."

Cameron shook her head as other guests invaded their space. Lex scanned the crowd until Daron waved him over.

"I need to make my rounds. Can you keep her company for fifteen minutes without antagonizing her?" Lex asked.

"Of course." Eric stepped forward so someone could pass behind him.

She scowled at Lex. "Not that I need to be entertained while you're busy."

"You know that's not what I meant." He kissed her cheek.

"I'll be on my best behavior," Eric teased, as Lex gave him a warning glare, then disappeared into the group of people chatting behind her.

"Yeah right," Cameron said with an attitude.

Her chest pressed against his as a group squeezed past her and Eric held her waist.

"Let's move closer to the VIP section, so we can have more room." Eric pointed to the open space near an empty roped off area.

Cameron made her way through the crowd but was forced to stop when someone cut her off. For someone concerned about an attack, the place was packed to the gills.

Eric bumped into her backside. The closeness caused him to react in a way that was obvious to her.

"If you keep putting your boobs and that gorgeous ass on me. It'll be me Lex will be trying to fight," Eric whispered into her ear.

"It's not my fault this place is overflowing with folks." Cameron moved again, surprised that Eric being that close hadn't set off any tingling sensations in her body. That concerned her a bit, that she wasn't having a physical reaction to his touch, especially since she had several to Daron's. Her gaze immediately connected with Daron's and a shiver shot down her spine. Shit. She broke eye contact as she threaded through the guests.

They finally reached the roped off area with plush seating and a private service crew. "What happened in Daron's office earlier?"

"I'm free to speak?"

"Yes." He removed his earpiece then reached into his pocket. She assumed to turn something off. "You've got two minutes before I have to check-in."

She scanned the room. "What shift is JD on?"

"This one, why?" Eric glanced at his watch.

"What time does it end?" She peered at Lex. He was engaged in conversation with Daron and a man she didn't recognize. Tia and Mac hovered by the buffet, standing a little too close to each other for casual friends. How stupid could the woman be? She had the top man but was hung up on one of his minions.

"In forty-five minutes. Why?" He gave her a devious look with a sensual smile. "I'm more than willing to keep you occupied until his shift's over. No need to mingle with peons."

She hit him in the chest with her purse. "I need to discretely say bye to him."

"He'll be in the back on the grounds a half hour before his shift ends. Don't do anything stupid," Eric cautioned her sternly.

"We already talked. He told me not to get involved and I won't."

"Cool," he said, putting his earpiece back in.

Cameron had planned to take the rear walkway between the main house and the second pool. She'd run into a little less traffic that way but still had to make it past Steve. Most people milling about the grounds didn't realize there was a lower level walkway on the other side of the bush. Those late-night walks were paying off.

He leaned in, saying, "I'll cover you on the camera for fifteen minutes tops. When you see Steve, that's your opportunity."

"Thanks." She stepped to the side as he reached into his pocket. "Now it's time for me to go make my rounds."

Her gaze settled on Daron, as he weaved in and out of the crowd, chatting up a few of the guests.

She gave Eric's arm a reassuring pat, then crossed the room to Tia.

"Isn't it amazing how well the party turned out, considering the hiccup in the plan," Tia raved, beaming as if she'd just been crowned pageant queen.

Cameron plastered on a fake grin as if she cared.

Prescott approached them and slid his arms around Tia's waist then attempted to do the same for Cameron. "Ladies."

"Tia, I'll catch up with you a little later." Cameron avoided Prescott's touch and aimed for the bar.

She thought back to Daron calling her into his office. Contrary to his statement, it wasn't to be his eyes and ears. Daron was playing the game full-on. She ordered a Black Widow Cocktail, then scanned the location for key personnel.

Lex and Daron were together still. Lex gave her an apologetic look.

Tia was now talking to a group of ladies, who wore outfits just as revealing as her own.

Mac and Prescott were no longer in the room.

Cameron noticed all the players in action as she made small talk with those who managed to halt her progress.

Steve entered from the staff door, heading toward Daron, Lex, and their elite guests.

Cameron took that as her cue and placed the drink on a tray and walked toward the exit before Eric left the security room.

"Tandria," Steve bellowed over the music and conversation.

She pretended she hadn't heard him and slipped through the people in her path. Steve managed to block her way when she was almost at the exit. "Hey," Cameron said, feigning surprise at seeing him.

"Enjoying yourself?" He put a finger against his ear. Eric must have been saying something to him. Steve stepped forward, glancing in the direction of the bar.

"I'll catch you later. You've got work to do." She slipped behind him and bolted toward the door leading to the outer passageway. Cameron moved into the shadows of the alcove near the door, opened her purse, and put rubber soles on over her heels. Then, she shimmied out of her dress, flipped it on the black side, slid the purse over her head, and sprinted down the black stone path.

When she finally laid eyes on JD, he was standing with a short Latino man. She gave a warning signal they perfected when they were younger— a low whistle of the song Funky Town. JD's head whipped toward the sound.

"Hey Angelo, check a little further down the way," he said, gesturing to the smaller house near the edge of the property. "I'll take the other way and meet you back in five."

On the stairs in between the bushes leading up to the grounds, she waited and gave another indicator so he could find her. He sauntered down the sidewalk until he reached her spot.

"Hey," Cameron said as he angled his body halfway facing her.

"What's going on?" JD asked, concern in his voice but his gaze stayed on the grounds.

She leaned on the banister and stood on the last two steps. "Nothing right now. But I need you to stay away from the party once your shift is over. That's when things are going heat up."

JD stared down at her. "Is that really necessary?"

"Something's supposed to happen tonight. Whatever it is, I'd prefer you to be as far away as possible," she requested as JD scanned the area over her shoulder.

"How about a compromise? I still have to eat. Thirty minutes, tops. I'll stay somewhere close to you." JD gave her those puppy-dog eyes that used to work on her mother.

"Okay," she conceded, trying not to smile. Enduring another forty-five minutes of the party wouldn't kill her. "But not a second longer," she warned. "I'm heading out tomorrow. I wanted to say goodbye now, since we won't have a chance later."

"Soon as I complete this assignment, I'll come see you," JD promised.

"You'd better," she teased, slapping a hand on his arm. "I didn't do all this for you not to remember my name."

JD smiled at her. "It's great to know you still have my back."

"Always." Cameron twisted her bangle watch. "My time's up."

"Be careful, Cam." JD turned his back to the stairs.

The Warden wasn't a danger to JD. Yet, she was still leery of leaving. Her cousin's knack for being in the wrong place at the wrong time had her worried. If he made it through the next hour, he'd be on a plane to Illinois in the morning. Then Jason wouldn't have to worry about her interfering.

"See you soon." JD glanced back and widened his smile as he took long strides up the concrete.

She shook her head. I guess that is his way of telling me I don't need to linger. Cameron ran the opposite way on the path leading to the door. She returned to the shadows of the alcove, flipped her dress back to the red side, slid the protective soles off from over her heels, then readjusted her hair and turned her glasses camera back on. She was about to step out and slip back inside when a familiar voice above, said, "Who's watching the grounds?"

She jumped on the stone ledge and held herself up to see who was with him. Prescott, Mac, and another person with one blue eye and one brown that she didn't recognize, were in a huddle beyond the bushes. She lowered herself, put the sole back over her heels, then lifted herself back up, to listen and watch.

"JD and Angelo on the water side. Pedro and Lenny on the dry side," Mac replied.

"Let's make JD the fall guy. Daron would never believe Angelo had the intelligence to pull this off, let alone the balls," Prescott stated. "JD would be more convincing."

Cameron's heart pounded in her chest as her mind flooded with possible action plans.

"Prescott," Mac shifted, glancing around. "We shouldn't talk—"

"Cameras and mics are off in this section," Prescott informed them. "And I haven't met anyone who could get past Steve."

"We got less than fifteen minutes to make it happen, boys," the third man announced.

Cameron debated running to JD while they talked, but based on where they stood, they'd still make it to him before she did.

"I'll call when I'm in place. Mac, make sure Angelo witnesses the shooting," Prescott instructed.

The guy surveyed the area and kept looking over his shoulder. "Your boat is in place."

"Remember," Prescott turned to the guy she didn't recognize. "Get JD out of here and on the other boat. If he gets killed, we might as well tell Daron what we're up to. Keep JD safe at all cost. If he's found dead, we have no cover for the next two months."

"We need Daron to be searching for JD, not someone else," Mac concurred.

"I want my men in the car with JD … shit." Prescott stared at his watch. "We need this to happen before they switch to the next shift."

They hurried away in different directions. Cameron jumped down from the ledge, running to the passage leading back to the house. She flung the door open, hitting Steve in the back. "Get Eric down to the water now!"

"Tandria—" Steve frowned.

"Don't ask any questions. Just do it, dammit," Cameron ordered, and took off in the opposite direction.

CHAPTER 30

Cameron's feet pounded against the pavement as she ran up the steps where she'd met JD earlier. She raced across the grass in time to see Prescott approaching JD from the opposite side. *Prescott's boat must be docked at the neighboring house.*

Before she reached her cousin, Prescott said, "I heard a gunshot."

Gunfire rang out a second later as Mac and Angelo came up from across the lawn. Mac yanked Angelo's head down. Prescott's hands went to his chest and he splayed back toward the water. JD lifted the gun in the direction of the gunfire then spun around to see Prescott falling.

Cameron didn't miss that Mac didn't let Angelo's head up until JD had shifted his gun in Prescott's direction.

As she sprinted toward JD, Mac sent Angelo toward the mansion.

She could tell her cousin still didn't quite know what happened. He lay on the ground, reaching for Prescott's sinking body.

"JD," she yelled, moving at top speed.

He raised his head and from his distressed expression, JD knew he was in trouble. He got to his feet and as he sprinted her way, two huge goons chased him down and grabbed him. They held him on both sides, half dragging his struggling body toward the back parking lot.

Cameron flung a card at each man and hit the targets. They released JD long enough to pull the cards out and toss them. Seconds later, their bodies hit the ground.

A black van screeched, the doors opened, and two burly men hopped out. One grabbed JD, using him as a shield while the other man motioned for him to go. The van sped off with JD inside.

Cameron reached into her purse and pulled out a drug-laced fan.

"You're going to take me out with that?" the man who stayed behind asked. He chuckled, cracking his huge knuckles.

Letting him land a punch would be like getting hit with a cement block. Cameron would rather shoot him than fight him, but the fan would have to do. She pushed the button and the blade emerged. Darting forward, she stabbed him in the gut, then opened the fan and sliced him twice across the chest.

"That's all you got?" He swiped her weapon away.

She hit him in the gut, then kicked him in the chest. He stumbled and lunged at her, but she stepped out of his reach. He swung at her face. She ducked. He snatched her by the arm, his other hand wrapped around her neck, squeezing so tight she couldn't breathe.

Cameron's feet lifted off the ground. She gulped for air while fighting to remove his hand and inhale.

His eyes went blank before his body pitched forward. She moved out of his hold, gasping as he hit the pavement with a thud when the drug finally kicked in.

Six of Daron's men came running across the back lawn. Cameron raced to the neighbor's place maneuvering to the area where Prescott was being pulled into a boat. The van the goons hauled JD off in had returned. They snatched up the guy she took down, then peeled off. A second van appeared, following the first one out of the guest parking lot. Daron's men fired at both vehicles but didn't slow their movement.

Cameron bolted across the lawn, heading for the valet stand. Glancing back at the house, she realized the attendees were totally unaware of the madness happening on the grounds. She swiped a set of keys off the valet stand then hit the alarm to locate the vehicle.

Eric blocked her path to a silver Lexus. "Where the hell do you think you're going?"

"I don't have time for this." She moved around him.

Eric snatched the keys from her hand and tossed them on the trunk of the car she was about to "borrow". He pushed her toward Daron's Phantom. "I'll drive."

She wanted to argue but now wasn't the time. She climbed in.

As Eric slid behind the wheel, two more black vans pulled out. "Are we following them?"

"No, we're catching up with the first two, before the split in the road."

"Yeah, I'm trying." Eric made headway and was close to the two vehicles trailing their intended targets easily, but they blocked both lanes. He shifted to the right and so did the vans. He moved to the left, and they changed lanes.

"Give me your gun." She lowered her window.

He took his eyes off the road for a second then handed over a Glock.

Sliding her body halfway outside, Cameron rested her butt on the window bracing her legs against the door. She fired two solid shots at the tires, then got back into her seat, buckling up. The van to the right fought to keep control and hit the one next to it then drifted lanes. The one to the left picked up speed to avoid being hit again. Eric gunned the engine, holding a steady course as the damaged van veered to the right again. The rest of the drivers had the presence of mind to give them space.

Bullets rained on the Phantom as Eric gained on the second van, then blew past it. Two remaining vans rode parallel. One dropped behind, continuing to switch positions along the roadway until they reached a spattering of cars further ahead. Cameron kept her eye on the one JD was in. "The first one is the target. Focus on the one with damage on the back."

As the traffic become heavier, one van turned down a side road and the other kept straight. Eric asked, "Are you going to tell me what happened out there?"

"Concentrate on the one that just turned." She hated being in the passenger seat.

Before she could mention the distance between them, Eric said, "I'm turning."

They drove about five minutes before a slower vehicle merged into Eric's lane.

She hit the dashboard when Eric slowed. "Don't let them get away." The van made another quick turn. "You should've let me drive."

"Chill! They're most likely heading for the airport."

No, turn here." Access to the Bay had to be somewhere close.

As he rounded the corner, she caught sight of the vehicle. Eric followed her directions. Three men were dragging JD up the concrete sidewalk.

The van peeled away, passing the Phantom on its way out.

"Let me out a little farther up the road. Go before the boat pulls out," she ordered, glancing at the bangle on her wrist.

Unbuckling her seat belt, she slid off her purse and shoes. A Mitsubishi did a U-turn in the middle of the street, cutting Eric off. He hit the brakes, and Cameron jumped out.

"Tandria," Eric yelled.

Cameron bolted up the pathway, rounding the corner to see the goons haul JD onto the speedboat then pull away from the dock. She dived into the dark water, swimming at a furious pace. When the boat gained momentum, she kicked harder until she was as close as possible. She threw the bangle at the boat, hoping she wouldn't miss from her position, then swam back to the dock.

Eric helped her out of the water. Gripping her by both arms, he stared into her eyes. "Are you crazy?"

Cameron wiped the hair out of her face.

"What would you have done if you had made the boat?"

She rushed toward the Phantom. "I would've handled the situation."

Cameron gave him an evil glare as she tried to get her heart rate to a normal level. Her biggest comfort was she knew that they didn't want to kill her cousin yet.

"Thanks for the reassurance, but three to one," Eric fussed at her side. "Those odds are better than others I've faced."

"I know you're a kick-ass type of girl, but these are dangerous men," Eric scolded her.

"I'm going to say this only once more. I could have handled it." She was tired of wasting time arguing with him. "Ask my brother."

Eric kept in step with her rapid pace. "What?"

"My brother didn't fill you in on my black-sheep past?" If he had, then Eric would know she didn't need to fight them all. Only one, to acquire his weapon and take out the rest.

"Hey—"

"I need your phone." She held out her hand. He hesitated before giving it up. She dialed the number and said, "It's raining fish."

Moments after she heard the words, 'We're on it', she hung up then deleted the number from the call list. Eric would have to log into his account to find out what number she dialed, and he didn't have that kind of time.

"You can start explaining," Eric demanded as they got into the Phantom.

She ignored Eric's question, mentally strategizing her next steps. "We need to get back to Daron's. How long will it take to get through his inquisition and get a boat?"

"If you evade his questions, like you're doing mine ... " Eric glanced at her. "It's going to take a while."

"Can you get me a speedboat?" Her team should be on the move. She'd know shortly if her bracelet had done its job.

"Seeing you'll get one whether I help you or not, the answer is yes."

"Contact my brother and have him waiting at an address I'll give you. Tell him if he doesn't show, he'd better hope he sees me before I see him," Cameron threatened.

"I'll relay the message." Eric stopped at a light. "This may be your only opportunity to tell me what's going on. So, start talking."

She recapped what played out with Prescott and JD. "What's happening in two months with Daron's business?"

"He goes international."

"He's already international," she shot back as her wet body shivered from the cold air blowing inside the car. She switched on the heat.

"Let's say he's linking up with someone who will make his international business on the level with the domestic operations," Eric replied as he upped the temperature. "Why?"

Her phone in her purse on the floor pinged. She grabbed it and checked the messages in that hidden app on the phone. Her team would be able to track them. *Fingers crossed it's not in a location that they'll notice.* "They're keeping JD alive for two months."

Eric lowered the windows, allowing the warm air to flow inside. "Daron's going to try to find and kill JD. He may not like Prescott but—"

"If Daron thought Prescott was dead," she paused as she slipped her shoes on, "he'd be still searching for a traitor as well as my cousin."

"What's the plan to get JD? One that won't get us all killed," Eric said sternly.

Cameron only distributed the details she needed him and her brother to know. By the time Eric turned on the street leading to Daron's mansion, she had Eric convinced her plan would work.

She picked up her purse and secured the contents. "Let me know when you have what I need."

"I'm on it after I check in with security," Eric stated. He slowed as they neared the area that had served as VIP Valet parking. Cameron was out of the Phantom before he could put it in park. She didn't make it to the huge black front door before it opened.

"What in the hell happened?" Daron blocked the threshold. His facial expression was stern; like a father whose daughter had just broken curfew with her no-good boyfriend.

"You want the details here?" Cameron questioned as she reached him, and Eric trotted to catch up.

Daron grabbed her arm as she tried to get past him. "You look like a drowned rat."

"Oh, thanks for the news flash," she shot back, waiting for him to release her arm.

"Go to security," Daron ordered as Eric crossed the threshold. "Get Steve up to speed. I want to talk with Tandria first. I'll deal with you later."

He held her arm with a firm grip as he half-walked-half-dragged her into his office. He slammed the door and locked it, then released her arm. "Have a seat."

Cameron glanced down at her wet clothes. "It's best I stand."

"Have a seat, dammit." Daron dropped into the chair behind his desk. "What in the hell happened and why were you there?"

She looked at the clock. "I can't say."

"JD's a dead man. *I can't allow* ... What?" He questioned as if he'd finally processed what she said.

"I'm not saying a word. Anyone could be listening." Cameron's focus shifted to the door. She was wasting time but if Prescott had left a present in Daron's office, she couldn't risk something being said to endanger her cousin.

"Tandria." Daron snatched a black tablet device and waved it over his desk first before doing a sweep of the entire room. "It's clear. Now talk."

She walked to the edge of his desk, glancing at the painting on the wall avoiding eyes. "The short version?" Cameron asked.

"Come here." He placed the device on the edge of the desk. Cameron was caught off guard as Daron pulled her around to him. He slid her body between his legs then leaned on the desk. She steadied herself on his chest. A flash of heat engulfed her body, which she quickly blamed on the adrenaline pumping through her veins. "I want you to look me in the eye when you tell me everything."

Daron was superb at reading people. She couldn't take it for granted that he was unable to detect and tell the difference between the traitor and the person who was trying to put him in prison. She answered, "JD didn't kill Prescott."

"I'm listening." His face relaxed a bit, but his arms stayed firmly locked around her waist keeping her securely in place even as she tried to put some distance between them.

She told him most of the story, leaving out a few details such as the fact that they escaped by boat. "It's all a set up, but before you go off seeking revenge. I need a favor from you."

His hands dropped from her waist. "No."

"Hear me out." She pressed her hands against his chest to keep him from standing.

"No, you've—"

"Listen to me," Cameron snapped as she tried to remain calm, mentally filtering her words wisely so she wouldn't set him off. "You're not known for letting emotions cause you to make mistakes."

His eyes softened from the hard glare. "What do you want?"

"One week to track down the people holding JD," she pleaded. Daron going after Prescott would ensure JD's death.

"Why?"

She stepped back, not knowing if it was a wise move to tell him now that JD was her cousin. "I don't have time for this. Do what you will."

Cameron dashed to the door, twisted the lock then the knob. Daron caught up with her, placed his hand on the door, forcing it shut. His body pressed up against hers as he put his weight against the wood. "Hold on."

She spun toward him. "You've had months to figure out what Prescott was up to. I'm asking for a week."

Daron glanced down at her fist, which rested on his chest, then focused on her face. "Take Eric with you." He removed his hand from the door. "After you get back, we're going to have a long discussion."

"Fine. Don't repeat this conversation with anyone until we get back. Especially not Tia." She gave him the same stern look he'd given her earlier.

"Go." He had a mixture of admiration and desire in his eyes as he stepped back to allow her to leave. "Don't get yourself killed."

"As if you care."

Daron's lips twitched, but he didn't confirm or deny.

Cameron stood in the opening floored by the sensation, then paused. "Where's my luggage?"

"Back in your room."

"So you knew I was coming back?"

"We have some unfinished business and I'm not talking about your killer instinct, either."

She smiled then raced up the stairs, took off the wet dress, and tossed it on the bathroom floor. Standing in her biker shorts and low-cut top, she grabbed her makeup case and threw a few things into a bag. She pulled out the cross trainers and a jogging suit from the suitcase. She changed, then replaced the twist in her hair with a basic ponytail. Her phone beeped. She glanced at the text from Eric. I'M READY FOR YOU.

Cameron grabbed her gun and left the room. If anything happened to JD, Daron wouldn't be the one Prescott had to worry about.

CHAPTER 31

Hours later, a highly-impressed Eric watched as Tandria used high-tech equipment to track the speedboat's movement. She created a search radius map and sent it to Ryder, the man she'd been speaking to on the radio. Eric and Tandria had cautiously searched a couple islands at the tip of the targeted area after investigating which ones were on sale or being rented out. She avoided the ones that showed signs of normal living, so they didn't scare anyone.

His eyes went to the curvaceous beauty. Other agents had mentioned Jason's brothers but never a sister. Eric was already in with The Warden when Jason was assigned to the FBI team. Since he was undercover, Eric made drops in specific locations, quick phone calls and clandestine meetings where he never really saw Jason's face. Had Eric truly met him in person before they arrived in Miami, he would have known they were related. Based on the conversation, Jason wouldn't appreciate Eric asking her out.

I'll be damned if I let that stop me.

Eric slowly made his way back, wanting time to talk to her while she was semi-undistracted. "If Daron discovers that you and JD are related, he'll—"

"I'm telling him later this week." She tilted her head in a challenging fashion. "If not, later this evening."

Eric's head whipped in her direction. "What?"

"It's strategy. I'm going to avoid talking to Daron for a while." Tandria closed the laptop and slid it into a protective sleeve.

"You're going to tell him?" Eric raised his eyebrow as she slid a compact, lipstick, makeup kit, and mascara into her purse. They were all seemingly innocent items, but now he knew better. The compact helped her track the bracelet; the lipstick case amplified phone reception; the makeup kit was a long-range Wi-Fi device and the mascara was a flash drive.

"I plan to give Daron a few islands to check out," Tandria said and claimed the seat next to him at the wheel. "Before you attack the idea, we need the manpower to pinpoint where they are."

"That's a risk." Eric was concerned Tandria would set off the side of Daron that people feared. As long as he'd been with the man, the only bodies that he'd seen dropped were the ones who gave them no other choice. Every decision to take a life was weighed carefully.

"At this point, it's all a game of chance. Two months can fly by in the blink of an eye." She shifted her gaze, as if there was something she wasn't saying.

"In all honesty, you have less than a month," Eric reminded her as they neared a more populated area. "If Prescott's mole is in play and Mac is in the wind, he may turn up the heat on everything."

"This is best," Tandria announced in a tone that signaled the conversation was over.

Eric guided the boat to the dock and they headed to the Phantom. "Daron isn't going to let you walk away. Going against Jason, you have fallen headfirst into his business. This isn't child's play."

She slipped into the passenger seat. Meanwhile, her fingers rapidly tapped on her phone. Eric reached over, pressing the phone into her lap. "Do you know how long I've been working to take him down? While he's starting to suspect something, at least I'm paid to take the risk. Why don't you focus on being Jason's little sister? Let the professionals find JD."

"Make sure my brother meets me at this address or it won't be me getting left out." She handed him a piece of paper then buckled in.

"Whatever." Eric glanced down at the paper. "Whoa. You're going now?"

"Yes."

Eric texted the information to Jason. He wasn't invited, but there was no way Eric was going back to Daron's without her.

I haven't stayed alive by being dumb.

◆ ◆ ◆

Cameron unlocked the door to the condo her team rented. She hoped trusting her brother wasn't a mistake. Her team could do the job and wasn't bound by any red tape. She didn't want them caught between Daron, Prescott, and her brother's team. Eric followed her inside as she picked up the remote on the dining room table and switched on some R&B. Minutes later, a knock came at the door. She let Jason inside.

She gestured toward Eric. "Let's go into the dining room."

"Lead the way." He was focused on the area the team had converted into an office. A large, transparent dry-erase board and several laptop stations occupied the room.

She turned on the laptop, pulled the memory card out of her purse, then keyed in a few strokes. Jason was eerily silent. *Maybe he's scared to say too much for fear of pissing me off before I tell him why I asked him to be here.*

"Come over here," she said.

As they complied, the screen went blank, then several images popped up.

Jason and Eric watched the sequence of events the night JD was taken.

"We've got two weeks to find JD and bring Prescott down."

"Two weeks?" Jason asked, and he didn't sound optimistic.

"The meeting that Prescott thinks is two months away now has a two-week timetable." Cameron watched them exchange questioning looks.

"What?" Eric frowned, nearly glaring at her.

"Once that happens, the whole plan changes. Prescott will be working off pure instinct and semi-rational thinking."

"Prescott isn't known for leaving folks on this side of the grave," Eric said, leaning forward and resting his hands on the back of a chair.

Jason grabbed a chair from the dining room and pulled it up near hers. "How did you know about the change?"

"Because ... " She swapped out the memory card, showing Daron talking on the phone stating that Prescott might not be attending the meeting. He ended the conversation by saying, "See you in two weeks."

"Damn," Eric murmured, exchanging a concerned glance with Jason. "Prescott was supposed to fly overseas Monday and stay for a month trying to broker a transportation deal."

She handed her brother a copy of the map she'd marked up. "Here's the area where they could be hiding."

Jason studied the destinations for a moment. "Can we go over all the markings?"

Cameron nodded, explaining the map's key. The next hour they discussed how to find JD and get him out safely. At times, Jason stared at her with amazement and sometimes what seemed like regret.

"What?" she asked.

"You could have been an excellent agent."

She glanced at her watch, causing Eric to grimace. "I'm going to avoid a face to face with Daron for at least the next forty-eight hours, only calling in updates through Eric."

"But you're going back to Daron's?"

"Yes, but I'll be gone before Daron and I have a chance to speak." Cameron pursed her lips as she stood taking in Eric's what-the-hell side eye and tight-lipped frown. "Stop worrying. You don't have to go back without me."

Eric's shoulders dropped and he sighed. "Good."

"The day we have that meeting, I'll tell him that I'm JD's cousin," Cameron warned.

Jason's gaze narrowed to slits. "Which means he's going to be watching your every move."

"No more contact from me, which leaves you in charge." Cameron grabbed the documents, put them into a black bag, then slapped it into Jason's chest. "But I still want you to call me when you find JD."

"I will," Jason assured as he dropped the strap over his shoulder.

"My men are working with top of the line equipment you've never seen before. They all know who you are and what you do. Don't pull any power plays," she warned. "All I need you to do is track their progress and decide what's the next move."

"We've gone over this," Jason huffed then shot an impatient glare at Eric.

She folded her arms over her chest. "I need to make sure you understand."

"I understand completely," Jason replied with an exasperated sigh.

"Eric?" Cameron angled her body toward him and he nodded. "I'll fly out tonight. I need everybody on point."

Cameron escorted Jason to the door. She extracted a lightweight backpack from the closet.

Eric stepped across the threshold and waited.

She locked up, headed down the hall, then engaged the alarm on the condo from her cell. Jason wasn't going to get the opportunity to double back for those memory cards.

Texting Rob, she requested that someone switch everything in the condo to the other location. She glanced back and caught a moving shadow. *Is that Steve?*

The only way that could be true was if Daron gave instructions to track her movement.

CHAPTER 32

Eric's mouth went dry as he watched from the office couch as Daron slammed the drawer hard. The large abstract painting behind his desk shook. He inhaled and exhaled, wondering if he was taking his last breaths. Being in this situation made Eric feel like he was repeating the traumatic experience of revealing to his dad he wanted to become an actor and major in Visual and Performing arts. His dad sat him down for hours flipping between grilling him about the decision, lecturing him, to threatening his life. That day paled in comparison to the heated tongue lashing and nonverbal, but hostile, death threat, Daron was issuing now. Tandria had this man riled up.

"Why didn't you come straight back after returning the boat?" Daron leaned on the desk with the weapon tapping his thigh. Daron's grip on the gun could reduce it to ashes.

How did he know we made some other moves? Eric swallowed, wishing he'd been able to get some rest instead of selecting his words carefully, trying not to get himself killed. "Tandria was creating a map of the islands where Prescott could be on hiding out."

He took out the map and handed it over as Daron's cell vibrated. Daron glanced at his screen. "Conversation to be continued."

Daron was out of the office before he could say otherwise. Eric let his head drop forward, slowly breathing to restore his heart rate. He stood, then rushed to the security room.

Everybody was on rotation to watch Tandria. Daron had someone sitting in a Yukon outside the mansion and others stationed at every door. She was going to have a hard time leaving without an escort. Eric wanted to know more about the feisty hellion he'd come to know as Tandria. What was it about her that drew Daron in a way that had him handling this situation much differently than expected?

Daron didn't lack beautiful women. Based on how Daron was allowing Tandria to participate, he was convinced that Tia was on her way out and Tandria was on her way in. The idea of Daron and Tandria together bothered him. Yes, he was attracted to her but the reason went deeper than that. He couldn't put his finger on why.

Eric entered the security room as Steve asked, "What's Tandria doing?"

He locked on to the screen as she escaped over the terrace rail, climbed down the side of the house, dropping into the passageway between the main house and the cottage. She sprinted across the stone pavement.

"Where's she going?" Eric raced out as Steve called for the team to go after her. *She's going to get herself killed.*

Eric bolted down the corridor, attempting to reach her before anyone else. By the time she was in his line of sight, she was already on a motorcycle pulling away.

"Damn." Eric rested his hands on his thighs, trying to catch his breath. *Daron is not going to be happy.*

His cell phone rang. "I've got a flight to catch, but I'll check in later." She hung up before he could respond.

Eric shook his head, letting the men approaching know that she was gone. No one wanted to be the one to tell Daron. He certainly didn't. The man was laid back until someone pissed him off; then it was like stepping on a landmine. Daron had left the house shortly after his earlier interrogation and would return later. Eric was relieved, but he didn't think anyone would sleep easy that night.

♦ ♦ ♦

The silence in the house was extremely loud as Eric waited to be called back to the couch. He didn't want to think about what would happen if Daron somehow found Eric's second phone and discovered who he was. He switched it off and taped it to the bottom of the dresser in his room.

Everyone knew the moment Daron found out Tandria wasn't there. The walls of the mansion seemed to shake as Daron bellowed, "Eric, in my office now."

Eric had no idea what part of the house Daron was in, but he made his way quickly to the office. He once again found himself on the infamous hot seat. This time feeling like a child called into the principal's office. Daron was furious no one had physically seen Tandria in twenty-four hours. The vein in his neck threatened to burst through his skin.

Daron loomed over him. "Next time she calls, connect her directly to me."

"Okay." Eric exhaled a breath as Daron stalked away, knowing she wouldn't stay on long enough for that to happen. "Did you see the email I forwarded you?"

"Yeah, I got the information. Someone's checking into it." Daron snatched the tablet off the desk, clearly not pacified by the update. "You … follow up with me later."

Tia entered the room without knocking and the conversation transformed from hostile to pleasant.

"Beautiful as always," Eric said as he stood, kissing her on the cheek, grateful for the rescue. He highly doubted "follow up" were the original instructions Daron planned to issue.

Daron leaned on his desk. "Where did you disappear to this morning?"

"It's spa day," she beamed, stroking her arm as if the presence of silky skin made her point.

Daron's eyes narrowed with anger. "Did we not discuss you staying home?"

"I'll see you guys later." Eric fled the office, closing the door, only imagining what the conversation had turned into.

Daron didn't look like he was in the mood to tolerate anyone, especially not Tia.

Lex was heading to the office when he reached the door and did an about-face. Lex gave Eric the 'I'm-not-crazy' expression, then went into the kitchen. If Lex was avoiding Daron, things were worse than Eric thought.

CHAPTER 33

Tracking down Prescott was Cameron's top priority since her team was tasked with finding JD. He might lead her to JD quicker than searching the islands one by one. She had to resist the urge to slice and dice him then leave him choking on his own blood. If Prescott or Mac saw her coming, they'd head in the opposite direction. Her visit with Ada for a new look was for that exact reason. She wanted to be sure they couldn't see her coming.

Cameron reclined in the salon chair, staring at the top of the walnut cabinetry and shelving, waiting for Ada to put the finishing touches to her face. Cameron needed her new persona in place to meet Red, who had a location somewhere in New York where Prescott was expected to be.

"Voilà. We're done." Ada whipped the chair around to face a large framed mirror.

"Not bad at all. Beautiful artwork." Cameron tilted her head to one side then the other, studying the tattoos on her neck. "I got to get used to this mahogany ruff neck."

"I'm mad you made me cut that long pretty hair," Ada complained, snapping the latex gloves off her hands.

Instinctively, Cameron rubbed the newly-shaved back of her head then grabbed the studded bandana, tying off the rest of her hair so that only the shaved part was exposed. "It's only the very back portion, Ada." As long as her hair was down, no one would even know the back portion was shaved.

Ada beamed at her work as she released her own long brown hair from a tight bun. "If I hadn't done it myself, I'd swear it wasn't you."

"How long will this stuff hold?" Cameron asked, knowing Ada was always tweaking the formula.

"Forty-eight hours through rain, sleet or snow without maintenance." Ada grabbed a blue plastic bottle off the shelf. "If you want it off before then, this is the only thing that will work."

She had spent the last five hours making this transformation, choosing weighted undergarments to add some pounds and selecting appropriately sized clothes. Her long nails were now short an inch. "I'd gotten use to those damn claws."

Ada stepped back, admiring her work.

Cameron stared in the mirror at the stud in her nose and two earrings in her cartilage. She appeared fifty pounds heavier. Her eyes were amber and with the cosmetic tape now had a hint of Asian descent to their shape. The eyebrows were almost non-existent, and her lips had taken on a permanent frown.

"Now, the accessories are key to your new look," Ada reminded her.

She remembered the routine well. The upkeep was the main reason why she didn't use Ada to watch over JD. "I'll be fully dressed for the next forty-eight hours until I complete my mission."

"The skin tone and the face accent will last as long as you use these products to maintain them." Ada handed her a bag.

Picking up her cell, Cameron read the message that came in. "It's show time," she noted in a deep throaty voice with a slight New York accent like Ada's. Cameron wasn't sure about the accent yet. She would wait until she reached her location and decide.

"You're crazy." Ada called out to Cameron, who was doing an exaggerate pimp.

She smiled, leaving the master of disguises to her work.

♦ ♦ ♦

Hours later Cameron as "Gemma", sat in a popular nightclub across from the roped-off VIP section with glowing blue tables that matched the blue sparkle in the bars around the room. The place was packed from the moment she arrived until three hours later, as she waited to see if Red's information panned out. The blaring Hip Hop music had the clear tables vibrating to the sound.

Prescott, followed by Mac, maneuvered through people into the VIP lounge. His appearance had changed slightly, his hair was cut short making him look a lot more like the black side of his family than he did with the long hair. Prescott's eyes were now a normal shade of brown. Those superficial changes were enough to deceive those who didn't know him well, but not enough to avoid someone who had targeted him.

The gatekeeper led him to a table full of men.

The only thing keeping Prescott alive tonight was the fact he had JD. Red appeared at Cameron's side. His cinnamon skin seemed to glow under the lights as he tilted his head toward the dance floor.

She followed him into the sea of moving bodies. Cameron's position put her at a perfect angle to watch Prescott without appearing to do so. Red danced in front of her for a few minutes before he slid behind her, grabbing her around the waist.

"All these men are making big moves trying to knock out a power player. They're utilizing each other's resources to pull it off," he whispered into her ear. "The one to his right is trying to take Thad out of play and was key in helping him pull off the Florida stunt."

Cameron recognized the third man who was with him in Miami. Prescott greeted each man, his two bodyguards stepped back as he mingled.

Red spun around her and she danced closer to him, saying, "I'm listening."

"The Warden knew a local team would hit him, which is why he was supposed to fly out Monday instead of staying in town as planned." His gaze swept the people closest to them. Then something behind her must have caught his eye because his focus stayed over her shoulder for longer than it should.

"How do you know?" Cameron asked before he guided her through the crowd and off to the side of the club.

Red checked his watch. "Something's up. Let's go."

The VIP section had emptied. Red sauntered to the side entrance with Cameron. When they stood outside, Prescott was getting into a Bentley Mulsanne, then moments later he was merging into the traffic.

"Dammit, I hoped I'd be done with this tonight."

"We've been here before, but I always come through." Red pulled out his cell.

"I need to get close to him," Cameron said, following him down the street.

"If you tell me what you're after, I can—"

"His cell." Cameron needed to slip some tech on it, so she'd have a line on who he was communicating with and possibly a location on JD.

"Mmm. I'll run a source down to his location and let you know how we can make it happen." Red unlocked a black Ford Fusion. "I've known you for what? About six years now. I'm still not sure what you look like."

She checked her phone for updates. "Well, that's the nature of the business."

"Kimura," Red said as he drove off. "When are you going to get out of the game and enjoy your life?"

"When I nail Prescott and find JD." Cameron texted Greg an update.

"Are you serious this time?" Red asked, his eyes widened as he shot her a quick side eye.

"Yes. Now it's your turn to talk." She slipped the phone back in her pocket. "How do you know so much about The Warden's dealings?"

Red shrugged. "My sister was married to his brother."

She kept her expression neutral, but the news caught her off guard like a sudden torrential downpour on a sunny day.

"Yeah, until death did they part. Warden's game was always hi-tech," he said, honking at a cab that cut him off. "His brother was the thug, the enforcer, the facilitator of dirty dealings before he started running things."

She tucked that piece of history in the back of her mind.

"He was a legit businessman until his wife, and some dude she was sleeping with, took him for everything and left him for dead. Kind of a kick in the balls—the dude was also one of the business partners in some special community project Daron was on."

"What did they do?" Cameron asked, wanting more details.

Listening to the rest of story, it explained his lack of trust in women. "His brother was determined to pay them back for what they did."

She glanced out the window to get a line on where they were heading. Red pulled off the road into a warehouse, waiting for his source to get back to him.

"Did his brother take down the wife and lover?" she asked.

"He tried but was ambushed and died. Anyway, once The Warden took over the organization, he become a force to be reckoned with." Red parked the Fusion as the white overhead door rolled down.

"What's up with sentencing people?"

"The Warden wasn't a criminal, let alone violent," Red answered. "His brother was the hardcore one. So, The Warden set up the system that gave certain people a chance to live. If they stepped wrong during the time, then they'd be ... deleted." Red grabbed a few items before shutting off the vehicle.

She was surprised when he got out. Normally they would sit in the car until he received the information. She followed his lead, sliding out from the passenger side, but glanced over her shoulder to make sure they were alone. "Deleted, that's a nice way to put it."

"No." He chuckled, walking over to the wood stairs, leading up to what she assumed was an office. "Deleted from the list of people protected from The Warden's brother."

"Then, they were as good as dead," she said, leaning against the rail and viewing the area behind them.

"Possibly. He'd let his brother handle them his way. That varied, based on the situation," he said as he opened a wooden door. "After his brother's death, he was left in charge and things changed a bit."

"What part of the story are you not telling me?" Cameron entered the kitchen with a clear line of sight to the red exposed brick at the other end of the room. She moved to the side, unsure if she should take a seat at the island or the chocolate couch in the living room.

"I should've known I couldn't slip much past you," he said, motioning for her to follow.

She trailed him to a small room beyond the kitchen, without windows. On the far end, black metal shelves held numerous devices. "What's the real story?"

"Most of it's true, except The Enforcer isn't physically dead, only to the organization." He sat at a black metal table that ran along the wall, then powered up a computer. "He and The Warden switched roles. The Enforcer is living the life The Warden wanted and The Warden is living the life The Enforcer created."

"Now how'd that happen?" Cameron rested her elbow on a table.

"My sister was pregnant at the time The Enforcer almost died." Red focused on the screen as his thick fingers tapped in the login info. "The Warden told him that his parents didn't raise them in this type of environment and he shouldn't either. He insisted that his brother give his child the same opportunities they had growing up."

"Interesting," she said, intrigued by this little slice of Daron's background. She found it fascinating he was one of the good guys. Well, as least as good as the business would allow.

"That was over six years ago. From what my sister says, The Warden found them. The word is they've surgically altered their appearance, but he recognized the opportunity and has set a trap."

"Them, as in the wife and the lover." Cameron could feel her eyes widening with the revelation.

Red looked up at her and nodded.

She still felt like that wasn't the entire story but she wouldn't press. Mentally, she rifled through faces and names of all the people surrounding Daron. *Keep your enemies close.* "How close are you and The Warden?"

"He calls on me every now and again." Red gave her an impish smile.

"Mmm," she muttered as Red pointed toward the computer. "Did he recently call wanting to know about anyone?"

Red snickered as he tapped an index finger on the monitor.

She shifted her focus to figure out what he'd found.

"He requested info on a Tandria Jenkins. I haven't met her yet. But I hope to someday. She sounds like someone else I know."

Cameron laughed then scanned the report, noting a hotel address and room number. "If your contact is sure he's there, then that's where I need to be."

◆ ◆ ◆

Red dropped her off at a temporary living space. A small studio with twin beds and minimum furniture. Cameron changed clothes to soften her appearance, then braided her hair and slipped on a long black wig. She didn't need the hotel security all over her when she returned.

She took a cab to the hotel where Prescott was staying and hung around the crowded lobby. An hour later when he came out of the double glass doors of the restaurant, she hopped up from the plush blue chair where she'd been waiting. Her feet rapidly moved over the blue and gold carpet until she reached the tiled corridor leading to the restrooms.

Prescott was on his cell, moving at a casual pace in her direction. As she passed him, she bumped the arm with the phone, causing it to clatter to the tiled floor. She snatched it up, slipping the small clear patch on the underside before he could make a move. She had six hours to listen in and download data before the tech disintegrated.

She powered the phone down and handed it back to him. "Sorry."

"No problem." Prescott hit the power button, unknowingly activating the tech.

Cameron wished she could have put the permanent one on but couldn't risk him finding it. Her fingers were crossed he'd check in on JD within that time.

She headed to the restroom and stepped back as two women brushed past her. The space between the sink and the stalls could fit an entire dance floor. She was glad it was fairly empty as she walked to the sink farthest from the opening, slipped in an earpiece and dialed into the system to see if it worked.

"Maureen, did you get Daron to agree to it?" Prescott asked.

"Of course he did, darling," Maureen replied, in a voice that could send a diabetic into a coma as the line started breaking. "But ... He ..."

Cameron could hear a clicking as Maureen's words got choppy.

"Hold on a sec," Prescott said.

She glanced at the cell in her hand to make sure she was still connected, then took out the earpiece. The light was green so she knew it was receiving, she slid it back in position.

"Keep a cool head." Prescott's voice suddenly boomed in her ear. "There's no way for him to know who we really are."

"You need to change your appearance again," she shot back.

Prescott grunted. "That's too risky if our plan's going to work."

"I called to inform you that he's intensifying the search for JD. Tandria is MIA. Keep your eyes open," she warned. "We still don't know what's her angle."

Cameron stepped back into the hallway, reclaiming her spot in the lobby with a view of the entrance and the guest elevators. Prescott walked out of the lobby, standing in between the two sets of sliding glass doors.

"Listen, we've been in this for years. We're finally at the point where we can take his empire once again ... " Prescott paused as a group of women entered through the front doors. When they'd cleared the area, he continued, "Do not mess it up. Do *not* panic. The moment you do, we're both dead."

"I'm sorry but he's saying things that make me wonder if he knows." Her voice was a high-pitched whine.

"Until he confronts you directly, kept your mouth shut," Prescott commanded as the Mulsanne pulled up. "Alright, I need to go. Baby, remember once we do this, we're set for life. No more looking over our shoulders."

"I heard that before," she replied with an attitude. "Look where we are."

"You know what you need to do." Prescott headed out as the line clicked and got staticky. "Maureen ... Maureen."

"Yeah."

"Be ready to rock and roll when I get back to Miami."

Mac sat in the driver's seat as Prescott held up a finger to say he'd get there in a minute.

Cameron neared the concierge's desk and sent a warning text to Eric.

Anyone in Prescott's path to Daron's organization would be mowed down.

CHAPTER 34

Once Cameron saw Prescott drive off, she made her way up to his room and didn't care if any camera caught wind. Only one duffle bag with clothes sat on the striped comforter. The closet was empty. Nothing was in the place that could lead her to JD. She set up hidden motion-activated cameras and microphones then slid out and headed to a nearby bar to wait.

An hour later, her phone vibrated. The waitress placed a Guinness on the small square table and walked away. Cameron plugged in her earphones, turning the volume to max and listened as she watched the clear view inside of Prescott's room.

He threw a suitcase on the king-sized bed. Mac leaned on the desk, focused on his phone. "Sorry. The other fighters you'd hired said Daron wasn't the one who paid them."

"I should've done it when I first thought of it." Prescott unzipped the suitcase as Mac rolled a chair toward the desk. "It's funny. People call me Lucifer but Daron has been the devil in my life since senior year in high school."

"I didn't realize you two went back that far." Mac took the papers Prescott handed him.

"He probably doesn't either." Prescott grabbed a laptop and situated it in front of Mac.

"How's he your Lucifer?" Mac hit the power key and spun the chair, facing Prescott.

"He landed a scholarship into a program that should have been mine. Not only did he get a free ride, but it also helped establish his business," he said with a hate-filled voice. "I ended up selling my soul to the streets to get through college."

Mac turned toward the laptop and with pudgy fingers tapped on the keyboard. "Did he use his family influence or something?"

"I had that scholarship locked and loaded. My counselors saw to that. My biggest competition hadn't turned in any project notes to get feedback before the final submission." Prescott pulled four black metal boxes out of the suitcase. "Yet he ended up with it. By the time Daron entered his first year in college he'd already started his business. Just to add fuel to the fire, he managed to marry the woman I've been in love with since fifth grade."

"Must not have been successful, considering what he does now," Mac commented. "And he's clearly not married."

Prescott muttered something Cameron couldn't hear. "By his second year he was doing extremely well. He stole my life when he won that scholarship. I've been determined to take it back ever since."

"I thought you graduated." Mac grabbed a pen off the desk and wrote on the papers Prescott handed him.

"I did." Prescott balled his fist. "But my pops wouldn't pay tuition unless I worked for him."

Mac frowned. "What about his wife?"

"Let's just say I appealed to the wild side of her that she kept suppressed to win her back." He slammed his fists onto the bed. The duffle bag rolled off, hitting the floor.

Mac's head snapped in his direction. "What's wrong?"

"Daron is what's wrong," he growled. "I left my dad's business to get revenge." Prescott picked up the duffle and threw it next to the suitcase. "Now he's running my father's business."

"Wait." Mac stood, waving. "Whoa. How did that happen?"

"My father passed, so I left Troy in charge. When I put my plans for revenge in motion, I had no idea he was Daron's brother."

"How did you *not* know?"

"I didn't realize Bryant was his middle name, not his last name. That's on me, for not allowing my dad to show me the ropes like he wanted," Prescott said through clenched teeth.

"The way Daron's name is whispered in the street and people are willing to pay top dollar for a sit down … " Mac lowered himself back into the seat. "I thought … "

"He refused to sell or transport drugs and weapons yet still managed to make the business more profitable than my dad ever did." Prescott slammed the suitcase closed.

"But you can't compare the two," Mac frowned. "Your dad was shot when the FBI took down his sex trafficking business."

"Exactly my point. He managed to be extremely successful without those profitable segments. Lucky Bastard." Prescott pulled out his cell, swiping, typing, then sliding it into his pocket. "Pisses me off to see those ridiculously-priced seats filled at the arena and those business opportunities rolling in."

"Those transportation containers are the real money makers."

Prescott gave a wicked smile. "Once we obtain one and duplicate the unit, I'll be able to charge a larger fee to move weapons and drugs for my clients."

"By this time next week, they'll be clamoring to get to you." Mac turned, closing the laptop and returning the documents. "Is your girl ready to do her part tomorrow?"

"She'll handle her part." Prescott gave an evil smirk. "And I'm ready to take his life, his power, and my dad's business. If I put all segments within the organization back in play, I may not get the life I dreamed of, but I'll at least have the life my dad wanted for his family."

"I've confirmed your seat at the table at Mickey's meeting." Mac handed Prescott the laptop.

Prescott dumped the clothes in the suitcase and folded up the papers before sliding them into each black box. Then, he put them in the duffle bag. "Deliver these. If Mickey accepts our offer to host, we need to ensure we can accommodate him."

Cameron waved the waitress over to pay her tab as Prescott zipped up the suitcase and Mac left the room. *Who the hell is Mickey? He couldn't possibly be the international contact Prescott is expecting to meet in two months.*

She sent a text to Trenton asking if a phone can record its location without cell service. Maybe Prescott's phone location would lead to her cousin. Frustrated, she walked back to the hotel. Cameron tried to look at the feed again but the screen was black. Prescott must have walked Mac down to the car. Picking up speed, she headed back to Prescott's room. If she could make it and swipe the laptop out of the suitcase before he returned, maybe it would yield JD's location. She glanced at the syringe in her inner pocket. If not, she'd have to make Prescott talk.

When she let herself in again, the area had been emptied of personal effects. *Damn, Prescott was on the move again.* She removed her equipment. Her next best bet was following his female accomplice.

Eric still hadn't responded to the text.

♦ ♦ ♦

Later that night, Red and Cameron sat in a green booth in the back of a quiet restaurant owned by a mutual friend. Red confirmed Prescott had left town. Based on the time, it was a couple hours after he left the hotel. Red was waiting on her private flight confirmation and Ada to make it back to her shop, before dropping her off.

"The Warden knows more than he lets on." Red shifted his empty plate to the side. "Don't try to play him."

"Except for leaving out a few minor details, I've been on the up and up." Since he'd probably already called Red to verify who she was, there was no doubt it was time to tell Daron she was JD's cousin.

Red shook his head. "I'm trusting you know what you're doing."

"I trust you not to get me killed." Cameron checked her phone. People trusted Red's information because it was rarely wrong. "The meeting is coming soon."

"How did you know?" Red frowned. "Any information you don't work to get is usually a set up."

Why isn't he responding? Cameron checked her message screen again to make sure she hadn't missed one from Eric. She looked up at Red as she asked, "What?"

"You do know The Warden created some of the tech that you like to commandeer from me." Red leaned forward. "I mean it when I say his ex-wife and her lover will be the last people who will pull the wool over his eyes."

She wondered if the two weeks info she'd been given was indeed a set up. But why? "I'm honestly not trying to interfere."

"Being between you and The Warden is a delicate position for me. I'm trying to be helpful to both without betraying either of you," Red confessed, his gaze narrowed as he rested his chin in his hand. "I can do what I do and help you because of him."

"Don't worry, The Warden and I are on the same side of this situation." Cameron understood completely. She knew better than to force him to pick a side. The man hadn't been in the business all these years by making enemies out of his key alliances.

"Stay safe." Red's phone buzzed. He stood, putting money on the table.

He must have received confirmation. She grabbed her bag as he handed over a flash drive in a plastic baggie and said, "For The Warden."

"Wait. I forgot to ask you … " She tucked the new item away and followed him out. "Who is Mickey? Prescott mentioned him."

Red didn't answer the question until they were in the Fusion heading to Ada's. "It has to be Mickey Holiday, the dirty politician who has his hand in a lot of illegal pots."

The cars ahead of them slowed then stopped.

"I appreciate the help and I won't be darkening your doorstep after this," she stated as she tried not to get irritated by the slight traffic jam.

"Because you can go straight to the source and get your tech toys," Red teased.

Cameron chuckled as he pulled over. "I'm serious about retiring."

"Kimura," Red called out through his lowered window.

She leaned in to listen. "Here's another tidbit. The Warden is in Bishop's intimate circle."

Red merged into traffic, leaving Cameron stunned. Autumn had been sent in by Bishop to watch Daron's back, not to acquire information to use as a weapon against him. *Had Red already given Bishop's file to Daron? How much does Daron know about me and my aliases?* She'd have to deal with those issues later. Right now, she needed to get back before they made their next move.

CHAPTER 35

Daron pushed the frame of an abstract painting behind his desk to open and enter the secure room. The steel door shut behind him. Lex was sitting at the largest of the seven workstations with a laptop in front of the security monitors.

He may have been pretending to want to kill JD for shooting Prescott, but the anger at the fact his team had done such a terrible job keeping eyes on Tandria was real. They lost her before she reached Bishop's old place. If he hadn't known Bishop, he wouldn't have had a clue of her whereabouts.

Daron slipped on a pair of disposable gloves before grabbing the manila envelope next to Lex. He took a seat on the leather couch near the server. The people within his organization who had their own agenda would get what they had spent years on, but things wouldn't quite turn out as expected. If all went well, these were his last official days as The Warden.

Lex put his cell next to the laptop and spun the chair to face Daron. "Prescott has emerged."

"It's almost over." Daron reviewed the contents of the envelope. Only a select few who knew his identity would be aware he'd retired.

"Prescott doesn't have a clue this supposed 'international expansion' is about tying up loose ends for your departure from this business," Lex said, as he unlocked the cabinet under the desk.

"Or that the real negotiations have already started." Daron was attending to lock in a few future favors so his retirement plan wouldn't end with a bullet in the head or serving life in prison. He stood, walked over to the copier and slid the photo of Tandria from the pile. He stared at her image for a moment.

"Do you think Tandria passed the two-week timeline to Eric?"

"When Prescott snatched JD, the timeline ceased to be valid."

The idea of claiming Tandria as his woman once he closed the book on this chapter of his life appealed to him. None of the women who crossed his path had him desiring to risk it all for a chance at love again until Lex introduced him to Tandria. Autumn flashed in his mind. Maybe that statement wasn't exactly true. He felt that intense bond with her as well.

Bishop was at the event the night he'd met Autumn. What were the odds of the one woman in the room that drew his attention like a bee to honey would work for Bishop? Daron didn't have a picture of Autumn, especially at the angles Red would need to confirm that Autumn was another of Kimura's aliases. *Maybe it was wishful thinking to believe that our connection went much deeper than simple attraction.*

"I can't believe *my* Tandria is the infamous Kimura." Lex tossed him a flash drive, which Daron snatched in mid-air. "I'm curious to know how she helped you out."

Hearing his friend referring to Tandria as his, grated on Daron's nerves. Daron was days from being able to actively make sure that would never be true. "She's the reason Troy survived Prescott's ambush. Bishop sent her in."

Daron laid the papers on the scanner and inserted the drive. He remembered pulling up to the remote cabin as gunfire broke out. Seeing her in action through the window as Bishop held him back when he attempted to get out. He and Troy didn't always agree on Troy's life choices but he hadn't wanted to bury him next to their father, either.

"If you knew her through Bishop," Lex said, picking up a black briefcase from the floor and sliding several thick manila envelopes inside. "Why start a fight series to find her?"

"After Troy recovered, I wanted to personally thank her," Daron explained, as the papers swished through the copier. "By that time, she was in the hospital fighting for her life." He stuffed the originals back into the envelope.

Kimura was rumored to have died but Red mentioned in passing that Ada hadn't cleaned out the special locker they kept for that mysterious woman. With Bishop dealing with his own medical issues, it hadn't dawned on Daron to ask for her real name until it was too late.

"That still doesn't explain the fights." Lex grabbed the stack of papers from him.

"She'd been into underground fights before she came to work for Bishop." Daron pulled the flash drive out the copier. "I figured she might go back to it out of habit. At the very least, come across someone who knew her."

Lex closed the briefcase. "Why didn't you recognize her in the pics?"

"Tandria looks nothing like the woman I saw that day," Daron answered, slipping the flash drive into his pocket. "If she hadn't come in using my tech and talking with JD—"

"You wouldn't have suspected she was Kimura."

"Nope." He'd known Kimura would eventually show up for JD because of their history with Bishop. He picked up the photo of Tandria again, the sweet curve of her lips, the sparkle of her eyes, that dangerous glint he saw there, her intelligence—all made her extremely sexy.

"It's hard to believe she worked for Bishop." Lex closed the laptop and stuck it in with the envelopes.

"She did it for JD but clearly she's good at it. Bishop molded her into a lethal weapon," Daron said, scrolling through his messages. "Funny enough, Bishop created the handles Kimura and The Warden but Onyx, the one he created for himself, never stuck."

Bishop's advice was to never use his real name during meetings and to occasionally send people in his place to make it difficult for anyone to pin crimes on him. When he met with people, he was always a representative of The Warden—except with Bishop's associates. His entire plan had been built on that advice and it had saved him more times than he cared to count.

"I'm going to make that run as soon as I finish packing up." Lex placed another briefcase on the desk. "Should I put someone on Prescott?"

"No. We know where he'll turn up," Daron said as Lex took off his gloves. "And we won't be the one to take him out."

When Prescott took JD, Daron had expected Tandria to go after her cousin. She surprised him by hunting for Prescott instead. Daron wanted to give her a chance to save her cousin before setting off the next chain of events. But if it became a choice between his plan and JD's life, JD was in trouble. If it was only Daron's life on the line, he'd let things play out. The success or failure of his plan affected the lives of several people who were very close to him.

His tablet pinged.

Lex handed it to him and the message flashed. Tandria had landed.

"A few more days and we'll have a new norm," Lex said as he went into the hallway.

Daron lowered himself into a chair, placing the photo down on the desk. He watched the monitors and only looked away after Lex drove off the grounds.

The last five years of his life had been torture. The past twelve months had been a special kind of hell trying to make this moment happen. All the players in one place.

Steve's number appeared on his phone display.

"What's up?"

"Tandria is moving fast, heading in our direction," he announced.

Daron glanced at his watch. Eric and Pedro should have dropped Tia off to the Illinois transportation team and been on their flight back. He made a last-minute decision to send Tia away. She was nervous and jumpy lately, which made him uncomfortable. He trusted her even less than he had before. Sleeping next to her these days was impossible. With these meetings he'd scheduled, he needed sleep to have his wits about him, and she had tried to be a major distraction.

"Check with the transport team and get an update on Eric and Pedro," Daron said as he cautiously took the exit to the hallway and front door.

He stood in the threshold as Tandria barely let the Avalon stop before she hopped out and took long strides to the door.

"Is Tia here?" Tandria brushed past him into the house.

He closed the door behind her. "No."

She whirled to face him. "Where is she?"

"Eric and Pedro took her back home yesterday." Daron entered the living room and rested his palms on the back of the couch.

"Just the two of them?" She pulled out her phone.

"Yes." Daron peered at her, wondering why the sudden interest in Tia. "Is there a problem?"

"Yes." Tandria appeared to be texting, frustration etched on her face. "She's meeting Prescott today."

"Eric and Pedro can handle Prescott's men." Daron walked toward her. If Eric couldn't handle the situation, he'd call Steve or his other team.

"It's not the men I'm worried about." Tandria's eyes widened and her lips tightened.

Daron cursed. That was why Tia was being so difficult. Prescott must have had plans to meet her at the spa.

Somehow, Prescott had found out the meetings had been moved up. He dialed Eric's number. No answer. He tried Pedro. No answer. He called Steve.

"What's the status on Tia and the guys?" Steve gave an update and Daron shook his head, indicating to Tandria that they didn't make it.

She frowned.

Steve informed him he'd received a text saying they made it but the last known location of Eric's phone was Biscayne Bay.

"I'm pretty sure I know where they're taking them," Tandria announced.

"I'll call you back in a minute." Daron disconnected the call and focused on her hazel eyes. "Where?"

"The same place they're holding JD." Tandria appeared to be texting someone again. "I'll rescue JD and the guys. You handle what you need to here." Tandria's phone vibrated in her hand. She unlocked her screen and started typing again.

"Why should I trust you?"

She glared at him as if to say, "you already know that answer."

"Say it." Daron wanted to see if she'd tell him the truth.

"JD is my cousin."

"Fine, I need Prescott alive." His entire plan hinged on Prescott. As much as he wanted him dead, he'd be getting off too easy and he had other things to handle. This wasn't how he expected the conversation with Tandria to go. He wanted to be co-conspirators so they wouldn't mess each other up. Having to split their focus could be dangerous.

Tandria rushed for the door. "What about Tia?"

"Your call." Daron shrugged. "But I wouldn't mind if she received a Kimura-style beat down before you do whatever you decide."

Tandria stopped in her tracks. She glanced back at him over her shoulder, raised an eyebrow, nodded, then tossed something at him.

He caught it against his chest.

"From Red," she said, crossing the threshold.

The Avalon's wheels screeched as she pulled out. He glanced down at the flash drive then dialed Lex. "We've got a problem. Eric won't be in place."

Lex groaned. "Dammit the plan—"

"Let's hope Mickey's treacherous ass is still having his meeting." Daron knew Eric had almost all the information to take The Warden down.

"Let me find out if Eric's people are on point then I'll know if you'll need to go with the backup plan," Lex said.

Daron needed the FBI in place. He didn't know if bringing The Warden down was more important than saving one of their own. Eric was temporarily out of play. Prescott's meeting with Mickey would be the key to everything.

CHAPTER 36

The speedboat bounced as the hull sliced through the dark water, taking Cameron to meet up with Rob and Greg. Her team's attempt to breach the house had been interrupted by Prescott's arrival with additional guards. She attached a specialty device to her phone, then called her brother.

"Did Eric come your way?" she asked as they came close to the island. "He should've led you to JD."

"Wait. Eric's in trouble?" Jason cursed. "I left your men to search the island while I—"

"I don't care what you're doing," she snapped as they slowed, nearing their destination. "I'll be too busy trying to save JD and Eric to meddle in your affairs."

She disconnected the call, her legs slid over the side of the boat and her sneakers sank into the wet sand. Cameron trotted up the slight incline laying on the grassy ledge between Rob and Greg. The area near the house was well lit but all they had was moonlight and stars to light their area. Several other men that Greg brought along were a little further down near the other boats.

"Prescott stayed a couple of hours then left on the speedboat with Mac and a few guards." Rob handed her the tablet.

"Where is Tia?" Cameron stared at the brick house beyond the trees. Guarded by a minimum of ten men on the screen, four of them swept inside. Rob tapped the monitor to get images of the house from different angles.

"She returned to the house guarded by two giants," Greg answered.

Cameron handed the tablet back to Rob. "Anything else I should know before I go in?"

"A second boat came from the other side of the island." Rob tucked the tablet in his backpack. "We assumed it was with Prescott."

Her hope was that JD wasn't on that second boat. He, along with Eric and Pedro, would be dead after this meeting wrapped up. "Okay, let's move."

Cameron and her team swept into the rows of trees. The six guards continued to patrol the perimeter at regular intervals. Pulling the tranquilizer guns out, she took down each man from a distance. The moment their bodies hit the ground, she waved the two teams forward. They silently advanced toward the house.

She followed them, slapping tech devices on the trees until she reached the clearing. One team went to the front door and the other slid in via the back. She sprinted for the basement window. Pedro hung shirtless from the ceiling of what appeared to be a jail cell. His head was bowed and his body bruised and bloody. Gunfire blasted as her team entered the house. She used her gun to break the window, cleared the larger shards, and crouched to slip inside. The remaining glass scratched the material of her outfit as she lowered herself to the concrete but everything remained intact. Moving across the cold damp space toward Pedro, she peeked through the bars, expecting to see JD and Eric across the hall in a similar situation. *What kind of evil person kept jail cells in their basement?*

Pedro's eyes widened, he exhaled then gave her a slight smile.

Cutting Pedro down, she asked, "Can you walk?"

"Yeah." His eyes were glassy from the effects of whatever drug he'd been given. His face was puffy and bruised, but he swaggered her way.

"How we getting out?"

He stared at the window like there was no way he would make it through there. She took the bag off her back, wrapping what resembled black electric tape around the bars and the locks. The tape was designed to apply pressure then issue a small explosive charge. She stepped back, and the lock popped. Grabbing the bars, she pulled them open.

She rushed into the corridor in between the cells. "Where's JD and Eric?"

"Prescott has them," Pedro spoke slow as if the effort hurt.

He moaned as he staggered behind her down the hall trying to keep up with her pace. She put a finger to her mouth to tell him not to give away their location. The sound of movement she'd heard before ceased and the house suddenly became quiet. She moved her mouth closer to the microphone in her collar, "Guys, is this silence a good thing?"

"Yeah. We're searching for your boys," Greg informed her.

"I have Pedro. JD and Eric are with Prescott. Meet us at the boat." Cameron tipped through the basement pressing her body against the metal bars and instructing Pedro to do the same. She'd be a fool to assume all the guards were upstairs.

She held her hand up to get Pedro to halt his progress, then gave him a gun. "I need you to clear the stairs. I'll be behind you."

"Okay."

He was clearly in pain, so she didn't want to send him up without a means to protect himself.

She looked him in the eyes. He spoke as if he was fine but his eyes made her question his physical state. "Are you in any condition to hit a target?"

"Yes," Pedro answered, quickly. Too quickly, as if his ego were talking instead of common sense.

"Make sure I'm not one of them."

He grimaced when trying to smile.

The tags she'd put on the trees on the way to the house could only be seen with special glasses worn by her the team. She handed Pedro a pair, hoping he'd be able to see clearly given that his eyes were swollen.

"Follow the red dots on the trees. They'll lead you to the boat."

"Got it." Pedro winced as he slid them on.

"When I say go, take off," she directed, peeking into the living space in front of the stairs that led to the main level.

She stepped into the opening, knowing she wasn't about to fight the huge dude standing guard. Pulling out her cards, she threw two in his chest, then stepped out of his range. When he hit the ground, she yelled, "Go."

Pedro raced toward the stairs.

Cameron climbed them sideways to make sure the giant didn't miraculously get up and follow them. The drug on the card might not be enough to keep him knocked out for long, given his size.

Pedro was moving across the hall on the main level to the door when a pop echoed. As she hit the top of the stairs, a portion of the wall opened.

Tia stepped out of the space, in full view.

Cameron studied the reinforced door doubling as a wall. *Why would this fool come out?*

Tia aimed a gun and shot at Pedro who was almost to the threshold.

"You're not going anywhere," Tia said, in a high-pitched voice.

Pedro held his hands up, as if in surrender. Blood dripped from his upper arm where the bullet had grazed him. Cameron shielded Pedro with her body, keeping her focus on the new target and said, "Go."

Pedro resisted. "I'm not leaving you."

"I got this," she yelled.

"No."

"I'll shoot you myself if you don't," Cameron threatened, causing Pedro to reluctantly slide out the door.

Tia's face twisted as she waved the gun at her. "You had to come along and ruin everything."

"You should've stayed in the panic room." She debated shooting the woman. Since she couldn't take a kill shot, it was a risk. The distance between them would give Tia an opportunity to fire multiple shots.

"I can't allow you to keep interfering." Tia inched closer, heels clicking against the wood. "I was slowly winning Daron back before you came."

"You should've shot first and talked later." Cameron stepped forward and kicked the weapon out of Tia's hand. The Ruger skittered across the floor as Tia launched a series of well- placed punches.

Cameron dodged most of them. "Oh, so you want to fight? Your boyfriend put ... *Damn,* I guess I should clarify. *Daron* put in a request for you."

She returned with a jab to the face, then kicked Tia's knees, sending her sprawling to floor. Tia rolled and recovered, getting to her feet and taking a more determined stance. "Daron will be surprised that I'm more of a fighter than he expected."

Tia aimed a roundhouse kick toward Cameron's shoulder, but the blow didn't connect.

Cameron knocked Tia's leg down, punched her in the gut, and followed with a left hook to the jaw. "You're not ready."

Tia glanced at the Ruger as though trying to determine whether she could cover the distance. Her lapse gave Cameron an advantage and she grabbed Tia's hair. "Lesson. Hair down is rarely an advantage."

Cameron flung her to the floor, but Tia scurried to her feet, grabbed a nearby lamp and swung, but she jumped back.

"We see Pedro." Rob's voice echoed in her ear. "Where are you?"

She punched Tia several times and landed a kick to her chest that planted the woman against the wall. "Give me two minutes. I'm about to grant Daron's request."

Cameron flicked out two blades and Tia's eyes widened. She was going to wish she'd stayed in the panic room when Cameron was done with her.

◆ ◆ ◆

Daron knew his facial expression probably matched the disgust etched on Lex's face as he wrapped up the last of the loose ends. He nodded for Steve to take over supervising the group, then walked over to Lex and moved into the office. He was not happy to hear that Prescott had pushed the meeting up by a day.

They were in the process of moving Daron's hidden surveillance room and modifying security footage now. The mansion would be cleared out before the Feds hit. The only problem, everyone wasn't in a public location. So it would be difficult to take them down with Prescott.

"Tell Steve to put Nicco in charge." Daron unlocked the wall safe and cleared out the contents, dropping everything into a briefcase. "We need to go."

Lex walked over to the entrance of the hidden security room. "I'll tell Nicco to text us when it's done."

Daron whipped out his cell. "I'm calling to make the arrangements now."

A few minutes later, Steve emerged with Lex and all three of them headed for the Cadillac Escalade before taking the back exit off the property.

Steve's job was to watch Eric to make sure he didn't stumble upon information that would jeopardize anything. The illegal activities associated with the fights were the only thing Eric could attempt to tie them to, but Eric had no solid proof. Daron prevented anyone from recording the transaction for the few female fighters that he'd paid off personally because he thought they could be Kimura. What Eric did have led back to Prescott. Daron made sure that the meetings Eric attended were legal and above board.

His phone rang as he neared Barton G's restaurant. Lex and Steve waited near the door as he took the call. "Hey."

"Where's Prescott?" Tandria asked with venom in her voice.

"Tandria." Daron paused, then gently implored, "I need him alive."

She mumbled something he couldn't make out, then stated, "Pedro's safe, but he still has Eric and JD."

In the background, a call for a doctor echoed over a speaker system. Tandria had to be at the hospital.

"Then why are you at the hospital?"

"Took Pedro to assess his injuries. They're keeping him overnight, now back to Prescott. Where is he?"

Without a doubt, Prescott would be reaching out to her again. Daron was convinced Prescott was going to contact her because he wanted

Tandria on his team and in his bed.

He waved Lex over. "My systems are currently down. So, I can't tell you where he is, but I can tell you where he'll be."

"Text me the time and location," Tandria growled.

Daron looked at the information on Lex's phone, pausing to think of the consequences of giving it to her.

"What's with the silence?" Tandria asked. When he didn't answer, she added, "I won't kill him unless I'm forced to."

"It's coming to you now." Daron sent the text.

Lex looked at Daron, silently questioning if everything was okay.

Daron waved for them to go inside as he worked on arranging to send Tandria some back up. She could take care of herself, but she would have more elements to deal with in that room than just Prescott and his people. If she took Prescott out tonight, it would be difficult to leave her alias, Tandria, behind. From what he knew about Kimura and Bishop's story, she deserved an opportunity to retire and get a second chance at life.

Preferably…with him.

CHAPTER 37

Fear of failure hounded Cameron as she remembered Pedro's battered body in the hospital bed. Her chest felt like an elephant had used it for a reclining chair. She inhaled and exhaled, reminding herself to put all her energy into making her desired outcome a reality. Cameron doubted Tia would be in any condition to run before the authorities dealt with her. The only thing that had saved Tia's life was she had better use for her. Besides of all the crimes she could potentially end up behind bars for, she had no intention of letting Tia be the one that sent her to prison.

Her phone vibrated as she left the hospital. A text came through from Daron with the information on Prescott. Her brother's team probably had no clue Daron's location without Eric to keep them updated. Her phone pinged. She opened a message from Prescott inviting her to the mansion. The text stated he had an offer she couldn't refuse.

Jason had already shown her his number one priority was The Warden and his crew. She wasn't counting on him saving JD.

She texted Greg the update since she doubted Rob had made it back from his run. Cameron went on autopilot as she drove back to the condo. She rushed in, changed, then picked up a set of non-lethal weapons since

Prescott would never let her through the doors with a gun. She took her hair down, made sure it was hanging over her face and put on huge sunglasses. A contact was already working on removing all images of her that had been taken while at the compound and mansion. Hopefully it was enough to keep her off the FBI's radar. Trenton and Greg met her in front of the condo building with their guest. She walked out in a black jumpsuit with a wide beaded bracelet on each wrist.

"Damn, Baby Girl." Trenton's brown eyes widened and his jaw dropped while he stared at her as he held the door open. "Rob and Greg mentioned you changed styles, but I wasn't prepared."

She sat in the back seat next to Tia who was bound, gagged and probably sore as hell. Tia had what felt like hundreds of paper cuts all over her body. The cuts were sealed with liquid band-aid but any wrong move and Tia was feeling the pain again. "Well, I didn't expect your personal issues to keep you overseas for so long."

Trenton closed the door, and grimaced. "I'm back and ready to ride shotgun."

"Did you apply Ada's gift?" Cameron asked, checking to make sure the shade on Tia's window was pulled down.

"Yes, we put it on. Did you?" Trenton volleyed back as Greg drove to Daron's mansion.

"I barely had time to change and grab my weapons." She pulled a compact out of her bag and started applying the cream.

Greg took one hand off the wheel touched his face. "What's with having us put on makeup? Transparent or not, it feels weird."

"My brother will be there. I need your images to be distorted on film long enough for Bishop's FBI contact to retrieve and remove them permanently," Cameron answered.

Trenton glanced back at her. "What are our assignments?"

She explained what she needed them to do, which was make sure Eric and JD made it safely out of the compound. "Try not to do anything that my brother can pin on us. He might make good on his threat to haul me off to jail, and I know he wouldn't hesitate with the two of you."

While the volatile environment at the location wasn't ideal, at least she knew the layout. Daron had eyes inside, so she knew how many men were with him. At least she wasn't walking in blind. She realized how dangerous Prescott was now that she knew what had been done to Daron.

They pulled up to the neighbor's house a few feet from the mansion's property line, parked and rushed along the stone path between the mansion and the guest house to the entrance, Trenton on her side and Greg pulling Tia along.

The door opened as she approached.

Mac grinned, glancing at his watch. "Pleasure seeing you again."

"Yes, I'm early." Cameron stepped in close. "Do you have a problem with that?"

"No, beautiful." Mac moved back, allowing her to enter. He stared at Tia as she passed but said nothing.

She wondered what had happened to convince Prescott it was safe to come in and act like king of the castle. "Where's Prescott?"

"He's in the entertainment room. If you could wait in the foyer while he wraps up." Mac escorted them into the area near the pool tables that was separated from the rest of the room by a wall that was half glass, half concrete.

Prescott was meeting with a group of men. A few familiar faces. Trenton leaned on a pool table behind her. Greg kept Tia off to the side and out of Prescott's direct line of sight. Her phone vibrated as a text came in from Prescott. He wanted to change the time and location. She replied, *Too late. I'm here. Look up.* Prescott's head whipped up, and he sent her a wicked glare before typing. A lovely sight to see, but you didn't need back up.

She replied, Just here to make sure I don't do anything to get myself in trouble.

Glancing up, she saw Prescott waving her over.

Her phone vibrated again. She checked the text then said to them, "We need to go now."

"What happened?" Trenton asked.

"Daron texted me." Cameron kept her fake smile in place. "Jason's team is preparing to breach."

Trenton quickened his pace. She grabbed his arm, taking long strides but not wanting to appear as if she was rushing. Trenton followed suit.

"Be ready to get Eric," Cameron said to Trenton, then turned to Greg as she grabbed hold of Tia's arm. "Find Daron's guy and search for JD."

Eric sat off to the side near the back wall with his hands cuffed behind him. Some people left through the back door while others settled in for a drink. Prescott was positioned next to the hidden door leading to a tunnel to the side parking lot. He moved on the side of the table that was closer to Eric.

"Ah, you brought Daron's better half with you." Prescott stepped forward, running his hand through Tia's hair.

"What do you want?" Cameron questioned as Trenton positioned himself to her left near Eric. Greg kept walking toward the bar.

Prescott returned to his spot. He took a sip of dark liquor in a tumbler, while peering at her. "Always a straight shooter."

"Clearly, you're not." The next text coming to her cell would be her warning to move.

"You want to spare JD? Come work for me," Prescott offered.

Her phone vibrated. Jason's team was heading for the building. "Where is he?"

"He's nearby." Prescott waved the waitress over. "I'll release him once you agree. Eric here, is a sign of good faith."

"Well, Tia's mine." She released Tia who walked toward Prescott.

"Sorry, she's not a viable trade."

Tia's movement stopped and her eyes widened.

"She was good enough to be your lover and your partner in crime, but not good enough to be an offer of good faith?" Cameron frowned. After all he did to be with this woman, him not attempting to save her life wasn't a good sign.

"Oh, I love her, immensely." Prescott pulled her to him. "Which is why her betrayal cut so deep."

"Let's get back to why I'm here." Cameron realized Tia couldn't be used as a negotiating tool and she didn't have time to waste.

Prescott grabbed a knife from the table and stabbed Tia several times before Cameron could get to her. "You shouldn't have tried to convince Daron to retire and build a life with you. That wasn't a part of the plan."

Eric rose from the chair and was quickly pushed back down by the guards.

Trenton gave her a what-the-hell stare as he shifted closer to Eric.

Cameron froze as Tia's body stilled. "Is this how partnership works with you?"

If he could do this to Tia without blinking an eye, what did that mean for JD?

"Only when you're not loyal." He lowered Tia into a nearby chair as tears rolled down her face. Prescott kissed her forehead then stepped back, took a napkin, wiped the blood off the knife and laid it next to his glass. "As I was saying, I'll release JD *if* you come work for me."

Her eyes went to Tia's blood on his cuff. She hesitated slightly, pretending to consider the offer. "Okay," Cameron answered, knowing they didn't have much time.

"Minimum three years. Still okay?" Prescott smiled as the wait staff refilled his glass and placed the bottle on the table barely looking Tia's way.

She agreed, glancing at Tia's lifeless body.

He motioned for his guys to help Eric up.

A loud boom filled the room, causing the glassware on the table to shake.

People scurried for the back exit. Prescott's men clambered for the hidden door, pulling Eric along with them.

She grabbed Prescott's shoulder as he raced to follow, giving Trenton an opportunity to go after Eric.

Prescott swung his arm backward, attempting to knock her arm away.

She released her hold, then grabbed his shoulder again. His other guard came to his aid. She kicked him back, and his body crashed into the table.

Grabbing her wand off her belt, she extended it, then whacked Prescott across the back. She retracted the device then ran, jumping on the table.

As Mac raced for the exit, she leaped into his path.

Prescott pulled out a Glock and aimed it at her, but Cameron yanked Mac forward into the path of the bullet.

"Tandria, it doesn't have to be this way," Prescott said.

She shoved Mac into Prescott, grabbed the bottle off the table, and slammed it into the hand with the firearm.

Mac dropped to the floor.

Cameron grunted as Prescott hit her side and caused her to stumble over Mac's arm.

Prescott hightailed it to the passageway as the glass between the foyer and the entertainment room shattered.

Cameron was hot on his tail, knowing she had to reach him before he could hit the button to lock her out.

He turned, hand raised, but stopped short of hitting the lock mechanism at the sight of her at the threshold, then took off down the long white corridor. Cameron's palm slammed down on the lock, then she raced after him. She didn't need one of Jason's men shooting her in the back.

"Eric's safe," Trenton spoke in her ear.

Prescott ran like he'd been a sprinter in a former life. She lunged at him.

He groaned as he hit the stone floor. He rolled, flung her to the ground, slammed his elbow to her ribs, then scrambled to his feet. Cameron was glad he was in escape mode. She had put herself at a distinct disadvantage by taking him to the floor. She sprang to her feet and continued the chase.

"You're not going anywhere." Cameron, still waiting for word that Greg had found JD and he was safe, felt a knot building in her stomach at the thought that JD wasn't on the property.

Prescott pivoted and swung a fist at her face. She blocked it, punched him in the chest then followed with a fury of blows to the face. Cameron felt the sting as he managed to get a few punches in. Blocking some of her jabs, Prescott ducked underneath her punch, then lifted her off the ground, banging her body on the hood of a car parked in the back lot. She groaned as pain radiated up her back.

She fought to slide her arm between their bodies. Cameron grabbed the bead off her bracelet, stabbing him in the side. He knocked her hand away. *Dammit! He didn't get enough to put him out.*

"Prescott, we've got to go," a husky voice yelled off to the side.

He tried to stand, but Cameron locked her legs around him. Her body lifted from the hood with his. "We haven't finished our negotiations," she said.

"What are you doing?" He slammed her body down again. The hood caved around her.

"Giving you time to think," she shot back.

"Freeze," a voice ordered.

Both Prescott and Cameron looked over at the weapons drawn and aimed at them.

"Stand up slowly," the man nearest to them commanded.

She unlocked her legs, searching for her brother's face among the four agents.

He wasn't.

In the time it took to blink, bullets rained down on the damaged vehicle.

Cameron immediately ducked behind the car. Prescott took off running toward a white cargo van. She stood to go after him, but someone yanked her backwards.

Prescott collapsed as he reached the van. That was all Cameron saw before her vision was blocked by the car, as someone held her in a tight grip.

By the sound of the screeching tires, Cameron assumed his partners in crime had pulled him inside the van. Four agents zipped past her, springing toward the vehicle.

She peered over the hood to see the back of the van in the distance.

Prescott got away. She slammed her fist into the metal then turned, glaring at her brother.

"Sorry little sister you're not getting killed today." Jason gave her a stern stare. "Not on my watch."

CHAPTER 38

The beeping of machines grew distant as Eric walked into the waiting area of the emergency room. To his surprise, when he had called Daron from the nurses' station, he learned he was already at the hospital. He hesitated slightly at the sight of Lex and Daron in the waiting room chairs. He expected them to be with Pedro. Eric had fared better than Pedro. He was only a little battered and bruised, but his pride was hurt for falling for Tia's ruse.

Tia had pretended to be nauseous to get him to pull over. When she got back in the car, she asked him to wait a minute. He noticed the nose plugs seconds before she released the gas. When he woke up, both he and Pedro were in cells facing each other and hanging from the ceiling by both hands.

Eric lowered himself into the black chair across from Daron and Lex, grateful for Tandria's guy assisting in the escape. If Prescott's men had taken him back, he would have ended up in the hospital like Pedro … or worse like Tia. He tried not to think about earlier when Prescott used him as a punching bag as he ranted, showing that his hatred for Daron ran deep.

Tia was the only reason his face wasn't swollen and messed up like Pedro's. She insisted Daron wouldn't have responded well to any negotiation if there were outward signs of physical abuse.

Eric shook off the memory. Lex and Daron stared at him. Before he could acknowledge their stares, Tandria entered. The other two men rose to their feet.

"I'm okay." She waved Lex off. "I may smell like menthol for a while but I'm fine."

"I'll go get the car," Lex said before rushing out.

Daron fell in step with Tandria, who didn't bother stopping and kept moving toward the exit. "Where do you want us to take you?"

Eric walked a few steps behind. He was curious about where she was staying now that law enforcement was crawling all over the mansion. He noted the bruising on Tandria's back. Jason had forced his sister to go to the hospital with a threat to be her personal escort for the next few days, then personally drove Eric and Tandria there.

"Give me a minute." Tandria pulled out her cell, then her eyes shifted to him. "You must be feeling like crap. You haven't said a word."

"Thanks for saving my ass," Eric said. The real reason he was quiet was because he hadn't been updated on everything. He would stay in observation mode until he was looped back in by Daron or Lex.

Daron's cell vibrated. He took the call, easing down the circular sidewalk to the end of the drive.

"Seriously, how are you feeling?" she asked in a soft and caring tone he'd never heard from her.

"A little sore, but okay," Eric replied, glancing at Daron before returning his focus to Tandria. "I heard you almost got yourself killed today going after Prescott."

Tandria sneered. "You're one to talk."

"I meant it as a how are you doing, not as a dig." Eric noticed Jason come to a halt on the opposite side of the street, then changed direction moving away from them.

"I'm sorry," Tandria sighed. "I was hoping for a different ending to the day."

"Understood," Eric stated, as Daron made his way back.

Tandria's cell chimed.

"We'll—"

She held her finger up, then answered putting the call on speaker. "Hello."

"The offer is still on the table," Prescott proclaimed. "I want you on my team now more than ever."

"Text me the location. But if you don't play nice, I won't play nice." Tandria disconnected.

"Did you just hang up on him?" Daron asked, as Lex pulled up.

Eric opened her door and grinned. "That didn't sound like you were playing nice."

"Exactly. Prescott has no intention of doing so. Neither do I." She slid into the Cadillac Escalade waiting for them near the parked ambulance.

Eric got in behind her, wondering if the vehicle had been rented or Daron already had it tucked somewhere.

"I can't have him stringing me along," Tandria continued.

"What about JD?" he asked as Jason's Altima passed by the entrance while Daron settled into back seat.

Lex drove off as she continued, "Prescott isn't to be trusted. He likes what he can't have. If I give in too easily and he loses interest, JD's dead before I can get to him." Tandria's phone vibrated again.

"It's unfortunate but true," Daron agreed.

"Can you pull into the gas station ahead?" Tandria requested, frowning at the screen.

Lex maneuvered into the lane to get to the station. She released her seatbelt. "Daron, come walk with me."

Eric watched as they talked on the sidewalk. *What the hell does she have to say to him that she couldn't say in front of us?*

Daron pulled out his phone and spoke into it. He ended the call then typed something into his cell.

Lex's mobile chimed, breaking the silence inside the Escalade.

Eric glanced over at Lex as he checked the screen. Tandria and Daron were heading back. They quietly slid inside the vehicle.

No one else spoke as they drove.

What the hell was going on? Where are we going?

Twenty minutes later, Lex pulled into the cell phone waiting lot of the Miami International Airport and parked.

Steve rapped his knuckles on the window ten minutes later.

Daron lowered the glass and accepted two manila envelopes.

Glancing inside the largest one as Daron tilted its contents into his hand briefly, Eric noticed a plane ticket to Houston. He looked up in time to see a truck pull into the departure drop off.

Daron turned to him. "Are you up for handling a little business with Lex?"

"Yeah," Eric replied, though he'd preferred to rest. Daron handed him the smaller one of the two.

"We'll check in when we land," Daron said, as he and Tandria left the Escalade.

Eric slipped out the back and into the passenger seat, watching them enter through the sliding glass doors. *Why was Daron escorting Tandria to Houston?* By the expression on Lex's face, he wasn't thrilled with the new development, either.

Eric didn't like the idea of the two of them possibly taking on Prescott alone. He needed to get a message to Jason. Jason would have someone tracking him. Eric fingered the ID, cash, credit card, and a cell. He knew not to make the call on one of Daron's phones. He had to look for an opportunity to pass information along without ending up on the wrong side of the grave.

◆ ◆ ◆

Several hours later, Eric was booked into a luxury hotel, showered, changed, and prepared to meet Lex in the lobby. Eric stared at his luggage, a clear indicator that Daron knew the FBI was on to him. Now he was nervous about the business they'd be handling that evening. He departed the room, hoping to stop by the front desk or security to get a call out to Jason.

Lex stepped into Eric's line of sight as he neared the front desk.

"We're heading out that way." Lex pointed behind him to the valet parking door.

Eric moved aside to let Lex lead, since he wasn't too fond of Lex being behind him. Lex passed him, going down a flight of the stairs. As Eric hit the bottom, a thick fabric covered his head, blanketing him in darkness. His hands were pulled and locked behind his back. Eric struggled and connected with someone's face as his body was shoved into the trunk. Someone held his legs down, bound them, then closed the trunk.

The truck surged forward. Lex and Steve were talking but he couldn't make out what was being said. They had always been responsible for getting rid of Daron's problems. The thumping of his heart provided a background as he thrashed around trying to find something to use to break the restraints. The attempt to free himself had his bruised rib aching like a bitch.

He didn't know how long it was before the Escalade stopped moving. The trunk popped opened and Eric suspected he was someplace where no one could hear a sound. He resisted as they dragged him out of the trunk and carried him a few feet.

"It doesn't have to be like this," Eric said. The material over his head seemed to tighten around his face as he spoke.

His heart pounded as though it would break through his chest wall. Every scenario he ran through his head ended with him taking a bullet and seeing his ancestors a lot sooner than expected.

"Sorry Eric," Lex said, as the restraints were being cut. "You're not authorized to know where we're going."

The hood was yanked from his head. Eric stood in a room that looked similar to the security room at the mansion. The loud thumping of his heart slowed. *Authorized.* Eric knew a warning when he heard one.

"We're tracking Prescott." Steve glared at him, parted his lips to say more but someone shouted, "We've got movement."

Eric watched as Prescott and his men stormed a warehouse and gunned down several others. *This can't be good.*

The gunfire sounded like everything was happening in this very room and not something unfolding on the monitor. Eric tried to identify the industrial building. As the door of the warehouse blew open on the screen, Lex's head snapped toward Steve. The monitor had zoomed in to Prescott's face, then out to a black case in his hand.

Steve stepped away while Lex's gloved fingers flew over the keys where he stood.

Tandria needs to know. Eric pulled his cell. No service.

Lex slid Eric a flash drive then everything went black. One of them grabbed his arm to lead him back to the vehicle.

CHAPTER 39

Houston's heat slowly warmed Daron's skin as he and Tandria walked to the pickup area where his contact was waiting for him with a Tesla. The sky was so clear and blue, the prediction of rainstorms was hard to believe. Tandria's team said Prescott was in Texas, even though she was supposed to meet him in two days in Wisconsin. Daron should have sent Eric or Lex, but didn't want either one of them alone and unmonitored, for his own selfish reason.

Daron took the keys from the Latino man who then headed back to the Hummer that was parked behind the Tesla. He opened the door for Tandria, watching his contacts pull off as she settled into the passenger's seat. Daron did a quick scan on the car with his tablet before sliding behind the wheel.

"I didn't expect you to come." Tandria buckled up.

"I needed Lex to handle other things," Daron said as they got underway.

"I could've come alone."

"You have an exact location?" he asked, turning up the air as the sun beamed through the window.

Tandria checked her phone again. "Not yet."

He had his team working on tracking Prescott as well. "I rented a hotel room where we can hole up until we've got the intel."

They rode in silence down the highway. He'd glanced over occasionally at Tandria, who seemed lost in thought. She was still gorgeous, although she looked tired. He felt an intense desire to comfort her but knew nothing short of getting JD back would suffice. When they arrived at their destination, he grabbed the keys to their room.

Daron scanned the area and found a Mexican Restaurant. "Do you want to walk and get something for us to bring back and eat?"

"Sure." Tandria aimed in that direction, cutting across a near empty parking lot.

By the time Daron paid for their food and received their order, it was drizzling. They rushed across to the hotel. When the reservationist said there was only one room left but it was small, he wasn't expecting this. The furniture was high-end but the space was extremely intimate, containing one king bed, two nightstands, and a flat screen television resting on a dresser.

Daron closed and locked the door, placing his food on the dresser. He went to the bathroom and came out with a large towel. He laid it over the bed, then placed their food on top. "Tell me about yourself. Let's start with your real name." He sat with his back to the headboard.

"Cameron Stone. I graduated high school by thirteen, college by sixteen and had a Master's by nineteen ..." she paused as she claimed a spot on the other side of him, then said, "You know what? Google me."

He pulled out his cell, typed, then read the first article. "Came out of college the same year as her oldest brother, Hawk. How was it growing up with three brothers and being the baby girl?"

"Mom finally had her girl so she wanted me in dance and gymnastic class, but I wanted to do martial arts with my brothers," Tandria answered as she opened her Styrofoam container.

"Clearly, there was a compromise." Daron sat his phone down, opened his utensil package, then continued scrolling. He glanced over, taking in her cleavage in the halter top. To imagine her fighting Prescott in that sexy jumpsuit was difficult, but the image of her slowly and seductively sliding it off painted a vivid picture in his mind. He attempted to rein in his thoughts and the sensual fantasy of the images that came across as he stared at his phone. "Does anyone else in your family know about your other life, besides JD?"

"My brothers do." She shifted her rice around, almost as if to make it an even layer. "My mother doesn't."

"All your brothers are in some form of law enforcement." Daron sat his cell on the bed and started eating the enchiladas.

"Yes, following in *their* father's footsteps." Her voice was laced with disdain.

"Their father? Obviously, there's a little tension between you and your dad."

"That's an understatement." Tandria stabbed at the burrito.

Daron took a few bites before unlocking his phone. "Interesting. Let me see what happened."

"You can't google that," Tandria said, frowning. "The incident is burned in my memory, but not in public records."

"Tandria. Tandria." Daron sighed.

She chewed and focused on something other than the conversation. He touched her arm. "Cameron."

She looked down at her empty container. "Yeah."

"Is that how you became JD's protector?" Daron asked, touching her had sent a jolt of lust through every part of his body that had him almost feeling guilty.

"Yeah."

Daron picked up their empty containers off the bed and trashed them.

Still feeling the heat from their contact, he took a moment to compose himself by washing his hands before taking his place on the bed again. "I'm curious, but if you don't want to talk about it. I understand."

Tandria relayed the story of JD getting badly beaten in jail, his mother not being able to afford bail and her going to work for Bishop to get him protection. Before Daron could comment, she inquired, "What did you do to JD? He's crediting you for his change."

He stretched out, folded his hands behind his head, then focused on the ceiling momentarily before turning his gaze on her. Tandria angled her body toward him, resting on her elbow, waiting.

"I told him what my mother said to me, the only person's approval he needed was his own." Daron rolled to his side, propping himself up to match Tandria's stance. "If he kept chasing everyone else's approval, he'd fool around and lose track of his dream."

"JD has a propensity for these situations because he's trying to prove himself." Tandria's gaze lowered to the bedding's paisley print, but he didn't miss the emotions brewing in her eyes.

"It makes him susceptible. Bishop mentioned it when he told me the story of Kimura," Daron explained, wishing he had an easy fix to remedy what troubled her.

Tandria sighed. "We talked about it before but … "

"Don't blame yourself." Daron tried to keep his focus away from the sadness in her eyes. "He wouldn't have received those words from you."

Tandria inhaled and exhaled quickly. "I never considered that trying to protect him probably fed into the problem."

"He appreciates you, but he doesn't want to keep putting you in that position of making those sacrifices for him." The glimpse of her softer side caused a surge of arousal that had the physical evidence of his attraction to her at an all-time high.

Tandria went silent. Her hazel orbs locked on to his as she gave him a slight smile. Daron could have sworn he almost saw a slight impression of dimples. As Daron witnessed the vulnerability, a strong need to create a safe space for her to simply be overcame him. She told him about the night that her father failed to make her feel protected.

He listened with rapt attention, and only wished he could be as honest with her as she was being with him.

Maybe down the road he'd get the opportunity to tell her everything. For now, he felt humbled that she trusted him with her secrets.

CHAPTER 40

Cameron's mind flashed back to the day that transformed her life and her goals dramatically as she told Daron about being left in jail by her father.

"I wasn't allowed to come home after we got out." She could feel her face tighten into a scowl.

"What?" Daron's jaw dropped.

"I ended up living with JD and my aunt." She stood and went to peek out the window.

She stroked the faint scar on her stomach where she took a knife to the gut after taking on someone harassing JD. Popping her right wrist, she thought about how she sprained it tussling with one of her aunt's boyfriends who had a problem keeping his hands to himself. After that, she kept up with her martial arts and weaponry classes, because she didn't have the luxury of getting rusty. Those incidents all happened within the first week, before her mom moved in with Aunt Renee for the summer.

Cameron returned to her spot on the bed.

"How old were you?" Daron's question brought her back to the present.

"Thirteen."

Daron's head reared back toward the headboard. "Damn. I ... "

"It's taken me years to realize that I didn't have to live this life. But we talked about this before ... " Cameron's thought trailed off as Daron laid his hand over hers. A simple but comforting gesture. She hadn't even told Nathan that story. The night she planned to tell him that, among other things, she'd been shot, which was another life-altering experience.

"Now your comment at the pool makes sense," Daron said, referring to her statement about leading a reactive life instead of a proactive one. "My mama used to say knowledge doesn't become wisdom until you apply it to life."

"Your mama was wise. It's interesting how one event can change your life, shift your focus, and have you walking in darkness."

Daron took her hand in his. "I'm confident that both of us will start to make decisions to create our best lives, instead of allowing the past to dictate our paths."

A sense of comfort, peace and contentment washed over her as she glanced up at him. Her body tingled as if she'd experienced an electric shock. The urge to wrap her arms around him was so strong, surreal, and frightening. Daron reached for her, pulling her into his arms. She laid her head on his chest. She had to remind herself what had brought them there. Daron had her wanting things she'd given up a long time ago. Cameron almost fell asleep, but shook herself, hopped off the bed, then rushed to the bathroom. Closing the door, she leaned on it as her eyes burned while she tried to hold back the tears and not think of what she'd lost—her family.

"Are you okay?" Daron knocked on the door. "Tandria ... Cameron."

Cameron inhaled and exhaled several times. "Yes."

She locked the door, turned on the faucet, and cupped the cold water before throwing it on her face. She yanked a towel off the rack and patted her skin.

"Autumn?" His voice filled with uncertainty. "You need me to get something?"

Cameron opened the door just enough to see him leaning on the edge of the dresser. "How long have you known?"

"The more time I spent with you the more I suspected, but now it's confirmed." Daron stepped closer to the opening. He reached in his jacket pocket, pulled out the envelop Steve had given him, then slid a plastic baggie out and handed it to her. "I never forgot you."

Her fingers curled around the plastic as she pushed the knob until the gap in the threshold was no more. The last thing she expected him to give her was the ring she lost that night. Her mind couldn't process the reason he would still be holding on to her jewelry. Cameron berated herself; she needed to focus on rescuing JD not contemplating pipe dreams.

A phone rang and Daron answered, but his words were muffled through the wood.

Get it together. Get it together.

She slipped the ring into her pocket then took a quick glance in the mirror before exiting the bathroom. Cameron refused to look at Daron when she reentered the small space.

"You good?" Daron stepped in her path, but she maneuvered to the nightstand creating a chasm between them.

She smiled. "Yeah, I ate too fast and made myself nauseous." Her phone vibrated. "We have a location."

The pouring rain greeted them at the door as they bolted to the Tesla. She programmed the address in the GPS as they drove out of the lot. They didn't make it far before they hit a flooded road and Texas Troopers were redirecting traffic. Daron detoured to an alternate route, but that road was flooded too.

Cameron slammed her hand against the dashboard. "Damn, we'd better turn back before we get stuck."

"JD probably isn't with Prescott anyway," Daron said as if it would comfort her as he maneuvered the Tesla back to the hotel.

Cameron dialed Greg. "The rain's got us blocked in. I need you to take one of the bulletproof vehicles and two of our throwaway bikes, grab my gear, and head to Wisconsin." She paused, mapping out the rest of the plan and transport that would keep them protected. "Make sure you stay a couple of towns over from Prescott's location and get me a room too."

The rain had slacked off by the time Daron pulled back into the parking space. "We'll check the roads in a couple of hours to see if they're any better."

She hopped out. "I want to check something. I'll be back."

Daron stared after her as he entered the side hallway.

Cameron stepped through the glass door of the front offices and moved quickly across the beige tiles. She rapped on the counter. The young man with an acne-riddled face glanced up and pushed long, sandy-brown hair out of his face.

"How may I help you?" He smiled, closing a comic book.

She leaned forward, hair dripping water all over the countertop. "I need another room for the night."

"Sorry, we sold the last room a couple of hours ago." He shifted his comic book. "If you can make it up a couple of blocks—"

"Thanks."

After the moment she had with Daron earlier, she wanted to know what her options were. Now, the only choice she had was to spend a night in that small room with a man who had her wanting more than sex. She needed that connection with someone who cared and made her feel comfortable. She noticed a pantry area and snatched a box of condoms off the hook. Cameron hesitated, debating the purchase as it meant acknowledging the inevitable.

She'd be a damn fool to go in unprepared. The last thing she needed was another decision to come back and bite her in the behind.

Maybe I need this thing out of my system.

Cameron returned to the room and found Daron on the phone pacing the floor. He was wrapped in a white bath towel, holding an upsetting conversation. Her eyes slowly inched from his full lips, to the broad shoulders, to the six pack. The front of his towel shifted as she took in the sight of him.

He gave her a tight-lipped half smile. "Let me know if anything changes."

"What's going on?" She tossed her purse on the dresser, then curled her fingers around the package of condoms in her pocket.

"Pedro had a complication, but he's out of surgery and stable now." Daron tossed his phone on the bed, ran a hand over his head.

Cameron tore her eyes from his pecs, but only for a moment. "Glad to hear that."

"Keep staring at me like that and we'll have a problem," Daron warned, giving her a searing gaze of his own.

She wanted to enjoy the night. Depending on what happened in the next forty-eight hours, she might not have another opportunity. No telling what length Prescott and his crew had gone to ensure their success. Cameron unbuttoned, then unzipped her wet jumpsuit and let it drop to the carpet. "Maybe it's the kind of problem I want to handle," she said, moving forward.

Daron held her shoulders, staring into her eyes. "Is this about me or are you having a last hoorah, just in case … "

Her eyes lowered to the colorful patterns on the carpet. Guilty as charged.

"Prescott won't be the one who kills Kimura." He kissed her on the forehead then picked up the soggy garment and placed it in her hand. "There's a large towel left in the bathroom."

Cameron smiled, more determined to have him. She tossed the condoms on the bed before she entered the bathroom and wrapped herself in a towel.

"Are you officially divorced?" she asked, remembering Red had mentioned he'd been married. She wasn't sure if it was Tia or Maureen that had been married to Daron.

"Yes." Daron averted his gaze and palmed a black device before moving out of her line of sight.

When she stepped out again, he was placing the square device on the back of the door. Cameron heard about Daron's security toys and had it been another time she would indulge her curiosity. Tonight, she was more interested in the man than his devices.

"I'm glad you're officially divorced." Cameron noted the hint of sadness in his eyes leading her to believe that Tia was indeed his ex-wife. She felt a tinge of guilt for hoping he didn't kill the mood by verbally bringing up her death.

"Didn't realize that would factor into this." He smirked as he turned to face her, folding his arms across his chest.

"I have my own personal rules that I don't break." She confessed, pressing her hands against his chest. "Being with a married man is one of them." She had to resist the urge to push him against the door and kiss him.

He made an attempt to move around her, but she blocked his path, placing her hands against his abs then stepping in front of him. "Let this be about us."

Sliding her hand behind the nape of his neck, she pulled him into a kiss.

He devoured her mouth like it was a delicious morsel of chocolate as her other hand traced the muscles in his back.

"I've been wanting to do that since forever." Daron lowered his lips again, deepening the kiss, demanding a response as passionate as his. Just as Cameron's knees caved, he scooped her up.

She wrapped her legs around his waist.

Someone tried the door handle and a series of beeps caused their heads to snap in its direction.

Cameron's legs dropped to the floor. As she went for a weapon in her purse, Daron held up one finger.

She froze midway to the dresser.

The device's screen lit up and the image appeared of the couple standing outside of the door.

"You're sure this is our room?" They looked down at the key packet before a red-headed woman popped the bald, burly man upside the head.

They moved away from the door and the screen went black.

Daron and Cameron exhaled.

"Where were we?" Daron inched closer to Cameron, then lifted her into his arms again and carried her to the bed. "Right about here."

"Mmm hmm," she managed to get out as he kissed her, then laid her on the mattress.

His lips traced the curve of her neck, inching toward her cleavage. His hand explored her body as his mouth gave attention to her breast. A breathy moan escaped her quivering lips—ones that longed to taste him as well.

Pushing him on his back, she kissed him, then slowly worked her way down his torso. She paused, feeling a sudden surge of emotion and a burning need.

"Having second thoughts?" Daron asked, lifting her chin up with an index finger so their gazes were locked.

"Not at all." She smiled seductively as she pulled his towel away from his waist. "It's yours for the taking."

Daron rolled her onto her back, nibbling her neck while lovingly caressing her breasts then tenderly stroking her abdomen, thighs, buttocks all the way to the soles of her feet. He gazed into her eyes then whispered, "I want to savor this."

He intensified the kiss as his fingers teased the delicate skin between her thighs.

"Yes," Cameron groaned as his lips worked their way to her breast and his tongue flicked over her taut nipples.

His warm mouth slowly worked down her torso, obliterating her senses. In one masterful move, he slid her legs over his shoulder replacing his fingers with his expert tongue. First he teased, tasted, then he ravished her as if he'd been in a desert for days and she was the only source of water.

She moaned as her body quivered and her head thrashed from side to side. She fought the urge to squeeze her thighs together, holding him prisoner as overwhelming sensations washed over her body.

Daron reached for the condoms and within moments prepared himself to enter her. She drew a sharp breath as he eased into her painstakingly slow, pausing and allowing her to adjust to his size. Soon each thrust intensified as she lifted hungrily, meeting each stroke. Sweet sensual torture flooded her body as he pushed her to the edge then slowed the pace and pulled her back. Cameron wasn't prepared for his passionate, yet tender, savoring of her body. The way Daron kissed, touched, and held her gave her a sense of belonging she'd craved for far too long.

The change in his breathing heightened her senses as he continued to rhythmically drive and retreat into her moist core. The sensations coursing through her body threatened to shatter her into a thousand pieces. Her moans mixed with his as she gripped the sheets, but he pulled her close as though not wanting them to be apart; even an inch was too much. Her body trembled as they both careened over the edge and straight into the abyss of ecstasy.

Daron collapsed, rolling to her side and reaching for her. They both lay quiet for a moment, waiting for their breathing to return to normal.

She smiled and curled into him.

Daron kissed her forehead, and she closed her eyes. She wished she could keep their connection about the physical act, as she had with some of her previous lovers. She hadn't dared to think she could have a normal life. A family. Him. The same man who saw the woman behind the aliases.

"You all right?" Daron swept a loose strand of hair from her forehead.

She opened her eyes and caught him studying her face. She didn't want to give the real answer to that question. "The day is just catching up with me," she replied, kissing his pecs as her hand slowly made its way from his chest to his abs. "But I'm ready for a no-holds-barred round two."

"I like the sound of that," Daron growled in a low, sexy tone that made her throb with desire.

The shrill ring of his cell grabbed their attention. He reached for the nightstand as her phone pinged in the distance.

Their moments of indulgence had ended.

He kissed her one more time, deeply. Disappointment flashed in his eyes.

She slid out of the bed and checked her messages. Cameron didn't miss that Daron asked if Eric's people were notified. Daron obviously knew Eric was FBI.

"Prescott was in Houston to steal four devices that can track radio communication up to 5300 feet each," Daron said, looking at her as her phone pinged again. "Prescott's already heading out of the city."

She glanced up at him. A dull ache in her back reminded her of the previous encounter with Prescott. "He moved the meeting up by a day."

Daron met her in the middle of the room, pulled her close, and kissed her passionately. "I'll arrange a private flight back to Chicago."

Cameron stepped from his hold and peered through a small opening of the curtain as he made the call. The rain had stopped and she hadn't even noticed. She stared at Daron's well-rounded behind and had to admit she was more distracted than she needed to be for the challenge ahead of them. She wasn't ready for the night to end or to go into battle with Prescott.

CHAPTER 41

The pressure of saving JD weighed her down like a concrete block tied to her ankle. She hadn't expected Daron to come with her after they landed in Chicago. He made a stop in Gurnee and picked up a suitcase before arriving at the hotel where her team had set up shop. Daron went into the mirrored closet to get the stand for the suitcase. She grabbed her duffle bag from the couch, opened it, and placed her weapons on the coffee table, checking them one by one.

"Bishop had me make those … for you?"

Cameron turned at the note of surprise in Daron's voice. He gestured to the gold wand in her hand and met her gaze head on.

She pushed the button to extend it, then twirled it in her hand, pressing another button to make the blades pop out. "I appreciate the genius who made it," she said with a slight smile. "It took me a while to master it, but once I did … "

"I told Bishop it would be difficult to use if you hit the buttons and your hand's in the wrong place." Daron stepped back.

"My biggest problem was taking it out of the training room and using it in the streets. I was used to the wand but triggering the blades wasn't natural." Cameron retracted the weapon and laid it on the table. She loved Bishop but hated the things he had to do in order to stay in power—like exploiting people's weakness and creating unusual weapons to torture the competition. If she hadn't, JD would've been prosecuted for a murder he didn't commit and his short period in jail would have become a full-fledged prison sentence.

"Here's some new toys to check out." Daron nodded toward the open suitcase on the stand.

She peered inside, then stared at him for a moment.

His only response was a wide smile.

She searched through, selecting items to add to her arsenal. Cameron picked up a weapon that looked similar to a gun.

"That's for shooting your bracelet's oblong bead," Daron explained, giving her a quick tutorial. "Warning. It's a prototype that hasn't been tested in the field."

Cameron placed the device with her other tools.

Prescott's plan probably involved taking her out so he could kill JD without worrying about her coming after him.

She grabbed her clothes and headed for the bathroom. By the time she changed and came back into the room, Daron was on the phone. She gave him a brief smile as she neared the desk, securing the weapons to her body.

"Are they all going to fit?" he asked.

She glanced back, gave him a suggestive smile and lowered her gaze to his groin. "Everything has a place."

Daron's low throaty chuckle echoed.

Her phone rang. She glanced at the screen, then answered Greg. "You're there?"

"We're here," Greg confirmed.

She snapped her fingers to pull Daron's attention away from his cell. "Are Lex and Eric in position?"

"They are," Daron answered.

"You meet them. I'll text the location," Cameron instructed Greg.

"I'll meet Trenton and Rob in the lobby." She disconnected, then texted over the information.

Daron disappeared into the bathroom as she grabbed the miscellaneous weapons. She slid the gold wand in a slot on the back of her shoulder and stored the black wand on the opposite shoulder. Cameron slipped the oblong bead bracelets on both wrists. Lifting a pant leg, she attached a holster with a knife to her ankle. Slipping into a pair of leather gloves, she put the cards into her pants pocket then zipped it. She holstered Daron's prototype weapon into the pocket where she normally carried her real gun.

Cameron kept her mind on the task at hand and not the plethora of emotions brought on by Daron.

The designer charcoal suit with black collarless dress shirt Daron wore, accentuated his great physique. The man was sexy.

She tore her eyes away from him. If she survived this, she'd have to deal with the issue she created in Houston. Cameron should have kept things in neutral territory until she addressed the file Bishop had given Daron, especially since he admitted he was well aware of her alter-identities.

"Change of plans. Did Steve come?" She scanned the area to make sure she hadn't missed anything.

Daron frowned. "Yes."

"You shouldn't come," she declared, coiling her plait and pinning it to her head. "I can't protect you and go after JD too."

"I don't need ... " Daron clamped down the rest of his statement and pulled out his phone.

She definitely didn't want to have to choose between saving his life or JD's.

Daron reached into the front pocket of the suitcase, then placed three ear plugs in the palm of her hand. "Press twice to activate them if you need to communicate with your team."

She closed her hand around them and nodded. "Thank you." With Prescott having a device that would intercept their transmissions, they couldn't risk giving him advance notice of their moves. This gift might help them all to get out alive. Daron was more than brilliant.

◆ ◆ ◆

The scent of grilled burgers and onions wafted in the air as Daron stared out the window watching the vehicles passing on the road. The restaurant buzzed with people talking, waitresses yelling orders to the cooks and silverware clinking against plates.

They were less than ten minutes from the cabin where Prescott and Tandria were meeting. Steve sat across from Daron, devouring his burger. Twiddling his thumbs while she took on Prescott felt wrong. He was tempted to use his drone to stay up to date on the situation, but didn't want the machine to be a distraction. Lex and Eric were a couple of miles away, surveilling incoming traffic and searching the data, looking for any suspicious arrivals. Daron decided he and Steve would be on the opposite end of the road than where Greg had setup shop to be nearby as back up.

Tandria's comment about making conscious life decisions instead of making reactive ones flashed in Daron's mind.

Steve lightly knocked on the table. "Is there anything on your mind besides the obvious?"

"A comment Tandria made has me thinking about my mother. She warned me life would tarnish my gift in unexpected ways and returning its shine wouldn't be easy." Daron shifted his plate of an uneaten steak sandwich and waffle fries to the side.

Steve took a sip of Coke, then asked, "Was this after your father's death?

"Yeah. At the time I assumed she meant to keep moving forward and put some effort into the scholarship project." Daron paused, looking out the window for a moment. "Now I understand that she was talking about the future as well."

He reflected on everything that happened after his ex-wife's and former business associate's betrayal. His methods were unconventional but he hoped, in some small way, he'd made his mother proud. Despite what the world thought, he knew the truth about who he was.

"Bishop utilized Tandria's gift in the wrong way." Steve picked up his phone, frowned at the screen, then returned to eating.

"Some people's paths to their purpose are unconventional," Daron paused as he remembered her lying on his chest, "what she does with her future will speak her truth."

Daron focused on the passing traffic.

It probably wasn't the best idea to discuss her family history and become intimate before she prepared to do battle with Prescott. The way he connected with Tandria in Houston had him hopeful that maybe they could make a positive impact on people's lives … together.

Daron needed to refocus on creating something to interfere with Prescott's device.

"You're quiet again," Steve said, sticking some fries into his wide mouth.

Daron shifted his focus from the window to Steve. "Trying to figure out the best way to help Tandria out and not—"

"This is as close as we can get." Steve raised an eyebrow as he finished the fries on his plate. "Will she kill him?"

"Based on the weapons Tandria took with her, she isn't trying to kill Prescott unless it's necessary." Daron sipped his coffee as his cellphone rang.

"How far are you from Tandria?" Lex asked as soon as Daron answered, then informed him that Tandria was in trouble.

"Shit! We need to go." Daron was out of the booth in a flash.

Steve followed suit. "What happened?"

Daron dropped money on the table. "Prescott hired a sniper."

Steve popped the trunk on their vehicle to give Daron access.

He opened the suitcase inside, grabbed several items and slammed the trunk shut. The moment Daron's door closed, Steve peeled the Lexus out of the lot onto the road.

"What's the plan?" Steve asked.

Daron situated the prototype weapon for Tandria's oblongs beads, along with the case holding the beads, on the floor. He placed the tablet on his lap. "Let me get our eyes in the air first."

He programmed the drone to Tandria's location then lowered the window as the Lexus slowed. The drone rested in the palm of his hand. After touching the tablet to set the drone on its course, it slowly lifted from his hand and into the sky. Steve picked up speed again as Daron raised the window.

The drone was set on autopilot until it reached its destination, then Daron would manually take control. The next task was to figure out which earpiece she was wearing so he could get a message to her. He might have to activate them all, but his warning could get lost in the noise coming from the other two units.

"Once the drone locates the sniper's position, you'll have to take him out." Daron grabbed the case with the beads off the floor.

Steve nodded.

Daron was asking him to take a huge risk, considering law enforcement was heading their way. *Hopefully the prototype works, and Steve won't have to use lethal force.*

His tablet beeped, alerting him that the drone had reached the area. Daron switched the screen to be able to view the area. No activity at the cabin. He inhaled sharply.

Are we too late?

"What's wrong?" Steve asked, glancing at him.

Shifting the drone's position, Daron exhaled loudly. He watched on the screen as the Chevy Cruze turned onto the road. "It's not what I thought. She's navigating through the trees. Finding the sniper will be a challenge."

How far are we away? He pulled out his phone to check the time Lex had called.

"Find Tandria and tag her on the screen first," Steve explained, as he switched lanes to move around a slow car. "Then go above the trees and switch to heat signature mode. Once you do, you can go back to search for the sniper."

He was grateful for Steve's knowledge. Daron may have created some of the programming and modified the design, but he rarely used it. The way Tandria was cutting down Prescott's men on the live stream, they wouldn't make it in time.

After tagging Tandria, Daron found the shooter but he hadn't heard the alert to let him know they were within range to communicate via the earpieces. The thought of them not making it in time had a vise grip on his heart.

"We'll make it in time," Steve assured him.

From his lips to God's ear.

CHAPTER 42

This place had the same eerie feeling as the time Cameron was on assignment to extricate the son of one of Bishop's friends. Bird chirping blended with the distant background noise of cars passing on the road near the cabin. She rode the motorcycle slowly through the trees that weren't clustered together. From the other side of the property, Trenton approached the log cabin on the other motorcycle. She stopped as Rob inched the Cruze close to the front porch. The red door opened. Prescott stood at the edge of the top of the stone staircase.

Five men were posted to one side of the cabin and probably another five were hidden on the other side.

Cameron pulled out one of Daron's weapon, wishing she had a real gun. The fact that she couldn't kill anyone made this a difficult situation and increased her chances of ending up dead. Prescott descended the first few stairs with his shoulders pulled back and wearing a smug expression. As he did, the men on both sides of the cabin moved. Rob backed out of the driveway. The men advanced with guns pointed at the vehicle. The bullets hit the Chevy in a flurry. The air seeped out of the tires.

Cameron fired the protype at the men as she emerged from the trees. The first man glanced down at his chest, pulled out the bead, and stared at the needle. His body swayed, then hit the ground. Four more bodies dropped right after him. Weapons spun in her direction.

She gunned it then hopped off the motorcycle, sending it barreling toward Prescott's men. They looked like bowling pins falling as they jumped out of the way. The bike crashed into a tree and fell to the ground.

Cameron pulled out the cards and flung them at the closest man as a couple sprinted toward Rob. She grabbed her wand, extending it and knocked the gun out of the nearest guy's hand. Next, she swung the black pole at his head, causing him to duck. She rolled over the man's back, twirled the wand, and knocked the second attacker's weapon away. The first one stood straight as she kicked him hard in the torso, sending him sailing back toward the grass.

Her back was to the corner of the house, which kept Prescott and the trees in her line of sight as she swung the pole, forcing her attacker where she wanted him. The second man grabbed the gun, rising to his feet as the first attacker dodged another blow from the wand, which grazed his chin. He yelped in pain as he yanked the pole and she quickly retracted it, then threw several jab and upper cut combinations to his face and torso. Her move forced him to be on the defensive. She positioned her body in front of him so his partner couldn't get a shot.

Prescott's confidence would be his downfall. He was so sure his team would take her down that he hadn't bothered to leave. She threw him a glance as she dodged yet another jab.

Prescott was scanning the trees.

Something's off.

"Tandria, get down now," Daron yelled.

She dropped to the ground.

A bullet meant for her ripped into her opponent's chest. He gasped as he fell back.

His partner scrambled to the trees.

She wouldn't make it to cover. She grabbed the guy stretched out on the ground and rolled him to his side using him as cover.

Rob took off in the direction of the gunfire.

Multiple bullets hit the ground and the body. As soon as they halted, she'd have to run. The sniper would be repositioning to get a better shot. She could only hope Rob would be able to find the gunman before he took the kill shot.

Prescott had moved back inside the cabin. If he had a gun, she'd already be dead.

"Sniper has been neutralized," Daron relayed.

She rushed to her feet. Four more men passed Prescott on the porch as she sprinted for the trees.

The fallen branches crunched under the men's weight as they approached. Crouching low, she waited while loading the last of her beads into the gun. She stayed still as footsteps came closer. Cameron aimed high as the first man stepped into view. She made a run for the next tree in the direction of the cabin. Sounds from the destruction of dry foliage and branches under running feet caught her attention. She pulled a card out and flung it at the man coming from the left. Seconds later, her body was slammed into the rough bark of a tree.

"It's so sad that we won't be working together." Prescott gloated as he smashed his fist into her jaw.

She absorbed the blow, planted her knee in his chest, and pushed. He stumbled back, and she landed a kick on the side of his head.

Prescott came back with a hook that barely missed the tree as she ducked under it. He kneed her in the torso.

Fighting him brought back every ounce of training with her dad. Jake always said he'd never hold back because she was a girl.

She didn't miss the fact that Prescott's counter moves kept her in a tight space between him and the tree, making it more difficult for her to kick him again. She quickly maneuvered into a clearing. Prescott stumbled, giving Cameron an opportunity to put some distance between them. Only to find two of Prescott's men racing toward her.

Cameron reached in a pocket for cards but it was empty. *Shit.* Quinn and Hawk emerged from the tree line, moments before the men reached her, and tackled them. She was shocked to see her brothers. That distraction cost her as she turned back to face Prescott. He kicked her in the stomach, which sent her flying. She tripped on a branch, landing hard on her behind.

Prescott scrambled for a Glock laying in the grass. He pulled the trigger as she stood. Cameron went sailing a few feet from him as the bullet hit her stomach. She could hear her brothers yell 'No' as her body slammed against the ground.

"Times up," Prescott growled, not paying attention to her brothers who were reaching for their weapons. "You should've just accepted the offer."

At the sound of a click signaling he was out of ammo, Cameron jammed her foot in his stomach and got to her feet. She grabbed the gold wand, extended it to its full length and smashed it into his midsection. She slammed the wand into him at every angle, making sure to whack his legs especially hard. She couldn't take any more kicks to the torso.

Prescott couldn't get close enough to land any punches either. When he reached in with two hands, trying to take the wand, Cameron forced him back. She released the blades and he gasped as his bloody hands dropped from the wand.

She twirled it and sliced him across the chest several times before he stumbled out of her reach. She retracted the blades as the wand landed on his jaw. He came back with a left hook. Cameron ducked.

Grabbing the wand from the other side, she swung it like a bat, pummeling his shoulder as Prescott launched himself at her. The force sent him flying to the ground. She pushed the button to release the blade, stabbing him in the shoulder. Cameron dropped to his chest with her leg across his thigh.

"You should've released JD and went your merry little way," she growled, twisting the blade in his shoulder. Prescott screamed, struggling to pull the blade out.

Cameron yanked it out, then struck the ground within inches of each side of his neck repeatedly, daring him to move. Prescott's eyes widened, but he remained frozen in place. She lifted the wand, sending the blade flying toward the middle of his Adam's apple.

"No," Prescott yelled as his hand went up, grabbing the pole to stop its progress.

"Stop," Jason shouted. "We need him alive."

The tip of the blade was pressed firmly into Prescott's neck. Both of his bloody hands were now wrapped around the wand.

"Lift the blade now," Jason demanded as Quinn and Hawk handed off Prescott's men to the FBI agents.

She hesitated, but pressed the button to comply.

Jason rushed to Cameron and confined her hands behind her as two men lifted Prescott off the ground. Quinn and Hawk silently trailed them. She was perp-walked to a Suburban, placed in the backseat, and the doors locked.

Two large men ushered Prescott to an ambulance.

"What? Were you two just going to stand there and let her kill him." Jason fumed, scanning the area.

"He shot her." Quinn glared at Jason as if he'd lost his mind.

"Hell. He'd have been dead," Hawk's eyes narrowed, as he slid his thumbs under the straps of the bulletproof vest he wore, "and not had the chance to pull the trigger the second time if I hadn't shifted to get Quinn out the line of fire."

"What the hell are you two doing here anyway?" Jason gave the two brothers an intense stare down. "I had this handled."

"Did you?" Quinn turned his lip up and cut his eye over at Hawk before returning his gaze to Jason.

Hawk frowned. "You should've told us you needed help."

"Are you trying to get Cam killed?" Jason scanned the area. "It's one thing for one of the agents to look like the woman in question with connection to The Warden. But three?"

"Mom frightens us more than any criminal or higher up." Quinn stepped closer.

"She couldn't shake the feeling that something was wrong with Cam," Hawk added.

Quinn pulled out his phone swiping then typing. "We caught wind of this and came."

"Well, I'm going to need you to go because we don't want any problems." Jason opened the door to the back seat of the truck.

Cameron crept out to stand next to him. "Thanks guys."

Hawk gave her a hug. "Can we arrange to see you when you're not in a crisis?"

"We may be able to make that happen," Cameron said, wincing when she tried to smile.

Quinn's eyes widened, then he glanced up at the clouds.

"What?" Cameron looked up.

"I heard the words 'may be' and I thought the sky would collapse on itself." Quinn laughed.

"Funny." She pulled him in, wrapping her arms around him and giving a tight squeeze even though it hurt like hell.

"All right, we out." Hawk said, walking away.

Quinn gave a two-finger salute and fell in step with Hawk.

Jason leaned on the truck, tapping on one of her wands. "You managed to save JD's ass."

She was glad to hear it. Her team hadn't given her confirmation. "I can get out of your way now."

"Let me get someone to check you out." Jason touched her bruised jaw with his free hand.

She winced before knocking his hand away. "I'm good."

"Your friend Daron wasn't here when we arrived. Now everyone's calling Prescott The Warden." Jason peered into her eyes as if he was accusing her of knowing something. "Interesting."

"Shouldn't your boy, Eric, have the answers for you?" She snatched her wand from him and tucked it back into the pouch on her back.

"Whatever." Jason gritted his teeth. He pinched the top of his nose. "Don't stay too long." He stared at her for a few seconds before walking in the direction of a swarm of agents.

She caught Eric approaching in her peripheral, seconds before he fell in step with her.

"I know never to make you mad." His gaze roamed her injuries. "Seriously, how are you feeling?"

"I'm fine," she lied. Every muscle in her body was screaming at her.

"Maybe we could go out to dinner when things settle down."

Cameron gave him the side eye. She pulled off the bloody gloves, stuffed them in her pocket, and snapped it closed. "Working with my brother is a deal breaker."

 He stopped, grabbed her wrist, and pivoted to face her. "I hear you're going legit."

She glanced to Trenton, Rob, and JD who walked toward Greg and Lex. "I don't plan to cut ties with the people I've called friends for years."

Cameron studied his face for a reaction. He gave her his best poker face, but his eyes shifted away from her briefly. While she and Eric had chemistry, she felt more of a connection to Daron—one that she didn't fully comprehend.

"I understand." He moved closer to her. "It won't be an issue."

"You're addicted to this double life you're living. You want a woman who can handle it." Cameron understood from these couple of months of not being able to actively live her normal life, that the transition would be hard for her. "I'm not that woman."

"That's not true." Eric said, continuing at her side when she resumed walking. "At least not the way you're trying to make it sound."

She remembered how her mom was upset when Jason landed himself in the hospital after getting shot while under cover. She stepped back. "You live a dangerous life. I don't want my brother visiting to tell me you didn't make it or that you're missing."

Cameron took long strides toward the vehicle, while Eric trotted at her side. "Your mind is made up, but this is the first time I almost didn't make it out. It was an eye opener."

"There's a difference between an eye-opener and a game-changer. When I ended up in the hospital fighting for my life, I still stayed in." She stopped moving. Eric stepped in front of her as she emphasized, "Playing this role to try to save JD made me more committed to make the changes necessary to live a different life."

Eric grabbed her around the waist, lowering his mouth toward hers and kissing her lips.

She immediately pushed him back, ending the kiss.

"You're sure we can't make a go of this?" He gazed into her eyes as if he was searching for the answer.

"If you keep going on like this, one day, you'll find yourself in a similar scenario and your team won't know you're in trouble." She didn't want to think about what would have happened if Daron hadn't warned her earlier.

"If it occurs, I'll send you a S.O.S so you can come save me again," he teased as his hands dropped to his sides.

"Not funny. Stay safe." She looked past Eric to see Daron leaning on the Lexus beyond the taped-off area. His frown wasn't hard to miss.

"Is my job the real issue?" Eric's gaze flickered between Cameron and Daron, giving her an accusatory stare down.

She grabbed him by the arm, ignoring the pain shooting through her body. "We are a conflict of interest."

Besides, it wasn't the best idea dating law enforcement until that missing file was in hand and incinerated. When she glanced back to where Daron was, she was surprised that he'd disappeared. She was curious how Daron pegged Eric as law enforcement. His cover had been pretty solid.

Trenton nodded in the direction of the road. She slid into the passenger seat of a van disguised to look like the other news vehicles rolling in.

On the ride back to the hotel, Cameron listened to Trenton telling Greg how he rescued JD. She figured that seventy percent of the story was true since he was known for embellishing details.

This part of the ordeal was over, but until Cameron had the file in her hand, she couldn't truly be free.

CHAPTER 43

Watching Eric kissing Tandria killed what little high Daron experienced for managing to come out on top. He was confident that Houston had put them in a good place. Unfortunately, he couldn't wait to find out if she'd had a change of heart.

"You can't miss this meeting," Steve reminded, as Lex tossed over a set of keys.

"I know." Daron slipped into the backseat of a Mercedes Benz S 560 as Lex drove off in the other vehicle.

He had to stay diligent to his plan to ensure everything was in place so he'd stay out of prison and keep Prescott in and powerless. He also needed to make sure those he loved remained safe. That included …. Cameron.

Steve glanced back at him. Daron tilted his head forward, letting him know it was okay to head out. He took one last look at Tandria before settling in for the ride. He scrolled through his email. Nothing had changed.

"At least the Feds only seized the Florida property," Steve said, adjusting the camera on the dashboard.

"Not a bad deal since we expected to lose two out of the ten they were aware of."

Small sacrifices to have Prescott sitting in jail, awaiting trial for all the crimes he'd committed. Eric had built a good case.

"Eric didn't expect Prescott to become the face of the organization," Steve said as he turned into their meeting location.

Daron chuckled. "Probably not."

The parking lot was empty with dim lighting. Benches and picnic tables beyond a cluster of trees in a grass clearing were cloaked in darkness.

"I thought Eric might have gotten suspicions when we had him do that package hand off with Prescott." Another undercover agent participated in the illegal exchange, adding to the growing evidence needed to prosecute The Warden.

The name Warden would forever be associated with Prescott.

He wanted my life, he's got it. He'll wish he'd resisted the urge to take over.

Daron leaned back on the seat and waited for his guest to arrive. He was grateful his legal investments had now grown enough to maintain his lifestyle without extreme scrutiny. The rest of his money was spread out in several accounts overseas as a precaution.

The door opened and an older white man slid in next to him. "Warden."

Daron smirked, tapping on his phone to start recording. "Mr. Knight, didn't you hear The Warden has been captured?"

"Mmm hmm." He laughed. "You sure you don't want to enter witness protection?"

"Won't need it. The agreement was I take my brother's place in the business to lure Prescott back to the organization so that you could take him down. My brother has immunity. He and his family will be in witness protection."

Mr. Knight twisted the envelope in his hand. "If people find out you were working with the FBI ... "

"Who's going to tell them?" Daron asked. "The only people who knew were Steve, Lex, Maureen, you and two other higher ups."

Maureen was also an agent. Desiree's death led him to the real reason behind the agreement. Desiree wasn't trying to prosecute Prescott, she was trying to kill him. Daron had no idea Desiree was half-sister to Knight's daughter until after her death.

"When everyone uproots from that town, it'll look suspicious." He gave Daron a stern glare. "Especially when the organization stops running and the compound stop hosting events."

"Lex and Steve are staying and working the legal business I've established." Taking down Prescott hadn't done a thing to dismantle the organization, even though the Feds had enough information to do just that. The case was to trap Prescott. In the process, the pieces of the business already had rising stars trying to take over.

Knight glanced at Steve then back to Daron. "Can we take a walk?"

"Sure," Daron said.

Knight and Daron stepped out, converging at the front of the Benz. Mr. Knight moved further away from the vehicle. "You should reconsider being in the program."

"After seeing all the incompetent agents you sent my way *and* I know where my brother is relocated," Daron frowned, gripping his phone tightly, "I'd rather take my chances protecting myself."

"It's scary how good of a criminal you became, and bravo for taking out your ex-wife while bringing down her lover," he sneered as if he hadn't come to Daron after they had their faces altered. Knight halted a few feet from the bumper. He raised his eyebrow, giving Daron a once-over. "Your godfather, Bishop, would be proud of you."

"He'd have nothing to be proud of if you hadn't needed to use my connections on both sides of the fence to bring Prescott down," Daron growled. It was never his intention for Tia to die. Serve a prison term for her crimes, yes. Get stabbed to death by a man who claimed to love her. No. "You could've had my brother do this."

"Not without having a large body count." Knight pressed his lips together. "Plus, you've taken down more than just Prescott."

"We would've been done years ago if you had sent me more capable people." Daron clenched his jaw as he willed himself to calm down. After Eric proved himself to be capable, Daron gave him access to the organization and quickly promoted him up the ranks.

"You could've taken Thad, among others. I bet they're appreciative of the save." He handed Daron an envelope.

Daron looked inside it as they resumed walking. "You're one to talk. Risking my life and using your position to settle a personal vendetta."

Knight's skin went ghostly white as his head snapped toward Daron. "What are you talking about?"

"I don't get to return to my legal business as if nothing ever happened. I'm not going to be held in high esteem or be able to hide behind a badge for the dirt I did to catch a criminal, not like your undercover agents." Daron ceased walking, staying in the camera's range. "I'll be forever looking over my shoulder because you wanted Prescott punished for trafficking your daughter, getting her hooked on drugs, then killing her."

"I ... I ... " Knight stammered

"You thought I wouldn't find out." Daron glared at him, then tapped his shoulder with the envelope. "All I know is that this secret deal you made with me better not go the way of the wind now that you have him."

Knight fidgeted with his wedding ring. "It won't."

"If I find the Feds knocking at my door, know you'll go down before I will," Daron said in a low, intense tone.

"You've nothing to worry about," Knight reassured, but his eyes held a bit of trepidation.

Daron had a lot to worry about. To the few that knew him as The Warden, he was a criminal. Some hard-core, no-frills type of men would be made extremely nervous by all of the information he'd accumulated and the places he'd been in effort to bring Prescott to justice.

"Goodnight." Knight walked quickly to his vehicle.

Daron watched as the rear lights of his Infiniti faded into darkness.

Steve lowered the window as Daron got into the Benz. Minutes later, the drone hovered by Steve's window. He brought it in and handed it to Daron. "Where to next? Celebrating with the guys or driving to Tandria?"

"The guys." Daron glanced at his phone. "It'll be the last time we're all together for a while."

"You're sure?" Steve's gaze flicked to him before he drove off.

Daron nodded. "You left the package for her?"

"Yeah," Steve replied.

"If she wants to see me, then she'll reach out." Daron sighed, because he wasn't certain she would. Seems like Eric was trying to stake his claim. Would she be more attracted to a man in law enforcement or one she thought of as a criminal?

He had to put safeguards in place to protect all the parties involved while they made the transition. Lawyers were on standby. Eric's people would come their way eventually. Maureen was safely back home and moving on to the next job the FBI had for her.

◆ ◆ ◆

They entered a luxurious penthouse suite around ten that night where a trusted group of men were congregated. Some milled at a billiards table, others gathered in the seating area and a few hung around the bar.

Lex handed Daron and Steve a beer. "Everything's good?"

"Yeah," Steve replied.

"For now," Daron added as his phone chimed. He left the men in the penthouse, stepping into the carpeted hallway. Red approached him, holding out a manila folder and a thick white envelope.

"You know you didn't have to personally drop this off." Daron accepted the file from Red.

"Bishop insisted that it be done this way." Red clasped his hands in front of him.

Daron stared at the sealed manila file and envelope. "Why didn't you hand this over earlier?"

"Kimura had a special place in Bishop's heart." Red moved away to a spot close to a door marked 'staff'. "He trusted you to watch over her for him. But he didn't think you were ready yet."

Daron frowned. "I've been searching for her for years."

"He knew something more was going on with your search for Prescott and didn't want to confuse your priorities."   Red walked toward the elevator. "The contents might surprise you and the letter will shine a light on Bishop's motives."

Daron lifted the items. "Thanks."

"I should be thanking you." Red pressed the button, turning to face Daron. "My sister would've been doing time right along with your brother."

The elevator doors opened, and Red stepped inside.

Daron slipped into the penthouse, went up to his master suite, and locked the documents in the safe. He returned to the living room, where he and the men who went beyond the call of duty of friends, laughed and talked until two o'clock in the morning. Lex was the last to leave.

"Steve slipped out before I had a chance to say I really appreciate the sacrifices the two of you made." Daron moved to the bar and poured himself two fingers of The Glenlivet.

Lex smiled. "Man, if I hadn't said yes, I wouldn't be part owner of a restaurant and Boomerangs."

"That wasn't your retirement plan." Daron sipped smooth scotch.

"Retirement came early and I'm not mad about it." Lex pulled the cell from his pocket, checking it. "I'll let the chef do his thing at the Italian restaurant and I'll get to be creative with the bar food. It's perfect."

Daron sank into a tan leather chair. "But you'll always need security as long as you stay."

"And you hired the best," he countered. "If Steve can't keep these last few years from coming back and taking me out, then no one will. You're the one who's refusing protection." Lex frowned as he walked to the door.

"I'm also not staying, either," Daron said, knowing they felt it didn't matter where he moved; someone would manage to associate him with the organization.

His life. His risk to take.

"Daron." He paused at the door. "Is there something else going on?"

"Nope. Once we confirm we don't have any issue with fight night

that would have us sitting beside Prescott, we'll be in excellent shape."
Daron stood and lowered the scotch to a coaster on the walnut table.
While Knight had agreed to the fights as part of the strategy, Daron was
prepared for him if he tried to do something underhanded.

"Your expression doesn't reflect a man who managed to get the best
of the man who ruined his life, while keeping his brother out of prison."
Lex crossed his arms, resting a shoulder on the nearby wall.

Daron chuckled as he leaned back in the chair. "That's 'my ego being
slammed to the concrete' expression."

"Tandria?"

"Yes, indeed." Daron lifted the scotch to his lips and took a sip.
"Thought we had a moment. Clearly we didn't."

"Understood." Lex smiled, then paused at the door. "The one thing
we know about Tandria is, she doesn't operate like most of the women
we've met. She's full of surprises."

Lex was right. After doing battle with Prescott and saving her cousin,
he didn't expect them to sit on the phone for hours talking about their
future. Maybe a quick call or text here and there. He wanted to be honest
with her but considering her lifestyle, he didn't know how receptive
she'd be. He had to time the delivery of the information just right. Too
soon, she wouldn't give them a chance. Too late, she'd feel manipulated.
His attraction to her fascinated him. He'd always had a thing for women
who were considered good girls. She was definitely not in that category.

Daron thought he'd married one but look where that got him. With
Tandria, she'd already know going in that lying beside him could get
them killed. They both had histories that could come back and wreak
havoc. Any woman that would do what she did to protect and save her
cousin, was a woman he wanted by his side, especially if she was going
legit.

Regardless of what happened between them, he vowed to protect her
from anything Bishop had in that file.

CHAPTER 44

Cameron's mind was on making it back to Chicago to retrieve that file. Her team had stopped to shower, change, pack, grab something to eat, rest for a couple of hours, then finish the drive home. Trenton, Greg, and Rob entered their rooms a couple of doors down. JD lingered, escorting her to the door close to the stairwell.

"Thanks." JD gave her a gentle hug.

"You know I got you. Think about what we talked about on the way over." Cameron hoped JD took her offer to work for her seriously.

JD nodded and walked away.

Cameron entered the suite and pressed her back to the closed door. Her ribs were bruised and her torso and back were sore. What she wanted to do was soak in that special mix Bishop had created for her, not go another round with someone. She moved about the living room with a gold wand in hand, just in case she had company. She didn't hear any movements but her own.

A large envelope with Daron's business card taped to it was sitting on a coffee table. Even though she assumed it was one of Daron's people who delivered it, she checked the rest of the suite before opening the package and reading the note.

Red had warned her Daron knew more than he let on. She flipped through the money he'd paid her for the fights she won, plus a bonus for Tia and Prescott. He also apologized for destroying her recordings and thanked her for saving his brother.

"Call if you're interested in something more," Cameron read out loud, not surprised that he'd already changed his number.

Everything except the note went back into the envelope. She would deal with that later. The only thing she wanted was some painkillers and to soak in a jacuzzi tub. As the stream of water hit the porcelain full force, she pondered the note. She had to do some soul searching before she made the call, because he was asking for more than she was ready to give.

She needed to be sure her attraction to Daron wasn't because he reminded her of all the things she loved about her ex. Cameron turned on the jets and slipped into the Jacuzzi, knowing it wasn't fair to compare them on that basis. Nathan was in love with her. Daron was interested in pursuing the possibility. If Daron had been in love with her, he may not have trusted her ability only helping when absolutely necessary.

Cameron wasn't ready to find out firsthand. Not that she regretted Houston, but it wasn't the smartest move on her part, considering that Red had probably given Daron Bishop's file on her or he would soon. She needed to tread lightly. Not to mention she needed to go search for the last of Bishop's files once she returned to Chicago.

When the hot water became cold, she stepped out and got dressed. She powered on the television to find Prescott's mugshot on the news and the leading story was "The Warden has been captured." Cameron now understood why Daron needed Prescott alive and why her brother had been so frustrated. She was surprised that Jason hadn't hemmed her up at the scene. As far as she knew, he would've had to contact the local office for the operation. Whatever he did to make it happen, she was grateful. A series of knocks sounded on her door.

"Cam, it's me," JD called from the other side.

She let him in. "Hey."

"I wanted to talk to you in private before we hit the road." JD perched on the arm of the couch. He smiled, "I'm still amazed to see you with long hair and without contacts."

"Don't get used to it. Greg brought the clippers so I can get rid of it." Cameron ran her fingers through her hair. She'd been tempted to keep it a few more days to hide the purplish bruise on her cheek. Cosmetics would have to suffice.

"If you're serious about your new venture, I don't think you should," JD said.

She crossed her arms. "Why is that?"

"The short hair is Viper. Cameron is somewhere in between Viper and Tandria." JD stared at her. "Besides, I heard you lost a bet to auntie."

"You checked in with your mom, I see." She playfully shoved him before picking up the clippers from the coffee table. "Maybe you're right, but that's not why you came here."

JD stood and turned to her. "The Feds might be fooled, but we both know Daron is The Warden. Did you speak to him about releasing me?"

"No. That last time I talked to him about you, I wasn't even sure we were going to be able to save you." She put the clippers in the duffle bag. "Why?"

"Someone left a note." JD sounded a bit disappointed.

Cameron tilted her head. "I can't take credit, but it probably has more to do with his need to lay low for a while than anything else."

"Making sure you hadn't made any agreements." JD sighed, rubbing a hand across his five o'clock shadow.

She winced as she moved the wrong way, and gripped her side. "The only thing I negotiated was some time to rescue you."

"Good. Daron was different from anyone I'd worked with," he stated, then told her about the business classes he'd taken and the conversations he had with Daron that went far beyond generic pleasantries. "I still feel like I have something to prove."

"Not to me," Cameron said as JD's gaze fell on the envelope and the note Daron had sent.

"I have something to prove to myself. Which is why I'm turning down your offer," JD admitted, with a sheepish smile. "I want to try to make a go of my own dream."

"In that case, I wish you the best." She gave him a huge hug.

JD pulled away. "Now for the second thing I came here for. What's going on with you? I haven't seen you like this since the time you'd decided to tell Nathan who you really were."

"Let's not get into that." Cameron grabbed the scissors from the table and maneuvered around him to make it to the bathroom.

JD followed her, leaning in the doorway watching as she made the first snip. "At first, I thought it was Eric, with all the comments from the team about the chemistry between the two of you. Then some thought it was Lex. Until today, when I saw the way you looked at Daron, I knew."

"Knew what?" Cameron threw the severed hair in the garbage then twisted to cut off the other side.

JD stepped closer. "That you were in love with him."

"That's impossible," she scoffed. "I don't even know him, really." She tossed out the rest of her hair then checked out the new shoulder-length cut in the mirror.

He leaned on the sink. "Ahh, it must have caught you off-guard which is why you're in denial."

"No, I'm not," she shot back, chopping off a few more inches.

"I'm safe." JD smirked at her. "You can't use me as an excuse to dodge those feelings anymore."

Cameron waved the scissors at him. "I don't make excuses."

JD didn't move. "I saw Daron's note on the table. Did you call him?" She frowned. "Not yet."

"It's not like you not to face something head on." He tilted his head, staring at her, "Besides your dad. Speaking of Uncle Jake, you need to have a conversation with him."

"Why?"

"I did. Now I understand that we didn't have the entire story." JD leaned closer. "And you already missed too much time."

Cameron gave him a stern look.

"We've been so focused on being left behind, we never thought to ask how would all of us have fit in Uncle Jake's car in one trip."

Like CPR paddles to the chest, her cousin's statement sent high voltage waves to Cameron's heart. Six kids wouldn't have fit in his car. He would have had to make two trips. *Could he have been coming back for us? Why kick me out then?* Cameron shook off those thoughts. She needed to make sure Bishop's file was where she suspected before she deep dived into an emotional abyss. "Maybe I'll finally sit down with him, but I'm not ready right now."

"Don't wait too long. Your dad isn't getting any younger and I don't want you to regret never giving him a chance to say his peace."

"Then tell me."

"If you want the truth and the ability to question it, you need to go right to the source."

"Why did I pull your ass out of the fire?" Cameron lifted the scissors and pointed them up toward his neck.

JD pushed them down and kissed her on the cheek. "Because you love me."

"You'd better be glad, too," she teased, as he swept out of the bathroom.

◆ ◆ ◆

Hours later, Cameron entered a grey brick house with stone accents, wearing a long, black wig and huge sunglasses that certainly weren't needed at such a late hour. She couldn't believe she'd forgotten about this place. She maneuvered past the living room and into a kitchen with stark white-and-teal decor. In her defense, Bishop had her working more assignments at once than he'd ever had before. She pulled the pantry door open, then tugged the shelves forward to get to Bishop's special room.

She placed her palm on the scanner and felt a prick on her finger. *Damn, I hate this one.* Cameron didn't know Bishop had upgraded to this particular system. After processing her blood, the screen said, 'Welcome

Kimura. Select future access programming.' Cameron selected the palm read and question mode. The steel door popped open and she entered, scanning all of the boxes piled on the floor. This stop wasn't going to be as quick as she expected. The previously empty shelves were filled with gold bars, others had black boxes. She pulled one of the boxes off the shelf and found that it was filled with diamonds.

Several Banker's Boxes were scattered about. It would take her a few days to go through them without any help. Better to get the safe deposit key and check it tomorrow. She spent an hour sifting through the containers. As she moved to the desk, a file folder stuck out slightly from under one of the boxes. She pulled it out.

"Yes." Cameron cleared herself a seat, placing the items on the floor. She broke the sealed file and flipped through, engrossed in the details before stopping at a random page. Bishop had Trenton hire the assassin that took out Greg's first wife. The wife was helping the FBI build a case against Bishop.

She would have to dig deep to find out what Greg's wife possibly knew that would cause Bishop to remove her on the sly without even a whisper of rumor surrounding the hit. She wished that was it, but by the size of the file it was only the tip of Bishop's iceberg. She closed the file, preferring not to come across anything else tonight that could rock her entire existence.

Cameron opened the security vault which had even more gold bars and boxes. She placed the file in a void she'd created in the gold, covered it with more bars, then closed the vault. This was her secret until she had time to filter through it. At least she could breathe easy that it wasn't floating in the wind for someone else to find and use against them. Now, she just had to hope that Bishop was telling the truth about the dossier in Daron's possession and that there wasn't anything inside that could get her arrested.

Her phone vibrated as she secured the hidden room. Lex texted her that she could head over to see Daron. Lucky for her, he was staying in downtown Chicago and not somewhere near the compound.

Cameron leaned against the pantry door. Some of the emotional demons that she'd always been afraid would break through at the most inopportune moments, reared their heads. Seeing her dad after years of avoiding him had been hard. Thoughts of the events that ended things between her and Nathan. The fear of losing JD. Nearly dying. Bishop's issues that refused to die with him. Her chest heaved, while unwanted tears created a river down her cheeks. The last few months had been taxing and her soul was weary. She could hear her father telling her 'warrior princesses don't cry' and her mother yelling, 'yes, they do. They just kick some ass while they're doing it'. To this, she smiled.

Daron reminded her of all the desires that had been pushed to the back of the closet of her soul. She felt like she could breathe just a little easier.

Cameron wiped her tears, then dried her hands on her pants. She secured the house and walked out to the Jaguar associated with the alias who lived there.

She drove down Michigan Avenue, knowing she needed to take some time to simply deal with the emotions that had her out of sorts. She snatched off the wig as she neared the hotel and tucked it in the glove compartment.

Lex did a double take as she approached him in the lobby. She'd given him fair warning that her appearance had changed again. By his wide eyes and dropped jaw, her short bob and brown eyes had caught him off guard.

She was dressed in tight jeans and a baggy shirt that exposed one shoulder. He gave her a hug then smiled as she made her way to the elevator.

"Okay." Lex pressed the penthouse button. "I disengaged the alarm long enough for you to get to him."

"Thanks," she said as he stepped out. She'd had to call Red for Lex's new number but she didn't grill him on anything else.

When she was in front of Daron's door, she knocked then dialed the number he'd given her.

"Hello," he answered.

"Are you going to let me in?" Cameron positioned herself where he could see her through the peephole in case he hadn't attached his device to the back of the door as yet.

Daron was probably taking in the brown eyes and much shorter hair.

"Tandria?" Daron asked, sounding uncertain which made her chuckle.

Cameron knocked on the door as she answered, "Cameron Stone."

The door whipped open.

Daron smirked as he slid the Beretta into his waistband. "Full of surprises."

"You should get used to calling me by my government name," she said as Daron ran his fingers through her hair, causing a tingle of desire and need to ripple down her spine. He didn't say anything about her appearance, but from the way his eyes devoured her body, the slight changes didn't bother him in the least.

"I had to call a friend to track you down." She knew he'd figure it was Lex, otherwise his alarm system would've alerted him the moment she pressed the button for the penthouse level.

"You could've called and asked directly," Daron stated, stroking a finger across her cheek.

"Where's the fun in that?" She sauntered toward a russet couch near the fireplace, then paused to take in the modern décor that fit his personality. "I wanted to personally thank you for having my back yesterday."

Daron stepped closer to her, and her breathing hitched. "Is that all?"

"I'd like to know, do you have a *legal* business that sells the security system you used at the compound and mansion?" She put some distance between them by lowering herself on the couch. "As well as the one you utilized remotely in locations like hotels."

He covered the short distance, then situated himself in a spot in front of her. "If I need to create a business for you to purchase the security system in order to spend more time with you, consider it done."

She was interested in getting to know Daron better and learning why Bishop trusted him enough to hand over a file on Kimura.

"So we're clear, the only offer on the table besides the business, is friendship with a few perks." Cameron was hoping now that everything was over, she wouldn't feel a flutter of emotion that she wasn't quite ready to call love.

"As long as you understand I have every intention on developing this *friendship* into a *committed* relationship," Daron replied, giving her a wide smile.

"Your comment has been duly noted."

She had no choice but to slow things down. Not only because of the file but also to make sure they both remained true to their word. Their kind of lifestyles were habits that were embedded in the fabric of their personas. She wasn't sure if it would be that easy for either of them to walk away. Cameron needed to know if Daron was truly retired before getting too entangled.

"Then I have something for you." Daron disappeared up the stairs.

What I want, you don't need to leave the room for. Cameron chuckled to herself, loving the way the shirt stretched across his muscular back.

Minutes later, Daron descended to the lower level with a manila folder in hand. "Here," Daron said, extending the packet to her.

"Bishop's file." Cameron was surprised to see the seal wasn't broken. She immediately questioned why he gave it to her. Bishop instilled in her to be careful of small, seemingly-nice gestures or favors. Those were the ones that usually came back to issue the most damaging blows to someone's life.

"What I learn about you," Daron reclaimed his spot in front of her. "I don't want it to come from a dossier."

She broke the seal, flipping through to find article clippings about the prestigious internship and projects she worked on, as well as pictures of her volunteering at various programs. "Why did Bishop give you this?"

"I haven't read the letter that came with it yet," Daron admitted, as Cameron sat the file open to a picture of her volunteering to build a house for Habitat for Humanity on the table next to him. He glanced down at the image then back up at her. "Building a new future."

"What's next for you?" Cameron asked, as Daron flipped the file shut.

A glimmer of lust and desire lit in Daron's eyes as the corner of his mouth lifted and his gaze dropped to her breast then traveled down her body before returning to her face. "Indulging in some of the pleasures life has to offer."

She smiled back as Daron ventured to the bar and pulled out a bottle of champagne and two flute glasses.

For the first time in a while, Cameron wasn't dreading what would happen next. The base plan was completely above board and legal. Her second project was a slippery slope. She had to take some time to think about whether she was willing to get ensnared in her old lifestyle for the purpose of helping people.

"I hear JD is pursuing a career in the arts." Daron poured the bubbly liquid into the glasses.

"I look forward to him proving his friends and family wrong." Cameron tucked her worries about the future in the back of her mind; now was time to appreciate the here and now.

She took the glass Daron offered and lifted it in salute. "To enjoying retirement."

"To being open to love and all the possibilities life brings." Daron gave her a wicked grin as they touched glasses and took a sip, both keeping an eye on the other over the rim.

Cameron had been fighting most of her adult life. Now was time to use that energy toward doing her part to create her best life. In that moment, it was cherishing Daron's company, celebrating JD's newfound confidence, and having the last of Bishop's files. She sipped to her future and to being ready for whatever life dropped in it.

Daron extracted the glass from her hand, then set them both down on the countertop. His arm slid around her waist, gently pulling her to him. Studying Daron's handsome face as he lowered his lips to hers, she wondered if life would make her new lover, an ally or an enemy.

Either way she'd handle the situation if it ever became a problem. Until then, she'd remain cautiously optimistic.